Shepherd Lake

Also by Peter Rennebohm:
Be Not Afraid
French Lake
Blue Springs
Buried Lies

Shepherd Lake

Peter Rennebohm

Dedication

Dedicated to Shari. The nicest person I know.

First Edition: October 2015

Printed in the United States of America

Pre-press by:
North Star Press of St. Cloud, Inc.
P.O. Box 451
St. Cloud, Minnesota 56302

Published by:

"The sympathy a man feels
Toward all living creatures
Is what truly makes him a man"

~Albert Schweitzer

One

THEY WERE LATE. Frank Nash hated being late. He hurried to get ready. The duck opener was an important event in the life of the Nash boys—Frank and son, Charlie. Tradition called for a 12:00 p.m. start, and Nash knew if they were late, many of the local ducks would find a quiet pond someplace deep in the woods to hide-out.

Nash, Charlie, and weekend guest, Earl Foster, hurriedly loaded the twelve-foot row boat. A gunny sack full of duck decoys landed between the seats. Everything else—shotguns, shell bags, folding stools, and a five-gallon steel gas can were stashed wherever there was room. Foster stole a quick glance over his shoulder at the steel pontoon boat tied to the far side of the wooden dock. His gaze went from the small boat to the pontoon . . . and back.

"You sure we shouldn't take the pontoon, Frank?" Foster inquired, a bit apprehensive.

"Well, we could, I guess. But it's hard to hide and tough to maneuver when we set out the decoys," Nash replied. "Might have thought about that earlier, maybe, and gone out in the small boat to set the spread." Nash noticed Foster's worried gaze and finished with, "Don't worry, Earl. We'll be fine."

Charlie was excited. Duck hunting with his dad meant the world to the boy. It wasn't the shooting, exactly. Charlie really never liked killing things. He often passed on easy shots for just that reason. On the other hand, he really enjoyed watching his Golden Retriever, Taffy, retrieve downed birds. He was pretty sure he wouldn't hunt at all if it weren't for Taffy . . . and his dad.

"Come on, son," Nash said. "Let's get that motor on and get going."

Charlie picked up the six horsepower Johnson and stepped into the boat. Frank held the boat close so his son could mount the heavy motor. The back end of the boat dipped noticeably with the added weight. Charlie glanced down as the motor settled on the stern. The one-inch rubber drain plug was firmly in place, just as it should be.

"Plug in, Charlie?"

"Yep. We're all set, Dad." Proud he thought to check the plug, the boy smiled.

"Earl, put that life preserver on. Okay?" Frank suggested. His friend was no swimmer, and Nash knew it. "Time to go duck hunting."

Charlie stepped in, started the motor, and let it idle in neutral. Taffy hopped in and settled at Charlie's feet.

"Why don't you get in the bow, Earl." Frank watched as his friend stepped gingerly into the boat and sat on the wooden seat. A large man, well over two-hundred pounds, Earl Foster grabbed both sides of the boat to halt an unnerving, sudden sway. The boat continued to rock. "Whoa. You sure we're okay here, Frank?" Earl's voice trembled slightly.

"Yeah, we're good. Don't have far to go . . . just across the lake and a bit to the west," Nash replied. "It's that same area of the lake I told you about last week, Earl." He lowered himself into the boat and pushed away from the dock. "Let's go, Charlie. Head for that spit of land on the southwest corner."

Just as Charlie put the motor in gear, the bank of clouds rolling in obscured what had been a brilliant October sun. "Looks like rain, Dad," Charlie observed with concern.

"Yeah. That's not good. Ducks don't fly in the rain, son. Your Uncle Tom taught me that. Wind's always a good thing, but the birds hunker down when it's real wet. Could be wasting our time here. Maybe it's just a passing shower. We can hope, anyway."

Charlie eased out into the lake.

* * * * *

THE DAY HAD BEGUN with a clear sky and a warm southern breeze. Frank had invited his neighbor and the family CPA, Earl Foster, to the Nash's cabin at Shepherd Lake for the weekend. Their plan was to hunt grouse early Saturday morning, then ducks in the afternoon. Frank also wanted to re-visit an area across the lake he had explored a few weeks earlier while grouse hunting.

The duck opener in Minnesota was always an exciting time. Anticipation was half the fun. Hunting officially began at 12:00 p.m. on the first Saturday in October, so the three had spent that morning driving back roads hunting ruffed grouse.

The 4th was also Charlie's sixteenth birthday. He'd been driving with either his dad or mom on a learner's permit for the past year, but now he could legally drive by himself. All things considered, this was a very important and exciting day for Charlie Nash.

"Hold it, Charlie! I think I see something under that Tamarac over there," his dad called out.

Charlie coasted to a stop. He and his dad slipped from the Buick, loaded shotguns with #8 birdshot, and let Taffy out. "Find 'em, girl." Charlie pointed to the alders beneath the tamarack.

Taffy dashed away, tail wagging furiously. Suddenly she stopped. Downwind of the partridge, she couldn't see the bird, but knew exactly where it was hiding nonetheless; her tail was rock steady and floated parallel to the damp humus.

"Go ahead, Dad," Charlie whispered.

Frank looked at his son with eyebrows raised. "You sure?"

"Yeah. I want to watch Taffy on this." Truth for sure, but once again, Charlie balked at the idea of killing.

Frank walked ahead, gun raised. All at once, Taffy leapt into the thicket. A single grouse exploded skyward. The roar of wings caused Frank to flinch . . . he barely shouldered his 20 gauge. He tracked the bird and fired.

The partridge continued on. Its rapid wingbeat faded. Incredibly fast and nimble, it ducked behind a large spruce. Frank fired a second time . . . a desperate shot certainly, but sometimes a single pellet could bring down a grouse. No such luck this time, however.

"Damn!" Frank exclaimed. "Flew right behind a tree, Charlie."

"Yeah, I saw it, Dad. Too bad." Charlie secretly wondered if he was rooting for the bird or his dad. "Good job, girl." Charlie knelt to give his friend a pat and a hug.

Frank checked his watch. "Oh, oh. We better hightail it out of here, Charlie," ever mindful of the 12:00 duck opening. "Lost track of the time. If we don't hurry, we'll be late setting out the decoys."

They piled back into the new Buick, Charlie slid behind the wheel. Their stop for the elusive partridge slowed them up sufficiently, so that they now had to rush getting everything ready for the duck hunt.

"What's the hurry?" Foster asked.

"I hate being late for the opening, Earl. That's all. We'll have to really hustle when we get back to the cabin." Frank passed out birthday cupcakes left over from Charlie's birthday party the night before as he carefully glanced at Charlie behind the wheel.

Charlie spun the tires in the dry gravel as he pulled out.

Frank shot a look at his son.

"Oops. Sorry, Dad."

Nash smiled and looked away. "It's okay, son. No harm done."

They arrived back at the cabin at 11:00 a.m. Frank looked at the sky as he guided everyone inside to gather their gear. "Make sure you guys have rain gear and rubber boots," Frank said.

Earl Foster was new to the sport—or to any sort of hunting, actually. He was unsure what to expect and relied on his good friend for guidance regarding equipment and clothing.

"We could be wasting our time. But, I still want to show you that area across the lake where I found that box, Earl."

Foster brightened at the mention of the box Frank discovered a few weeks ago . . . specifically its contents.

Frank knew how miserable it could get sitting in a blind in a pouring rain. His friend would endure, however. Frank knew his friend well. They had been fraternity brothers and friends since college. An unlikely pair—Frank the ex-football star, Earl the brains of the fraternity and its president. Earl's friendship had endured throughout Frank's troubled drinking years, and he remained loyal and trusting. They were very close.

Charlie pulled on hip boots—a birthday gift from his dad. "Watch," the boy said. "We'll have our limit by two o'clock and we can go poke around that old building site you're so interested in, Dad."

Nash Senior wasn't convinced by his son's optimistic prediction, but didn't want to worry Foster any more than necessary. He sensed a definite uneasiness from his friend and business advisor. "Okay. Let's get going. We're going to be late if we don't step on it."

Nash slipped on his hip boots and watched as Earl wrestled with knee-high rubbers. When everyone had their coats on, he picked up his shotgun, shell bag, and lunch sack, and headed for the door.

Charlie whistled for Taffy, who appeared from beneath the dining table. A relatively small dog, Taffy was nine years old . . . still in her prime.

"Is she a good duck dog, Charlie?" Foster asked.

"She was bred to hunt, Mr. Foster. That's what the guy who sold her to us said, anyway. She really does love it. She's a strong swimmer, has a good nose, and most of the time anyway she mind's well." Taffy seemed to understand her master's words as her tail drooped just a bit. She wrinkled her upper lip in a weak smile.

"Okay, guys. Let's roll." Frank held the door for the pair, closed it behind him, and walked abreast of his son down to the lake.

They reached the dock. Shepherd Lake, a small, deep-water lake, was no more than a mile long by a half mile wide. It was located seven miles west of the small lumber town of Hackensack. Primarily a fishing lake, it was populated with sunfish, crappies, northern pike, and large-mouth bass. The Nash cabin was one of only three on the lake—all situated on the north side, recently constructed. The only road to the property wound through the forest from the east.

The Nash's had built their cabin in 1957, a couple years after the fortuitous events in Blue Springs, South Dakota. Charlie had been more than happy to help finance the cabin with a portion of his new-found wealth. The other two cabins were located on the east and west ends of the lake.

Nash's cabin sat on forty-three acres mid-way between the other two. All three parcels had been purchased shortly after the federal government opened up the area now known as the Chippewa National Forest to homesteading. A huge area of forest land had been closed off from the public both during and after the war.

The forest and lake had always been a bit mysterious. During World War II, local residents—the few that lived on the lone road from Hackensack—along with curious town folk, had been told that the government was experimenting with a top-secret project to create extremely valuable motor fuel from, of all things, sawdust.

In the early stages of this highly suspect development, the Army had been charged with securing the site and surrounding forest lands. Several local lumbermen had been hired to cut and harvest timber. Laborers from the CCC brought in to construct the various buildings, were shielded from the actual experimentation. All they knew was that the project required copious amounts of sawdust; that the resultant product—something called "ethanol"—could alter the course of the war.

The area was patrolled regularly by the Army's military police. The war had most people on edge, and whatever activity occurred in the woods on the south side of the lake was largely ignored by locals. All anyone knew was that the single road leading into the massive woods was being heavily patrolled by the Army, and any attempt to discover what was going on was forbidden.

Now, however, after the obligatory ten-year moratorium, the land was open to the public. Charlie and his dad had been grouse hunting over there a couple of times, and together explored most of the grounds comprising the abandoned military site. A few of the buildings remained untouched, padlocked, boarded shut. The single gravel road winding into the restricted area, now branched off for access to the north side of Shepherd Lake: Access for its new summer residents.

The distance between any of the three cabins on Shepherd Lake was significant. Seldom, did the Nash family hear or see either of their neighbors. Frank loved the privacy and seclusion. He cherished the quiet beauty of his woods. Towering white and red pine along with the scraggly, less desirable, jack pine comprised most of the woods. Occasional stands of birch and poplar lent a whitish contrast to the green forest.

Charlie spent many days exploring the woods around their cabin. As time permitted, longer forays across the lake were taken to search deeper into the federal land on the other side.

With both an inlet and outlet on each end of the lake, Shepherd was a clear lake—deep and cold. The west and southwest shores were mostly bog—swamp land with deep, sucking mud on the bottom. Scattered tamaracks, alders, spruce, and poplar dotted the wet, inland areas. Patches of wild rice were scattered around the lake—a favorite treat for local puddle ducks. It was near one of those beds on the south side of the lake that Nash intended to set out decoys.

Two

CHARLIE WRENCHED THE THROTTLE and sped across the lake. A few heavy raindrops began to fall. He looked at his father who had turned away from the rain and now faced his son. Frank, a large man with graying hair cut short, had a handsome face with the exception of his most prominent feature, a bent nose, broken numerous times in his football days with the University of Minnesota Golden Gophers. When shaving, Frank's battered face was a reminder of those years, but not in a negative way. Specific instances of a cleated foot or elbow slamming into his face were fondly recalled; Frank had loved playing football—no matter the price he had to pay.

He wiggled his nose now, as he thought back to his old coach, proud of his accomplishments on the gridiron, but not nearly as proud as he was of his son, Charlie.

He smiled, observing his son maneuver the small boat across the lake. In spite of the weather, Frank was enjoying this time with his son and best friend. He shouted, "Well, this is what duck hunting's all about, son."

The teenager smiled back. He idolized his father. After the events in South Dakota three years earlier, he and his dad had become very close. Prior to that—not so much. Frank's drunken behavior had in fact driven Charlie from their home—driven him, along with Taffy, to run far away to South Dakota.

Once sober, however, Frank allowed his son to grow in ways of his own choosing and refused to badger him ever again about playing football. Instead, he reveled in his son's skill as a hockey player and realized Charlie's real passion was on the ice . . . not on the football field.

In return for this new understanding, Charlie made every effort to spend time with his dad.

Things had worked out swimmingly, Frank thought. He had successfully come to grips with alcohol and had been dry for three years. Life was good for the ex-footballer.

Earl shifted positions to avoid the punishing rain. The boat tipped steeply as he did. Frank leaned in the opposite direction to correct the list.

"Careful, Earl," he warned. Nash had a prickly feeling at the base of his spine as he watched his son maneuver the boat. He had never gone out with more than two people in the old boat—whether for hunting or fishing; and couldn't recall ever loading the boat with quite as much gear. He studied how heavily the boat was loaded and wondered if they should have taken the pontoon instead. *Too big . . . too difficult to steer,* Nash thought. *We'll be okay . . .*

Taffy rose and pranced a bit. "Settle down, Taff. We'll be over there in a little bit," Charlie said. Rainwater began to run down his neck. Heavy drops slapped on the surface and looked eerily like water boiling in a shallow pan.

Charlie shivered and tightened his coat collar as he stared into the gloom. Always a bit small for his age, he finally grew a startling six inches that past summer, now measuring a shade under five-foot-eight. He had not yet achieved his father's stature—broad shoulders and deep chest, but the sport he had chosen didn't require muscle mass as did football.

Charlie was extremely happy in his current frame. His confidence expanded with the added height. Finally, he had grown to be as big as his friends and classmates. A good-looking kid with blue eyes and brown hair kept reasonably long as was the style, Charlie was athletic and coordinated in whatever he chose to do. He could, "play," and he played any game quite well. This innate ability to excel at whatever he attempted, gave him a great sense of confidence.

The rain pounded now, and thrummed on the bottom of the boat. All three hunters were soaked.

Charlie kept the motor at a moderate speed and steered a diagonal course across the black water. It took twenty minutes to reach the far, opposite shore. Frank's target was a favorite hunting spot, a short spit of land alongside a wild rice bed on the southwest side of the lake. The point they were going to hunt jutted out alongside a deep bay that curved inland for quite a distance.

Charlie coasted into shore and let Foster out. Taffy jumped out and raced up and down the reedy shoreline. Frank and Charlie rowed out to set out the two bags of decoys. When finished, they pulled into shore, hid the boat and walked to the blind.

It was after noon by the time everything was set. Frank pulled out an extra poncho and handed it to Foster. "Here. This should help a bit."

The hunters spent the afternoon hunkered down, watching for any movement. Though little was flying, they managed to shoot a few wood ducks. Charlie was fairly certain his dad had been the successful shooter. He knew he hadn't hit anything as he intentionally aimed high. He beamed at the job Taffy did swimming after the downed birds. As the afternoon wore on, the rain let up and became a light drizzle.

Oddly, there was no wind, and the temperature hovered at about forty degrees. All in all, conditions were tolerable, but neither Charlie nor his dad felt inclined to leave the blind to explore the old military site.

Earl Foster was curious about his friend's find, but he was too wet and miserable to suggest tramping in the sodden woods. *Maybe Sunday,* he thought. He scrunched deeper into his poncho, now fully convinced that duck hunting wasn't his cup of tea.

As daylight diminished, Foster suggested they should pack up and head back. "'Bout time to quit, Frank?" Hope filled his voice.

Even though Nash hadn't seen a duck for quite a while, he stubbornly wanted to wait until the very end, hoping for at least one more shot and a retrieve for Taffy. Nothing flew, however, and as darkness settled like a blanket, Nash knew they had to leave. "Okay. That's enough. Let's get back to the cabin and get dry."

Because Frank and Charlie intended to come back out in the morning, they decided to leave the two-dozen decoys out on the water. Frank doubted there would be any significant change in the wind direction, and, besides, all three were miserably wet and chilled. Foster quickly stepped into the boat and again settled in the front.

Taffy hopped in . . . as did Frank. He noticed a few inches of water had collected in the bottom of the boat, but without a can to bail, didn't give it another thought. He watched Charlie start the motor, put it in gear, and turn the throttle handle. Surprised that both his feet were now under water, Frank had a sudden flash of concern. His original estimate of only a few inches had been in error. At least six inches sloshed around the bottom of the boat, and the water level seemed to be rising.

Frank's heart sped as he looked around. They were already a hundred and fifty yards from shore—fully committed to continue across the lake. He couldn't see anything due to the blackness and rain slanting into his eyes, but he knew Charlie instinctively could point the boat in the right direction.

Just then, the motor sputtered, lost power, quit. Charlie looked at his father.

"Water in the gas?" Frank asked his voice nearly a shout.

Charlie shrugged and glanced down to check the rubber hose from the gas tank. "Hose is still attached," he yelled back.

The heavy boat drifted a short way. Charlie tugged on the rope. The motor caught. Then shot forward—rapidly. Strangely, the water in the bottom had deepened, even though the rain had lessened. Charlie watched in horror as a wave of water shifted from the back to the front of the boat, then back again. Within seconds, the bow was under water. Earl Foster was splashing about.

Like a submarine on a shallow dive, the small boat submerged. Water poured over the bow. Charlie and his dad looked at each other—eyes wide in astonishment and fear. Both knew there was nothing they could do to stop the boat from sinking. They would be swamped in seconds as it was. The boat settled as if a giant boulder had been dropped inside. For Charlie the world seemed to stop. He held his breath, waiting for something, anything to signal that what was happening to them really wasn't.

Everything seemed to slow down—like a movie in slow motion. Nash felt outside of himself—watching events unfold that he was a part of. He refused to accept what was happening. Bile lodged in his throat. He looked at his friend. Earl's face reflected the stone-cold terror Frank felt deep in his gut.

Foster looked to be in shock. Eyes wide—darting right and left—he couldn't grasp what was happening. All at once, all three understood with absolute certainty that their situation was dire. They were in serious trouble.

For a long time, no one spoke. Nothing happened. The only sound was Taffy paddling away from and around the sinking boat. The rain had quit. Taffy lunged, providing enough impetus for the boat to roll in the opposite direction.

Earl shouted just as the boat turned over. "Frank!"

All three were thrown out into the lake. Nash and Charlie managed to swim back and cling to the overturned craft. Earl grabbed for the bow. Taffy returned and furiously scrambled to climb on top of the overturned boat. Nash pushed her off with his free arm, for the boat kept sinking under the combined weight of three hunters and a dog.

Whatever flotation there was under the seats was not enough to support the hunters as well as the boat. The motor added to their danger, threatening the minimal buoyancy.

Earl yelled, "Frank! What're we going to do?"

Nash treaded water. "Charlie stay off the boat! It won't support all of us. Get your hunting coat off. Take off your hip boots." He struggled to remove his own, heavy coat.

Charlie began removing his hunting coat. It was very dark. Very quiet. He removed the coat, and suddenly felt Taffy clawing at his back. He pushed her away and yelled, "No! Get out of here!"

She did as she was told, but soon returned to claw her way onto the boat again. Only the very tip of the upturned bow was visible above the water line.

Charlie feared he'd have to do something about Taffy . . . she was endangering all of them. "Taffy! No! Go! Go on, girl."

She seemed to understand and remained close to her master . . . floating. Waiting. Tail waving and working as a rudder.

Frank knew they had to get the motor off. Earl was struggling to retain a slippery grip on the bow. He was coughing and sputtering and thrashing about.

"Charlie! Can you get the motor off?" his dad asked.

Charlie didn't have time to remove hip boots. "I'll try." He dove and began loosening the mounting screws. After three or four attempts, the motor finally fell away and the boat regained a bit more buoyancy.

It was clear, however, that the boat was too old and lacked sufficient flotation to support all three people. "We have to swim to shore!" Frank shouted.

"Frank. . . I, ah . . . I can't." Foster sputtered. He was breathing heavily—gasping for air. "I can't swim!"

It took a moment for Foster's declaration to register. Then Frank remembered: Earl couldn't swim a lick. Frank's brain spun out of control.

It never occurred to Charlie that anyone, particularly an adult, couldn't swim. Everyone he knew . . . Charlie included, could swim.

Foster had the only life jacket, so he was safe for the moment. Frank and Charlie treaded water. They were in the middle of the lake- —in absolute darkness. Taffy was confused. She kept crawling up on the boat.

"No!" Nash grabbed her by the collar and pulled her away. For a brief moment, he considered the unthinkable: He'd have to hold her head under water and drown her—otherwise, she might get everyone killed.

"Earl, the boat won't hold all of us." Nash's breath came in short bursts. "Charlie . . . and I . . . have to get . . . to shore. Stay here. I'll . . . come back . . . and get you." The calmness of his voice belied the terror he actually felt.

Nash had no idea how he was going to come back out for Foster. All he knew at that point was that Charlie and he had to leave, or they'd drown. "Charlie! Come on! Start swimming."

They left the relative safety of the overturned boat and splashed towards shore. Charlie tried a breast-stroke. As his arms grew heavy, he switched to a side-stroke. Hip boots filled with water and kept dragging him down.

Nash struggled as well . . . managed a sort of one-handed dog-paddle—pausing frequently to catch his breath. In the dark and gloom of the evening, he lost sight of Charlie. His heart froze. "Charlie? Charlie?" He spun around and stared into the darkness. "Charlie?" He had to keep going toward shore—had to find his son.

"Charlie? Charlie? Where are you?" Taffy paddled by. Alone. Nash couldn't see his son. He paused to listen. The only sound he heard was a loud ringing in his ears. His labored breathing masked any response from his son.

* * * * *

14

NASH'S VOICE CARRIED on the breeze. There was one other person on the lake that night and he heard all the voices. All the shouts. The man smiled. Dressed entirely in black, ghostlike and nearly invisible, he rose from a crouch behind a fallen log. He stretched. He was in no hurry now. Tall and slender, he easily blended with the alders, poplars, and spindly tamaracks. He stared into the dark. *Almost too easy,* he thought. Everything was working out according to his carefully crafted plan. His employer would be pleased.

Eventually, satisfied that his scuttling of the boat would have the desired result, and no one came ashore, he would vanish into the dark, wet forest. And if, by some stroke of luck any of the hunters managed to reach shore? Well, he knew exactly what to do in that unlikely scenario. He was prepared to deal with that.

The long hike back through the forest along the old logging road to his car would be laborious, but once his job was completed—the contract filled, he only needed to report back to the man with the money. A big payday would soon be his. But, for now, he continued to wait. To listen.

Three

harlie! Answer me, son," Nash called.
"I'm okay, Dad. I'm over here. Ahead of you." Charlie's voice
sounded from a distance.

Relieved, Nash paused to catch his breath.

Taffy had caught on that they were returning to shore and plowed ahead of her master. A strong swimmer, like all of her breed, she kept coming back to Charlie who was tiring and seemed to have little strength left to continue. His boots were full of water. Charlie decided he had to get them off before it was too late. His coat was already gone, so he unbuckled the boots from his belt, and taking huge gulps of air, submerged to slip them down his legs. Realizing that he could easily become entangled in the straps and might never re-surface, he reached for the surface. His mouth cleared. He inhaled deeply. One of the boots slipped off, but, out of breath and weakened from the effort, he gave up any attempt to remove the second one.

Taffy came back once more. This time, when she reversed her course, Charlie grabbed her tail. She turned her head . . . once, with a puzzled look, but continued toward shore, dragging Charlie in her wake.

With Taffy's strong strokes and Charlie's one-armed, side-stroke, they managed to gain on the shoreline. Taffy pulled while Charlie kicked. His grip on her tail never relaxed. Slowly, painstakingly, they closed in on shore.

It seemed to Charlie that it took forever, but finally he and Taffy reached the outer perimeter of the decoys. Winded, scared, and not at all certain what would happen next, he released Taffy's tail, grabbed three of the decoys, and tucked them under his stomach. Charlie paused momentarily and looked back for his dad. He thought he could hear splashing above the shouts from Foster out in the lake. "Frank! Please."

Charlie stared into the gloom. Then, faintly at first, he spotted his father some distance away. Foster's cries sounded fainter now.

"Help! I can't hold on much longer." Foster's plea for rescue filled the dark night.

Charlie knew he and his dad had to get to shore before they could entertain any hope of rescuing Foster. "Dad? Are you okay?"

"I'm fine, Charlie." Nash was breathing hard. "Need a minute to catch my breath's all."

Charlie strained to see his father. Alarmed by the raspy, tortured sound of his father's voice, the boy shouted encouragement. "You can do it, Dad! Grab a couple of decoys and wait a minute."

Nash tried swimming with the decoys, but the strings and lead weights created too much resistance. He left the decoys and continued on—stroking, kicking, dog-paddling. Exhausted and fearing he wouldn't have the strength to reach shore, Nash took a couple of hard strokes and then his feet touched soft bottom.

Charlie was waiting for him. They hugged briefly. "You okay, son?"

"I'm all right, Dad." They were alive. Charlie shuddered with joy and relief.

Their brief moment of euphoria ended abruptly, as Earl's, frantic call echoed from the dark.

"Frank! Frank . . ."

Foster was not particularly athletic. An over-weight accountant who at thirty-four was grossly out of shape, Nash was concerned about how long he could continue to hang onto the boat. He also worried about the pitiful lack of flotation beneath the seats on the old boat. "Hang on! I'll be right there!" Nash yelled.

As much as he hated the idea, Nash knew he had to go back out for his friend. He doubted the man could hold on while he and Charlie maneuvered their way around the lake.

Charlie and his dad staggered out of the water and collapsed on the shore. They clung to each other, shivering, hyperventilating. Happy to be alive.

"What are we going to do?" Charlie asked.

Nash took a quick inventory of their situation. They were on the far side of the lake. He either had to go back out and get Earl, or they somehow had to walk, swim, or crawl through the mud all the way around the west end of the lake to the only other cabin remotely close—directly across the lake.

Both Charlie and his Dad knew the lake well. The southwest end was a tamarack swamp—nothing but bog and muck. But the only way to reach help was around and through the swamp. Someone had to get to the cabin across the lake from where they were. Unsure if anybody was even home. Unsure of how long Earl would hold out. Nash couldn't see any lights through the murky night. He decided to send Charlie around to the cabin. But first, he had to try something.

"We have to find a log. A big one. Float it out to Earl. I'll bring him back while you go around this end of the lake to that cabin on the other side," Nash instructed.

They moved inland, searching for a suitable log. "Here, let's try this one!" Nash said, calling to his son. Nash picked up one end and Charlie took the other. They began carrying the log down to the water. Both could tell from the weight of the old wood that it was probably too saturated to be of much use; but they had to try. They dropped it in the water, and as feared, only a small portion of the log was visible above the water.

18

"This is never going to work," Nash said. "It won't support even one person. I'm going to have to swim back out." Nash wasn't anxious to dive into the darkness, but knew he had to try. "Don't worry, son. I'll be okay." His voice barely conveyed confidence.

Foster was still yelling. A good sign, but Nash had no idea how long he could last. He had to be cold and tired. Soon hypothermia would set in. He also didn't know how long the boat would remain even partially afloat. Time was running out. No one would come looking for them anytime soon. Nash began removing his hip boots.

"I'll go with you, Dad," Charlie said as he sat down to take off his remaining boot.

"No, Charlie. You have to start working your way around the lake."

"I'm a strong swimmer, Dad. I can help." The boot flopped in the water.

"No! You need to go for help." He looked at his son fondly . . . admiring his courage and at once grateful for having the clarity and sobriety to witness what Charlie had become.

Decision made, father and son hugged briefly. "Go on, Charlie. I'll see you soon. Promise."

Reluctantly, Charlie watched his father slip back into the dark water. Nash waved briefly, then paddled on out toward the middle of the lake. Charlie would have to walk, or crawl through the boggy swamp, a distance of at least three-quarters of a mile, to the other side of the lake until he reached the nearest cabin.

If no one was home, he'd use the phone if they had one, then borrow a boat and go back out on the lake. "Come on, Taffy. Let's go."

He quickly realized that walking through the brambles, deadfalls, and muck was impossible. He'd have to crawl and dog-paddle through the swamp. Taffy would swim. He dropped to all fours and slipped out into the water.

"Frank?" Foster's cry for help filled the night and Charlie with terror.

"Hang on, Earl. I'm . . . coming . . . to . . . get you." Nash called from the dark. It was the last time Charlie heard his father's voice that night.

Surprisingly, the water felt almost warm to Charlie after standing in the cool, wet night air. Half crawling, half swimming he made his way through the mud, the tall rushes, and over half sunken logs. Taffy led the way—oblivious to the nightmare unfolding. At one point, Charlie put his hand down on something hard. The object moved. *A large snapping turtle,* he thought. Charlie shuddered at the thought of the turtle grabbing one of his bare toes or fingers.

He slowly made his way around the lake. It seemed to Charlie that the trip took forever. *Please God! Don't let anything happen to Dad or Mr. Foster.* Charlie prayed as he plodded on . . .

* * * * *

IN TIME, FOSTER'S SHOUTS were not nearly as loud, or frequent. Charlie wanted to call out to his father, but knew he had to keep going. He was winded, tired, frightened, and concerned he wouldn't reach help in time.

After struggling through the swamp for a very long time, Charlie was spent. He didn't think he'd have the strength to go any farther. His efforts would be futile. His father and Mr. Foster wouldn't survive. Almost delirious with exhaustion, he thought, *I hate that boat . . . should have bought a new one . . . we had the money.* He cursed everything . . . and nothing.

Briefly in a moment of clarity, Charlie wondered why they'd sunk. Then he refocused on his effort and getting help.

Suddenly Taffy surged forward just as his head crashed into a wooden beam. He reached up. *A dock!* He couldn't believe it! *We made it. There has to be someone in the cabin.* He climbed on the wooden planks and looked up toward the darkened structure. *Please, please be home.*

Too late? He hadn't heard Foster's voice for quite some time. Nor his father's.

Charlie stood and faced the cabin. With great relief, he saw a faint light in the window. Charlie yelled, "We made it, Dad! Hang on!"

Taffy barked as the door to the cabin opened. Someone came running toward the dock. There was no sound from the middle of the lake. The sky was clear. Millions of stars shone overhead. It was deathly still.

Charlie shouted to his father, "Dad? Did you hear me, Dad? We made it! We'll be out to get you in a minute!"

Still no reply. Charlie collapsed in a heap. His mouth dry. His heart pounded. *No! Please, God! They have to be okay . . .*

The cabin owner reached the dock. Charlie quickly told him what happened . . . where to look for his father and Mr. Foster. The cabin owner's boat was in the water, but he had to go back to a shed to retrieve a motor. *It's taking too long,* Charlie thought. He began shivering and clung to his dog to share her warmth.

Charlie was too tired to move. Taffy sat rock still. Nose and ears alert to any sound from the others. Exhausted herself, she faced the darkness. Ears back, hair on her neck up, she whined softly.

The cabin owner finally got the motor mounted, started it up, and headed off into the darkness towards the middle of the lake. Charlie waited intently—listening, hoping that he'd hear a yell back that both men had been rescued—that both had been found. Safe. Alive.

The sound of the motor died, and stillness again filled the night. A faint knock from the wooden oars sounded. After that, Charlie heard nothing—only his own shallow, raspy breathing and Taffy's sudden, low whine.

It was too quiet . . . much too quiet.

* * * * *

Charlie was helped into the cabin that night by the owner's wife and daughter. He was wrapped in blankets and given a mug of steaming, brandy-laden coffee. The boy was too tired to think straight. Slightly drunk and delirious, nothing happening seemed at all real.

He faced the door, expectantly. Adrenalin spent, Charlie began to shake uncontrollably. He wanted to go to sleep, and awake later to learn that the horror had simply been a bad dream.

Taffy, curled at her master's feet, shivering. She was an immense measure of comfort to the boy. More than simply a pet, she was part of the family. They had been through a lot together in the last few years. Now, they waited for word of Charlie's father and friend Earl Foster.

After a long while, the cabin door opened. Charlie raised his head from his chest. He heard the sound of footsteps entering the room, and looked up from beneath a blanket tightly wrapped around his upper body.

It was the cabin owner. Charlie stood and peered around the man, looking for his father. There was no one with him. Trembling, pale-faced, Charlie looked into the man's face. Hopeful.

Eyes cast down, the man struggled for words.

Charlie waited. No one spoke. The rain started up again and pattered against the thin roof.

The cabin owner straightened, cleared his throat, and quietly said, "I'm sorry, son."

Four

IN THE SPRING OF 1942, the war in Europe was going badly for the Allies. Britain and the United States began secretly developing plans for the re-occupation of Europe. Their plan had serious obstacles to overcome, however. German U-boats were inflicting heavy losses on the Allies. Troop and cargo ships were constantly under attack as they attempted crossing the North Atlantic.

Air support for the Allied ships was thin, at best. The limited range of aircraft hindered efforts to provide adequate protection for the vessels. Many planes ditched in the North Atlantic as their fuel ran out before reaching and defending the cargo ships. Something had to be done or the war would surely be lost.

The so-called "Mid-Atlantic Air Gap" was a very real problem for the Allies. An alternative plan favored by Winston Churchill envisioned large, floating platforms to support air-craft landings in the mid-Atlantic, ones large enough to maintain a squadron of protective fighter planes. The size and scope Churchill envisioned went way beyond even the largest aircraft carrier of the period. As much as ten to fifteen times as big. And, as had already been proven, the carriers currently in service all floundered in the heavy North Atlantic seas. Something else had to be done.

This seemingly preposterous idea was hatched by Churchill's chief of Combined Operations, Lord Louis Mountbatten. He was charged with developing such a floating platform. Project "Habakkuk" was thus born. The name derived from a Biblical passage from the Book of Habakkuk:

*"Behold ye among the heathen, and regard, and wonder marvelously:
For I will work a work in your days, which ye will not believe, though
it be told to you."*

In the early stages of planning, Mountbatten believed the American aviator Howard Hughes would be the perfect man to spearhead the project. Initial, top secrete inquiries soon detailed Hughes struggles with an early dementia few people knew about. Hughes was crossed off the list.

Mountbatten turned to his chief engineer, Geoffrey Pyke, who was fond of quoting the Bible, including passages from the Habakkuk. Pyke was given a green light to proceed. He tinkered and experimented with all sorts of ideas regarding the ideal material to support such a gigantic floating island Pyke would eventually create from blocks of ice and, of all things, sawdust. He envisioned building an actual iceberg from this very material. Ultimately, all involved believed Habakkuk had a real chance to succeed.

Pyke's task: Create and build a vessel approximately 2,500 feet long and 350 feet wide, with a deck-to-keel depth of 200 feet, and walls four feet thick. It was to have a draft of 150 feet, and displacement of 2,000,000 tons or more, constructed from 500,000 blocks of ice created from a mixture of wood pulp (sawdust) and water. The product later came to be known as "Pykrete," named after its inventor.

After months of secret experimentation, Mountbatten and Pyke were satisfied that the test results were all positive. They were ready to present the first samples of Pykrete to Prime Minister Churchill. Mountbatten trembled with excitement as he loaded the final samples in insulated crates, and trucked with them to Churchill's country home, Chequers.

When Mountbatten arrived, he was shown into the entry hall. He reported to the clerk in attendance, "I have with me a small parcel of great importance."

He was told to wait in the parlor. A member of Churchill's staff appeared a while later and apologized, advising that the Prime Minister was at that moment indisposed. He was, "bathing in a soaking tub."

"Good," said Mountbatten. He could wait no longer. Without invitation, he left the parlor and bounded up the stairs. "That's exactly where I want him to be," he shouted.

Mountbatten entered the steaming bathroom to find Churchill in the tub. "I have," Mountbatten explained, "a block of a new material I would like to put in your bath."

Mountbatten opened his parcel and dropped its contents between the prime minister's bare legs. It was a rather colorless and ugly chunk of Pykrete. Churchill's cigar twitched noticeably as the cold cube bobbed between his hairless legs.

Churchill and Mountbatten stared at the chunk intently. They looked deep into the steaming depths of bath water. The ice was not melting. It floated half in and half out of the soapy water.

"Pykrete is a super-ice," Mountbatten explained. "It is strengthened tremendously by mixing a slurry of fourteen percent wood pulp." He fairly beamed with the news.

"Continue," Churchill requested as he stepped from the tub. Personal assistants scrambled to towel the prime minister.

"The mechanical strength of this material is quite remarkable, sir. For instance, a 7.69 millimeter rifle bullet, when fired into pure ice, will penetrate to a depth of about thirty-six centimeters. Fired into this Pykrete material, it will penetrate less than half as far—about the same distance as a bullet fired into brickwork." Mountbatten waited for a response from his commander.

"In other words, you envision a vessel thick enough to withstand the enemies' torpedoes? Bombs as well?" Churchill inquired.

"Yes, sir. To both. Additionally, if a chunk is broken off the vessel, the ship will be a floating sea of raw material ready to repair any damage, immediately," Mountbatten replied. "The crew will be equipped to continue manufacturing Pykrete as required, while at sea." After a brief pause, he stated, "Virtually indestructible, sir."

Mountbatten went on to explain that it would take months . . . years, even for the Pykrete to melt. Furthermore, Mountbatten said, "In battle, the ice ships, or ice-bergs, could put their onboard refrigeration systems to good use by spraying super-cooled water at enemy ships, icing their hatches shut, clogging their guns, and freezing hapless sailors to death." Mountbatten's brown eyes twinkled at such horrifying images.

Churchill, ever the pragmatist, held off opining regarding Mountbatten's final boast. He was dubious, but nonetheless, willing to gamble on Mountbatten's idea.

"Excellent," Churchill replied. "Continue on, my good man, and now if you don't mind, I'd like to towel and complete my dress . . ."

The ship's deep draft would keep it out of most harbors. It would have limited maneuverability but be capable of up to ten knots cruising using twenty-six electric drive General Electric motors mounted in separate external compartments. Normal, internal ships engines would have generated too much heat for such an ice-craft.

Inside the vessel, a large refrigeration unit would maintain the integrity of the Pykrete and prevent dangerous melting. Its armaments would include forty two-barreled, 4.5-inch dual-purpose turrets, and numerous anti-aircraft guns. It would house an airstrip and up to 150 twin-engine bombers or any number and combination of fighter planes. The berg would carry immense quantities of valuable aviation fuel to re-supply Allied bombers crossing the Atlantic.

The Habakkuk was imagined to be virtually *un-sinkable* as it would have been a streamlined iceberg—or floating island. Kept afloat by the buoyancy of its construction materials, and highly resistant to damage by virtue of its sheer bulk. It was projected to take seventy million dollars and roughly 8,000 men working eight months to build. However, both Churchill and President Roosevelt, who ultimately would partner on the project, both desired proof positive that the idea had merit: That it would indeed, *float.* That it could be propelled and navigated.

The two leaders commanded that two test *islands* be built to verify the validity of Mountbatten's hypothesis that it would work without question. Why two? If one test site was compromised; i.e, if the enemy somehow managed to discover the plan and sabotage the project at one site, the other would surely be completed. Also, by building two, the leaders would be doubly certain that the real Habakkuk would indeed work as planned.

Churchill instructed his staff to begin work immediately and construct such a test island at Lake Louise, Alberta, Canada. This small prototype was to be constructed at Patricia Lake, measuring sixty feet by thirty feet, weighing in at 1,000 tons, and kept frozen by two, fifty-horsepower motors.

Similarly, President Roosevelt assigned General Richard Abdelkader to construct an identical test-model at a secret location in a very cold region of the United States; an area with easy access to harvestable timber, and of course, a hidden lake. The area chosen—later to be known as the Chippewa National Forest, was selected in Northern Minnesota. It was an area familiar to General Abdelkader, as he had grown up in a small town a short distance from the site.

The forest land provided seclusion, extremely cold winter weather, an unlimited supply of pulp wood for the Pykrete, a deep, fresh-water lake, and could be easily guarded from prying eyes as it was situated in a largely, unpopulated area. Construction of the prototype island would take place on the shores of a small, unnamed lake deep in the forest.

Abdelkader was instructed to maintain the utmost secrecy and security, and to mask the true intent of their work. The government came up with a bogus explanation that was so far-fetched, it was almost believable: Creating a new fuel made from sawdust. To all who inquired about the sudden activity in the area west of Hackensack, and the hiring of local residents, the government explanation given out was simple: They were experimenting with building an alternative fuel refinery to manufacture *ethanol*.

Five

A S BOTH PROJECTS GOT underway in late 1942 and early 1943, problems arose almost immediately: Namely, a binder coupled with a melt-retardant was required to mix with the sawdust slurry. Otherwise, the Pykrete failed suspension tests and began to melt too soon. Ideally, scientists envisioned a single material that would serve both purposes. Chemists and physicists from both the USA and Great Britain huddled and finally came up with a solution. An extremely rare and costly raw material, rhodium, could be added to the slurry to sustain its ability to withstand fracturing under stress and extend the Pykrete's melting point by a factor of eight.

While the sawdust was in a fourteen percent slurry, small quantities of this rare mineral had to be introduced. The rhodium would have to be added in a pulverized, powder form to increase the slurry mix by two percent. The metallurgists and chemists faced one more monumental problem: rhodium was only available as a by-product of gold and silver ore. It had to be mined out of the precious metals.

Rhodium was first discovered in 1803 by William Hyde Wollaston, soon after his discovery of palladium. Rhodium had to be precipitated out of the gold or silver by a very complicated chemical process. The end result was a rare element; a hard, silvery metal with a high reflectance, that did not form an oxide, and with an extremely high melting point. The material when pulverized from small blocks, was exactly what Mountbatten and Abdelkader needed to mix in with Pyke's slurry.

Only small quantities were required per cubic foot of ice. The rhodium was separated, melted down, and poured into thin, wafer-like half-inch thick squares. It was readily transportable in wrapped packages of twenty-four per wrap and stored in secure lockers. The wafers were easily pulverized on site, as needed.

Veins of rhodium-rich ore were available four-hundred miles to the west, from the mines in and around Deadwood, South Dakota. Mountbatten's source for rhodium would be the gold-rich mines from the area around Haines, Alaska.

General Abdelkader would have to oversee two separate projects: both veiled in secrecy, both critical to the war effort in 1943: Mining and transporting the rhodium from South Dakota and also building a prototype "island" deep in the woods of Northern Minnesota on the shores of a small, deep-water lake, away from any and all prying eyes.

Abdelkader divided his time between Deadwood and Minnesota. He recruited his former first sergeant, a no-nonsense, battle-tested Army veteran, Barstow Fistric, to head up the construction and logging. Fistric hired a local logger, Early Ducet, to oversee the lumbering phase and ensure an adequate supply of sawdust for the Pykrete mixture.

Ducet was thrilled to be involved. Denied enlistment into the Marines because the last two fingers on his left hand were missing, Ducet felt honored to serve his country in a different way, by working for General Abdelkader. A loner, Ducet lived nearby, managing to eke out a living by logging and trapping in the winter, and milling the lumber during the summer. Ducet looked every bit a backwoods logger: tall, with dark eyes, coal black hair, and prominent ears that projected quite a ways from the side of his head. Ducet was no stranger to hard work. The general certainly picked the right man in that regard.

Once the CCC crew left the project site, Ducet, his loggers, and a handful of scientists and engineers would be the only non-military individuals working on the project. First Sergeant Fistric was charged with keeping an eye on Ducet and riding herd on all the others involved in the project.

Ducet, in charge of the logging operation, had no knowledge of Abdelkader's true mission. As far as he knew, he was involved in creating enough sawdust from poplar, spruce, and maple to supply the scientists' huge appetite.

In time, the rhodium was successfully mined and precipitated out of the precious gold and limited silver ore. The valuable mineral was then smelted into the small, square wafers. The gold and silver were returned to the Deadwood Mining Company, and Abdelkader took charge of the rhodium. None of the Deadwood Mining Company personnel had knowledge of the strange powder mined from their gold ore. Nor did they care.

Abdelkader personally supervised the loading of the mineral into a wooden shipping crate, and accompanied the shipment by freight train back to Minnesota. Off-loaded onto one of the Army's deuce-and-a-halfs, the packages of wafers wrapped in wax paper were trucked to the site and stored in a secure location near the camp. A contingent of armed soldiers accompanied the truck to protect the valuable load. The rhodium was carefully guarded day and night.

Large trucks were a constant presence for many weeks on the dusty back roads west of Hackensack. Heavy construction materials, shop equipment, portable generators and refrigeration equipment, all had to be hauled in and set up. Lumber from local yards was the first to arrive and promptly fashioned into required barracks, a mess hall, a small HQ for the general and Fistric, along with various other structures to house machinery and equipment. It took the better part of six months to clear a site deep in the woods and set up all equipment required to actually begin the manufacture of Pykrete.

General Abdelkader traveled back and forth from the project to Deadwood until actual construction of the prototype was underway. He decided early on that the small lake where they would launch their iceberg required a name. He chose Shepherd Lake. He thought the name to be exceptionally appropriate.

"Why Shepherd?" Fistric inquired.

"Its genesis is an especially poignant passage from the Bible, First Sergeant. I felt it appropriate given the nature of the finished product and all the floating island will mean to the war effort."

"Yes, sir. Very appropriate. And what was the Biblical reference?"

"Jeremiah. Chapter 49, verse 19. *'And who is that Shepherd that will stand against me?'* Thought that pretty much fit our circumstance. The ice boat in its final form will indeed *Shepherd* our boys across the Atlantic."

"I'd say it's a perfect choice, General."

"Thank you, First Sergeant. That will be all for now."

Abdelkader already envisioned additional stars on his shoulders . . . perhaps pinned by Roosevelt himself. The general permitted a slight smile to crease his thin lips. He carried himself as he imagined the great generals in history, might have. He had height—well over six feet. Broad shouldered, heavy chested, his posture was erect at all times. Dark-brown eyes closely set but deep in their sockets hid much of what the general was thinking. Seldom showing emotion, his feelings were kept close—except when risen to anger. A picture he had seen of General Patton became his model. His command would be patterned much like the great Patton's.

As the project moved forward and Adelkader's prototype began to take on a discernable form, the general dreamt constantly of the day when his commander in chief would pin a glorious medal on his chest. A third star for his collar was a certainty, and together he and FDR would together witness the launch of the *H.M.S. Habakkuk.*

With that goal in mind, Abdelkader drove his soldiers and scientists relentlessly, wanting to be the first to finish his prototype. He knew he needed Mountbatten's successful prototype as well, but if he finished first, his president would surely reward his hard work. He obsessed over the process that would lead to his personally overseeing construction of the Habakkuk; his dream would be fulfilled.

Abdelkader needn't have worried about how quickly Mountbatten would build his iceberg. Both men proceeded apace. The Lake Louise project was disguised as a floating boathouse. By late autumn of 1943, Mountbatten began testing the berg's ability to withstand shock from bullets fired at close range. The Pykrete blocks exceeded all expectations. Mountbatten was excited about the quality of the tests, and ever the perfectionist, continued testing relentlessly.

Churchill grew inpatient, though. The prime minister anxiously awaited word from Mountbatten that either test iceberg was in all aspects a success. That they could begin actual construction of the first Habakkuk.

General Abdelkader, never shy about cutting corners, prodded Fistric to finish his tests, and complete the project. The first sergeant implored his team of engineers to work around the clock to finish ahead of the British team. It was no secret that his general would not be content with anything but a first place finish. The crews struggled to finish.

* * * * *

IN THE END, HOWEVER, the H.M.S. Habakkuk would never be built. By 1944, land-based aircraft were attaining longer ranges, U-boats were being hunted down faster, and the United States was gaining numerous island footholds in the Pacific—all contributing to a reduced need for a vast, floating airfield. And, of much greater significance, deep within the newly built Pentagon was the knowledge that America already had a secret weapon in development to be used against Japan—an end to the war that would be brought about not by *ice*, but by *fire*.

Lord Mountbatten accepted the news that Habakkuk would never be built, with grace and dignity. On the other side of the ocean, however, the same could not be said for General Richard Abdelkader. The general was furious. Frustrated and bitter beyond words that all his hard work was for naught, he felt betrayed by his government and by FDR.

Abdelkader vowed that all his efforts would not go unrewarded. He devised a plan to line his pockets as due compensation for his loyalty and devotion. The general reported to his superiors various, "difficulties" inherent in closing down the site at Shepherd Lake. He enlisted his trusted first sergeant to make preparations to carry out his plan.

The general felt certain that if he could stall his superiors long enough, and as the US became more deeply involved in war on two fronts—the Pacific and the Atlantic, the War Department would lose track of the Shepherd Lake project.

In the end, he doubted anyone would dig very deep to uncover what he was really about.

Abdelkader *eventually* filed all the necessary paperwork required to shutter the highly secret war-project. He and Fistric stayed on to supervise the dismantling of the construction site. The floating island was uncovered and left to wither and melt under the hot, summer sun in 1944.

Early Ducet was sent packing. All military personnel were shipped to their home bases. General Richard Abdelkader promptly retired, as did Barstow Fistric, his aide and confidant. As the general's plan had been laid out, both men would, for all intents, vanish.

The project site on Shepherd Lake, became a tiny spot on a map of Minnesota within the boundaries of what later became the Chippewa National Forest. For security reasons, the project site was officially closed to the public for a period of ten years after the war. The only road into the area west of Hackensack was closed, and a twelve-foot gate was constructed to halt any traffic into the area.

Early Ducet was summarily deputized by the Cass County sheriff to patrol the area and discourage visitors. Ducet lived nearby and proved to be a willing guardian of the property. The loyal logger accepted the job with little reluctance. Over the years, he managed to keep most interlopers and hunters away from the Shepherd Lake site.

Of equal interest, and without a doubt of greater significance, no trace of the Shepherd Lake rhodium stash was ever found. Records of its transport to Fort Knox had been properly filed, and all indications were that the valuable packages were shipped to the federal depository by truck shortly after the shutdown in 1944.

The rhodium never arrived. Because of the intense focus on the war effort at that time, interest in locating the valuable rhodium was nil. In time, not a single member of the Defense Department ever pursued the valuable missing shipment. No one even knew of its existence. It was almost predictable. The extremely valuable box of wafers were lost in a paper shuffle. No one cared about the rhodium—except for the two men who stole it.

The two prototype ice-ships: One at Lake Louise, the other at Shepherd Lake, were abandoned. Though complete enough for testing, they never were. Both would not melt until the end of the following summer. The remaining rhodium for the Patricia Lake project was gathered and shipped back to Britain. The cache from Minnesota never re-appeared.

Six

December 1, 1960
West High School
Minneapolis, Minnesota

RAIN AND SLEET BLEW down Hennepin Avenue at a steady pace. It clouded the teen's thick, horn-rimmed glasses. He struggled to protect the stack of books under one arm. The free arm was held over his head . . . weak protection from the rain. His lenses had fogged, and he could barely see. Traffic on Hennepin Avenue was steady at 7:45 a.m. on that Monday morning. The slender boy hurried along the sidewalk.

Oblivious to the two boys creeping up behind him, the youth had no time to react. His books were knocked from the crook of his arm. They scattered on the wet pavement.

"Hey, four-eyes! You dropped your books," one of the boys teased.

"Yeah. What's your problem, anyway, pussy?" the older of the two barked. His mouth twisted into a cruel grin as he anticipated more mischief at the lone boy's expense.

Russell Posey turned to face his tormentors, knowing immediately it was the Slocum brothers—Vernon and Louis. He'd encountered this pair before.

A hand slapped at his glasses. Posey's head snapped to one side as Vernon's fat paw struck his cheek. The sound of flesh-on-flesh scared

Posey more than the blow actually hurt. Accustomed to years of bullying, Russell Posey had managed to develop something of a thick skin—at least to the verbal taunts. His ancestors hadn't done the boy any favors when it came to the family name, either. Posey longed for the day when he would turn eighteen and legally change his last name.

In the meantime, Posey had managed to develop a certain skill at protecting himself from serious injury, once the beatings began. He was a survivor, and even though he had grown accustomed to physical confrontations, he still disliked violence—intensely. Particularly when leveled at his own body.

He managed to endure the name calling and beatings, but right now his face hurt like crazy from the first blow. His heavy, black glasses flew from his face and landed next to his books on the hard, wet concrete. Almost blind without the lenses, he stooped to retrieve his glasses. Vernon stepped close and kicked at them savagely. The glasses separated into two pieces and skidded further away. And then—the final indignity: A wet, black engineer boot planted in Posey's back. He was pinned to the wet pavement with a resigned grunt.

"You'll never make it through the year, you wimp," the older Slocum shouted. "What a loser . . ."

"Well, if this is any indication of what's ahead at good old West High, you may be right," the blond-haired boy offered. Posey's weak attempt at humor went unnoticed by the Slocums. He wiped his bloody lip and inhaled deeply, ready for what was surely coming next.

Across the street, a fourth boy had witnessed the entire attack. About to enter school, he instead left his books beneath the overhang above the steps, darted between cars to cross the street at a full run, jumped the curb, and grabbed Vernon's arm just as he was about to deliver another blow to Posey's head.

"Leave him alone, Slocum," the new boy quietly demanded. He twisted the boy's arm and held fast.

36

"Hey, let go my arm," Vernon wailed.

"Yeah, why don't you mind your own business, Nash?" Louis Slocum said, as he took a tentative step toward Nash.

"That's enough," Charlie Nash said.

"Oh, uh, okay. You gonna stop us, Nash?" Vernon sneered. "You and what army, punk?" He straightened to his full six-foot height and clenched both fists. "You a tough guy now, Nash? Besides a hot-shot hockey player?"

The shorter boy stood his ground and replied, "Not really, but he didn't do anything to you so why don't you leave him be?" The words flowed evenly, calculatingly, and without rancor. His voice betrayed little of the mounting rage building inside his wiry frame, however.

Charlie Nash had grown familiar with this angry feeling lately; much like pus from a festering boil surging through his veins. He seldom displayed the pure rage he lived with—except when provoked, as now. His eyes drifted from one antagonist to another, carefully calculating his next move. He relaxed his shoulders and moved gently on to the balls of his feet.

The younger Slocum separated. The antagonists stood on either side of Posey's defender. Tension rose.

Posey felt compelled to speak. "Hey. It's okay. Really. I'll just pick up my books. . ." He glanced at his attackers and finished with, ". . . or not." He watched the Slocum's slip around into position.

The younger Slocum stuck a leg behind Posey and shoved him backward to the pavement. Posey's head bounced off the concrete. A dazzling display of multi-colored stars whizzed before his eyes. At the same time, Vernon Slocum swung a large fist at Charlie, but missed. The smaller boy had seen the punch coming and leaned back.

Slocum reeled, lost his balance entirely as his errant swing carried him past Charlie. As he turned for another shot, a rock-hard fist from Charlie slammed into his nose instead.

All the boys heard the sound of collapsing cartilage. Slocum dropped like a stone—holding his bleeding, broken nose.

Charlie turned to Louis and in the blink of an eye, two punches—one to the gut, and a second to the soft tissue on the side of his neck, drove the fight from him. Louis joined his brother on the ground.

Vernon regained his footing and charged head first into Charlie. The top of his head struck the smaller boy in the back. Without seeming to notice, he in turn flung up his elbow, whipped his upper torso around, and smacked the older boy in the ear. Slocum collapsed in a heap. This time he did not get up.

Posey stood in awe. He watched as the boy took a deep breath, unclenched his fists, and bent to retrieve Posey's broken glasses. "Here, you'll probably need these," he said and handed over the broken pieces. "Hope you can fix 'em."

"Some adhesive tape should work. Happened before." Posey replied. "My name's Russell. What's yours?"

"Charlie Nash," the boy replied and bent to retrieve the scattered books.

"Nice to meet you. Seen you play hockey. Thanks for the help." Posey gingerly fingered the painful lump forming on the back of his head.

"No problem." Nash turned to the Slocums. "Those two've had this coming for a long time. Kinda been waiting to have a go at those jerks for a lot of years." Charlie eyed the Slocums as he spoke.

"Watch your back, Nash," Vernon Slocum snarled as he and his brother crept away.

"Anytime, Slocum," Charlie replied. "Come on, Russ. We'll be late for school." Charlie flexed his hand and glanced down at rapidly swelling knuckles.

Posey noticed. "You okay?"

"Yeah. I'll be fine."

They walked to the corner and crossed Hennepin to West High School. "You just move here, Russell? Haven't seen you around before."

"Yeah. My dad was transferred from Indianapolis. We moved into Kenwood a month ago."

"Oh? Where?" Nash asked.

"Sheridan Avenue. . . near the railroad yards."

"No kiddin'? That's so cool. My grandmother lives on Sheridan too. We live down by Kenwood School. On Oliver, just a few blocks away."

"Uh, well maybe we'll see each other again," Posey offered hopefully.

"Yeah. For sure," Nash answered. "You a junior?"

"Yep."

"Me too. Maybe we'll have some classes together." Charlie Nash held the door for Posey, and the two boys slipped into the school.

* * * * *

A DARK, PLYMOUTH SEDAN parked across from West High School came to life. The tall man at the wheel had witnessed the entire fight. He smiled wryly and with just a touch of admiration. *Tough little shit,* he thought. *Have to remember that . . .*

He made a U-turn and drove to the Rainbow Café on the corner of Hennepin and Lake Street. He parked and went inside. His employer's instructions had been specific: Observe the Nash boy, but under no circumstance was he to engage the kid. He had been instructed to phone his employer every few days. He was due to make that call.

He stepped into the phone booth, dialed the number, and waited. The phone was answered by a woman, "Hello?" Her voice soft, sexy, he thought. *Wonder what she looks like?*

"It's me. Let me talk to him," the man said. He waited.

39

"Yes? What can you report?" A male voice asked.

"Kid got into a fight this morning defending some other kid. I'd say the two guys he cleaned up on are pissed off and will probably want to retaliate at some point."

"Make sure they don't. But, keep it quiet. Understand?" the voice on the other end said.

"Consider it done."

"I'm getting closer and closer to the target, so it won't be long. Turns out there may be more of a reward for our efforts than we thought."

"Yeah? How so?"

"Something else turned up. Not sure what, exactly. Kid won't let me see it, but he's got something valuable stashed someplace . . . maybe in the old man's safe deposit. Anyway, I found some notes in Foster's desk. Metallurgical results. Reads like it's some mysterious, very valuable mineral, I think. Not sure how much there is, but it was all supposed to be hush, hush. Could be very, very valuable. So we are on task. I'm getting close to the target, but need you to make sure the boy doesn't interfere. Everything's falling into place after your superb work last fall. Call me tomorrow. And keep an eye on the kid."

"You got it. By the way, you were supposed to pay me double, remember? The envelope was light."

"Yeah, I know." The man paused. "You sure about body number two? They couldn't find him, you know."

"Yeah. I'm positive. Whacked him on the head when he came back to shore . . . he fell back in the water. If the blow didn't kill him . . . he drowned. Count on it. And get me paid. Do you have any idea how hard it was putting that deal together? No comment? Well, let's set the record straight, Boss Man. I had to reconnoiter from some shitty old maps at the County Courthouse. Then, I have to walk forever on some long forgotten road—through the rain, to the area they were hunting.

And then, cleverly sabotage the boat to make it look like a tragic accident. 'Course it didn't hurt to have all that rain to help fill the boat. So, don't even think about shorting me on this one, Boss Man, or I'll come lookin' for you. I won't be in a very good mood either."

"I'll mail it tonight," the voice said. "Same PO box?"

"Yes. Goodbye," the man said.

"Take care of any interference," the voice instructed.

"Count on it . . ."

He hung up, stepped from the booth, and settled on a stool at the counter. "Fried egg sandwich, miss."

The waitress nodded and put the order in.

Kinda cute, he thought as he watched the waitress tuck a stray strand of auburn hair behind her ear. *Looks a bit like a librarian. Maybe I'll hang around here for a while . . . see what comes up.*

Seven

IT HAD BEEN A NIGHTMARE of a fall and winter for Charlie Nash. After the tragic events at Shepherd Lake the previous October, the teenager had slipped into a deep, stifling depression. He could barely remember anything after the accident.

Divers from the Cass County Sheriff's Office had been unable to find his father's body and determined that, because the lake was so deep, the body sank to a depth they couldn't search. Perhaps weighted down forever by boots and hunting gear.

The lake froze soon after the accident, and the authorities felt they didn't have sufficient funds to continue the search over the winter. They recovered Earl Foster's body with a life jacket wrapped around his neck. He floated to shore. Frank Nash's body was never recovered.

A memorial service was held in mid-December at Lake of the Isles Lutheran Church, the same church where Charlie had been confirmed. Charlie's mother and grandmother felt it important to have the service before Christmas. The church was across from Lake of the Isles, where Charlie spent summers playing ball on the grasslands surrounding the lake, and winters playing hockey. Charlie spent many, many days there as a much younger boy playing cowboys and Indians over on one of the lake's two islands with his neighborhood gang. He relished those days. It all seemed to be so far away from this sad day . . .

Now back in the old church, but for a much different reason. He glanced at the pew to his left where he had sat with his parents a few years ago for his confirmation. A knot formed in his chest. His eyes watered as the reality of why they were here hit him. Hard.

The service was a blur. Devastated by the loss of his father and ridden with guilt, Charlie floated in a dark world, a place he remembered all too well when he had run away from home as a twelve-year-old. He was unable to shake the depression he now felt.

The funeral was attended by hundreds of friends and well-wishers. There were still many adoring fans who remembered, "Fearless Frankie" Nash and his gridiron exploits.

Charlie's good friend, Quill Purdue, Quill's wife, Maggie, son, Cort, and his wife, Maxine Purdue, and their daughter, Sarah, all made the long drive from Blue Springs, South Dakota, to attend the service. Charlie felt a small measure of comfort by their presence. While struck by how cute Sarah had become and managed to gracefully grow into her body, his bitterness permitted little appreciation of her beauty.

In addition, Charlie's longtime friend, Penny Tercel remained close by during the funeral, and at Charlie's urging, sat next to him during the service. Penny was feeling warmly possessive about her close friend at that moment. They had been very good friends for many years. She held his hand now, and squeezed tightly as the pastor spoke glowingly about Frank Nash.

Penny and Charlie had been friends since early childhood, and as they both grew up, what was once merely an innocent friendship had naturally blossomed into the potential for something more. But, what, exactly, neither teen could or would verbalize. The former tomboy, Penny, who played hockey with Charlie and his buddies, had, in her own right, grown into a strikingly attractive young lady. Penny had gladly accompanied Charlie to various school functions during their sophomore year, and while neither teen could put into words what exactly their relationship had evolved to, they enjoyed each other's company immensely.

At this moment, Penny felt compelled to hang onto Charlie. Especially after being introduced to his comely friend from South Dakota, Sarah Purdue. Penny had heard about Sarah—mainly from Charlie's mother. The relationship between Charlie and Sarah had never been of concern to Penny until this moment when she finally met Sarah.

Penny thought Sarah Purdue was every bit as nice as Charlie's mother had said. Still, she felt a new and unfamiliar sense of propriety when it came to her childhood buddy. She was jealous. This feeling was new, maddening but, at the same time, strangely wonderful.

Charlie did not recognize all the emotions flowing from Penny. While he had occasionally wondered if he and Penny could ever have a typical, boy-girl relationship, right now his thoughts and feelings all focused on his father. That is, his father's tragic death. Suddenly he felt he had to get away. He was having trouble breathing and began sweating. He tugged at his collar.

Penny noticed his discomfort. "You okay?" she whispered.

"No." He started to rise, but Penny tugged him back.

"Wait. Pastor's almost done," she said.

Once the service was finished, guests lined up to pass through a reception line before heading to a light lunch laid out in the fellowship hall. Penny led him to the head of the line and helped him through the ordeal. She faithfully remained at his side.

Charlie shook one last hand. He had to leave. "I'll be back in a minute, Penn." Charlie slipped out of the line and darted away. His arm ached from shaking so many hands. Eyes blurred. He had barely been able to mumble intelligible greetings to the well-wishers. He retreated down into the church kitchen. He needed to be alone.

His old friend, Quill Purdue, found him there a short time later. "Charlie? You okay, son?" Quill inquired as he draped an arm around the boy's shoulder. He waited for a reply. Charlie was silent. "Don't do this, Charlie. Your dad wouldn't want this from you."

Charlie lowered his head and choked out, "I can't help it, Quill. I . . . I just feel so . . . I don't know . . . lost. It's worse than when I ran away."

"Look at me son." He lifted the boy's chin and looked directly into his blue eyes. "You have to get past all this. Your mother needs you now more than ever. In time, things will ease a bit. I know about your pain, son. Remember my grandson, Justin?" Quill's eyes glistened with the remembrance of the death of his grandson back on the farm at Blue Springs.

"I remember, Quill, but this . . . this is different. On top of everything else, it was my fault, Quill, and . . . and, that . . . hurts. It hurts so much," Charlie replied, choking back tears of anguish.

"Come here, Charlie. Sit down." Purdue had once been a tall man. Now, age had taken a toll . . . he stooped a bit, and his shoulders slumped. Pure white hair, worn long, feathered his ears and framed a kindly, leathery face sun-burned from many days in the orchard.

The old man and his young friend sat on a couple of folding chairs in a relatively quiet corner of the warm kitchen. Church volunteers scurried about cleaning dishes and washing serving platters. They shook heads and nodded knowingly, but chose to let Charlie and Quill keep their conversation private.

"First of all, the accident was not your fault. It was raining . . . hard, remember?"

"Yeah, but what about the plug? I checked that before we left, Quill." Charlie paused, then continued. "At least I think I did. Don't know how it came loose . . . Everything's so foggy."

"The plug could easily have dislodged, son. The boat was old, the plug just as old. It probably didn't fit very tight, you know?"

Charlie breathed deeply, looked at his old friend and said, "But, I should have stayed with Dad, Quill . . . or, or gone back out with him to get Mr. Foster."

"No, you shouldn't have, Charlie. You would probably have drowned. Your father knew what he was doing. He wanted you to stay safe. He trusted you to get to the other side of the lake. You did." Quill laid a heavy hand on Charlie's arm. "Look at me, son." He waited for Charlie to match his gaze.

"The accident was a sum of events, Charlie. Whatever happened was beyond your control. That boat was twenty years old. It sank. They found almost no flotation under the seats. It couldn't support two men, but you or your father had no way of knowing that." Purdue waited for a response from the distraught boy.

Charlie studied his older friend. Something he had said triggered a remembrance. A brief spark in his blue eyes shown. He sat straight and said, "No. That's not right, Quill. There was always a bunch of foam stuck under each seat. I used to see pieces of it in the bottom of the boat . . . from the mice. They nested in there. One time I felt under my seat to see what was there and felt a big chunk of foam." His voice adamant.

Purdue considered the boys words and carefully replied, "Well, then something happened to the flotation under those seats, Charlie. Time, I suspect. Or, the mice you mentioned—must have chewed most of it up over the winter." There could be no other explanation, the old man believed.

Charlie considered Quill's reasoning with a worried look. "I don't know, Quill. Something's not right. I just . . . I don't know, it feels all wrong to me."

In spite of the old man's attempts to relieve Charlie's guilt, Quill could see he wasn't having any success. *Time for a diversion*, Quill decided.

Charlie looked over the kitchen at the church ladies as they busily continued banging pans and dishes during their cleanup.

"Lemme tell you a story, son. Might help sort all this out. If not, it's a fun story anyway. Okay?"

"Sure."

"This is a true story about a friend of mine. His name's Bill." Quill cleared his throat and adjusted his rump on the hard chair.

"This is about Bill's parents. An older couple. Seems the father never drove a car. At least Bill never *saw* his father drive one."

"Never?"

"Nope. Never. Father's name was Bert and said he quit driving in 1927 when he was forty-five. Last car he drove was a 1926 Whippet. 'In those days,' Bert said, 'to drive a car you had to do lots of things with your hands, and more things with your feet, and look every which way. So, I decided I could walk through life and enjoy it, or drive through it . . . and miss it.'

"'Oh, bullshit,' Bert's wife said. She had been listening. 'You hit a horse.'

"'Well, there was that, too,' the old man replied.

"So, Bill, grew up in a household without a car. Whenever Bill asked why all the neighbors had cars, and they didn't, their mother said, 'No one in this family drives. Period.'

"But one day when Bill turned sixteen, the father decided it was time they had a family auto. So in 1946, the father bought a used Chevrolet. A stick shift of course—four-door model, white with fender skirts. Loaded. But what was peculiar was that because neither of the parents drove, it became Bill's car."

"Now, having a car and not being able to drive it didn't bother old Bert, but it didn't make sense to the mother. So, in 1947 when she was seventy years old, she asked a friend to teach her to drive. Bert gave his okay to the project but insisted they practice in a nearby cemetery. 'Who can your mother hurt in a cemetery?' Bert asked.

"Anyway, for the next many years, until she was eighty-three, the mother, Agnes was her name . . . She was the driver for her husband. Neither she nor her husband had any sense of direction, but Bert loaded up on maps. They seldom left the city, but he appointed himself navigator. It seemed to work according to Bill.

"After he retired, Bert almost always accompanied Agnes whenever she drove, even if he had no reason to go along. If she were going to the beauty parlor, he'd sit in the car and read or take a stroll. If it was summer, he'd wander into a nearby saloon to listen to the Cubs game on the radio.

"In the evening, then, when Bill would stop by, he'd explain, 'Cubs lost again. The millionaire on second base made a bad throw to the millionaire on first base, so the multi-millionaire on third base scored.'" Quill paused as Charlie snickered.

"Okay, so now you see what kind of guy old Bert is, right?"

Charlie nodded knowingly, a smile creased his lips. "Sharp. A thinker."

"Yep. Once when Bert was ninety-five and Agnes was still driving, the old man said to Bill, 'You want to know the secret to a long life?'

"'I guess so,' Bill said somewhat dubiously, knowing the answer would probably be something bizarre.

"'No left turns,' the father declared.

"'What?' Bill asked.

"'No left turns,' he repeated. 'Listen up. Several years ago, your mother and I read an article that said most accidents that happen to old people occur when they turn *left* into oncoming traffic. See, as you get older, your eyesight worsens. You lose your depth perception,' he said. 'So, your mother and I decided never again to make a left turn.'

"'What?' Bill asked again incredulously.

"'Yep. No left turns. Think about it. Three rights are the same as a left—it eventually gets you headed the same way . . . just a block away is all. And that's a lot safer than making lefts. So, we always make three rights.'"

Quill paused waiting for Charlie's reaction. By now the teenager had straightened and his eyes sparkled. He seemed eager to hear the conclusion to this peculiar parable. "Okay, keep going," Charlie said.

Satisfied he was having an impact, Quill continued. "So, Bill says to his father, 'You're kidding right?' He turned to his mother for support. 'No,' she said. 'Your father's correct. We make three rights. No left turns. Ever. It works.' But, then she added, 'Except when your father loses count.'

"'Loses count?' Bill asked.

"'Yes,' his father lamented. 'That sometimes happens. But it's not a problem. You just make seven rights, and you're okay again.'"

"Of course, Bill couldn't resist digging further and asked, 'Do you ever go for eleven?'

"'Oh, no' Bert said. 'If we miss it at seven, we just come home and call it a bad day. Besides, nothing in life is so important it can't be put off until another day . . . or another week.'"

Charlie was smiling broadly now. So was Quill. "I don't know what the moral to all this is, Charlie, but maybe if you remember this, 'No left turn' strategy when you're up against a tough situation, well, it might help you get past it . . . maybe lead you to make some other choice, ya know? Seems to me you're at a place like that now, son, and you oughta think about three rights instead of taking a left."

Neither Quill nor Charlie spoke for a long time. Quill's friendship meant the world to the boy, and the old man's stories always left Charlie feeling smarter, wiser even, for some time after. "Thanks, Quill." He reached out and shook the older man's hand. Charlie fought against an urge to slip back into his earlier gray mood.

Quill held on to Charlie for a long time. His time with the boy back on the road to Blue Springs a few years earlier, had been extremely meaningful to him. Charlie was special and the old man was very fond of the boy, as well as his family. "Come on, Charlie. Let's get back to your mother," Quill suggested. He draped an arm over the boy's shoulders and squeezed him close. Their brief embrace meant much to both.

Charlie felt a bit better, but primarily it was due to seeing his very good friend again. The events out in South Dakota had been at once terrifying and nightmarish, but they resulted in a wonderfully warm and memorable relationship with Quill.

They went upstairs. Charlie rejoined his mother and Penny. Marsha Nash was very fond of the neighbor girl Charlie had grown up with. She and the Tercels had often privately discussed whether or not Charlie and Penny might someday become a, "couple." Marsha looked at her son now and noticed the two teens holding hands. Her heart swelled. She caught Penny's eye and winked. Penny blushed and leaned a bit closer to Charlie.

As that sad day drew to a close, Charlie said his good-byes to everyone, and walked the Purdue family to the old station wagon. He thanked everyone for coming. Sarah, who was a year older, pulled Charlie to one side and said, "Charlie? I think your friend has a serious crush on you." She poked him in the arm. "Huh? You two dating?"

To that point, Charlie hadn't noticed that a great deal had changed between himself and Penny. However, he considered what their hand-holding meant, and of course was aware of both his mother and the Tercel's not-so-subtle comments about, "Charlie and Penny." He wasn't certain he was ready for that involvement.

"Nah . . . Penny's just a good friend, Sarah." As he spoke the words, he felt dishonest. Deep down, he knew the relationship he and Penny had was more than just being, "friends."

But, this was all unfamiliar territory, and the teen was uncomfortable talking about any of it . . . especially with Sarah. He wondered later if others held the same thoughts about himself and Penny, and made a note to ask his friend Posey what he thought.

For now, he tried to dismiss Sarah's comment, with a casual, "By the way, Quill tells me you're going steady, Sarah? Is Cort okay with that?"

Sarah leaned close. She whispered, "Hush. I'm not sure Mom has told him."

"What's his name?"

"Tom . . . uh, Tommy."

Charlie smiled and prodded a bit. "And?"

Sarah laughed. "What?"

"Tell me about him," Charlie insisted.

"Well, he's a senior too. Captain of the basketball team. He has a full scholarship to South Dakota State." She was clearly proud of her boyfriend.

"That's great, Sarah," Charlie said and meant it. Sarah was a neat girl, and he wanted nothing but good things for Quill's only grandchild. She had suffered greatly during the events at Blue Springs, and Charlie was very pleased she'd recovered and was having a good life now.

So, having successfully deflected attention back to Sarah, and away from himself, Charlie finished with, "I won't tell your dad. Go on and get in the car. Maybe I'll see you out at the ranch this summer."

"Bye, Charlie. I hope so. Then you can meet, Tommy." She gave him a kiss on the cheek and climbed in the car. She rolled down the window, and finished with, "Penny's very nice . . . you be nice to her. Hear?" They all waved as the station wagon pulled away.

The rekindling of that warmth with the Purdues and other family members at the service proved to be short-lived, however. The sadness and bitterness he had been feeling would return . . . and deepen. Nothing he tried as a diversion—even a maniacal devotion to hockey could alleviate his pain. Having made the West High varsity hockey team in his sophomore year had done wonders for his confidence, but after his father's death, his attitude still teetered between relatively easy to be with to being a total pain in the butt.

Posey confirmed that his relationship with Penny publicly seemed to be more than just, "casual." Hearing that, Charlie promptly avoided further contact with his childhood friend for quite some time. He wasn't ready for such a commitment. As he thought about the subject, it felt more like he'd been following a prescription laid out for him by others. Charlie was smart enough to have sensed long ago how much everyone expected that he and Penny would be together throughout high school—and beyond. It was this expectation he rebelled against. A very similar reaction to what he felt about his father's fervent wish for Charlie to follow in his footsteps as a football player.

Both subjects never seemed to allow for a free choice in Charlie's mind. And now, when it came to the subject of his relationship with Penny, it felt as if he had lost all voice in the matter. It was not entirely his choice. It was too easy. This seemed to be one of Quill's, "left turns" into traffic.

Decision made, he stopped seeing Penny without saying a word. He avoided her in school, around the neighborhood, and wouldn't answer the phone when she called.

Penny took the rejection quite hard. She tried talking to Charlie to find out what she had done to upset him, but he avoided her. He refused to even talk to her other than to lamely claim, "he was too busy with hockey." Penny was crushed. Her relationship with Charlie had been very important and meaningful to her, and his sudden rejection left her feeling lost and bewildered.

In fact, Charlie had stepped off a dangerous emotional ledge. The choices and decisions he had been making were flawed, but the sixteen-year-old was helpless to halt the free-fall. He rebuffed all attempts to bring him out of his self-imposed isolation . . . isolation from family, most friends, and of course, Penny Tercel.

Penny gave up all attempts to talk to her friend, and avoided Charlie for the next few months. If they were about to meet in the halls, she turned away and headed in the other direction. Many times in the past they had walked to and from school together. They no longer did, and wouldn't speak to each other again for weeks and weeks.

* * * * *

"HELLO?" THE VOICE on the phone said.

"It's me. Is he in?"

"Just a minute."

"Yes?" the man answered. "What have you to report?"

"Got the envelope today. Still a bit light though, my friend."

"What? We agreed on six thousand . . . three apiece, right?"

"Uh, uh. No. You forget how I had to go muckin' around in that god-forsakin' swamp . . . chasing through the woods and stumbling around in the dark. Are you shittin' me? It's five a piece and cheap at that," The man stated.

"All right. All right. I'm a little short right now. This is taking longer than I thought. Give me a couple weeks. I've almost reached a point where I'll have control of everything . . . be patient, Splinter."

"Hey! No names, remember?" Tambor Splinter was fanatical about his employers' not using his real name. "Call me Victor if you have to call me anything."

"Sorry. I forgot. Okay, Victor it is. Anyway, what's been going on?"

"I attended the service for Nash. The kid spent much of the time with an old guy named Purdue and holdin' hands with his girlfriend. Not sure who Purdue is. Drives a station wagon with South Dakota plates."

"I know about him. The boy traveled with Purdue out to South Dakota. They're close, I'm told. The girl's Penny Tercel. Might be a way to use her to get what we need. I'll keep track of her."

"Well, if this Purdue gets in the way, then what?"

"Do what you have to do, but only if necessary."

"Got it. What else?"

"What about the other two kids? The ones he got in a fight with?" the voice asked.

"Done . . . won't bother anyone for a while. Add two grand to what you owe me, Boss Man. Let's wrap this up pretty soon. I'm getting bored.

Nervous. Don't like being exposed this long. Pretty soon I'll have to move on . . . got other offers."

"Right. We're close. I promise."

"Better be. I'll phone in a couple of days. Going to the kid's hockey game tonight . . . he's actually pretty good . . . has a future in college I'd say, unless something happens along the way. Know what I mean?"

The man now known as Victor hung up. He strolled down the block . . . He rolled his new name around in his head. *Kinda' like that,* Splinter thought. *Best one I've used yet . . .*

Eight

IT WASN'T LONG BEFORE Charlie formed a new, constant friendship with Russell Posey. They had walked home together that rainy, sleety Monday after the confrontation with the Slocum brothers, and spent much of that following winter developing a strong bond.

Charlie's time and energy was focused on hockey that winter. Daily practices and numerous games around the city as he traveled with his high school team to various venues.

As a junior, he quickly developed into one of West High School's leading scorers. He was fast, had very soft, clever hands, and loved to work the puck back and forth with his line mates, John (Morrie) Peyson and John (Shelly) Shelton.

But, Charlie continued to brood about the loss of his father. Ridden with guilt that he should have done more that rainy night in October, Charlie's sour mood affected most of his behavior. Hockey and help from his close friends saw him escape that reality sometimes. He was most at peace when on the ice. It seemed that only then could he lose himself in the game he loved.

As the winter season moved along, it became evident that Charlie's team, the "Cowboys," would have a difficult time moving past the Minneapolis City Conference playoffs to the prize all Minnesota hockey players coveted: the state tournament held in St Paul. The boys on the team all had hope, however.

The team's coach, Tom Warner, was also the high school biology teacher. Charlie enjoyed Mr. Warner's classes, and at times received favorable treatment because of hockey. Mr. Warner was well aware of the tragic events of the previous fall and went out of his way to make sure the Nash boy didn't have to deal with any more than he was capable of handling.

Charlie soon developed a strong attachment for Warner. When he learned of the coach's extensive hockey background, including a career at Dartmouth College, a Winter Olympic stint, and a pro-tryout, Charlie had a new hero. Warner knew and understood the game of hockey, and while the kids he worked with in the West High area came from varied environments, every now and then a few boys appeared for tryouts with certain innate, natural abilities. Warner could recognize pure talent when he saw it, and he quickly spotted glimpses of that unique talent in the Nash boy.

"I just hope he doesn't get derailed by his father's death," Warner commented to one of his two assistant coaches. "He's got too much talent to waste, Ben."

Ben Addison, a recent college graduate and former hockey player for the University of Minnesota Gophers, nodded his assent. "I agree, Coach. He's a natural. Really fast, and I love his play-making. Actually, I have a hard time keeping up with him when you and I scrimmage with them."

"You think he's Division One talent?" Warner asked, knowing that Addison, as a recent graduate, had a better take on what was required to play college hockey in 1960 than he did.

"Maybe, Coach. Depends on how he matures . . . needs to grow some, I think. A bit too light right now. He's a tough little mutt, though. Competitive as hell. Won't back down, that's for sure."

"Yeah, but that temper of his could detract from his overall game. Not sure he can get past his father's death and lose all that anger. If he loses focus now . . . " Coach's voice trailed off.

"Yeah, he's been taking too many penalties, Coach. We need him on the ice—not in the penalty box."

"You know, sometimes I think he goes out of his way to get into a scrap. He can't play like that and hope to move up to the next level," Warner said.

"Maybe have a little talk with him, Coach?" Addison suggested.

"Yeah. Might be a good idea. He's a real likeable kid when he's not pissed-off. I'd like to see how far we can go in the conference playoffs, and we need him to be at the top of his game." Warner concluded with, "I'll have a little chat with Charlie after class tomorrow."

Charlie and Posey soon discovered that even though their backgrounds were quite different, they shared many of the same interests. Both loved the outdoors, were amused by many of the same things in life—mostly people related, had developing interests in the opposite sex—but little experience, and both loved the game of hockey. Posey merely as a fan and observer, however.

Their other commonality was an almost total freedom to do whatever they pleased. Posey's parents gave the boy free reign to pretty much go where he wanted and when. Charlie's mom was too distracted by her own interests—including a growing involvement with the new family financial advisor, Duane Silk. Dealing with her own grief, she failed to pay much attention to her son.

So, whenever Charlie wasn't either practicing, traveling with the team, or playing games for the Cowboys, he and Posey hung together. It was a friendship that rapidly grew and developed.

Coach Warner pulled Charlie aside one day after class, as he had promised. "Charlie, can I talk to you for a minute?"

"Sure, Coach." Charlie stepped out of the line of departing students.

"Have a seat, son," Warner offered.

Charlie sat in the chair next to Warner's desk. He laid his books down on the corner and waited.

"Big game Friday, Charlie. If we can't get past Southwest, our season's over."

Charlie was well aware of the importance of the up-coming game, but not what Coach was leading to. He waited for more information.

"You have the potential to be a very good, college-level hockey player, Charlie." Warner paused to test the boy's reaction. He knew he was venturing into treacherous waters regarding the boy's psyche. "Potentially," he added.

Charlie's face reddened. He was both embarrassed, and thrilled to hear such encouragement coming from someone like Coach Warner. He didn't know what to say. He coughed, and waited again.

"Did you hear what I said, son?"

"Yes, Coach . . . but I'm not real big, ya know. Probably a real long shot, right?"

"That's the potential I mentioned, Charlie. Yes. You think you'd like to play college hockey?"

"Sure. Who wouldn't?" His voice rose a fraction as he considered such a thing. But then, negative thoughts crept back. "No telling if I'm going to grow much, though. My dad was pretty big . . ." Charlie choked and couldn't continue as he spoke about his father.

Warner studied the boy and decided to jump in with both feet. "I'm not talking about how big you are or aren't, Charlie. Whether you grow more between now and your senior year is irrelevant. I'm talking about your attitude: Both on and off the ice." Warner hesitated and observed Charlie's reaction. The boy's eyes glistened and bore into the older man's.

"I'm not sure what . . ." Charlie began. He was confused.

"Horse crap, Charlie!" Warner blurted. "You know exactly what I'm talking about. Ever since your father's accident, you've been going around like a bomb just waiting for a fuse to set it off. You are far too good a player to take those stupid, cheap penalties and waste your time in the box."

"But . . . I thought . . ."

"I'm not buying any more excuses. Get over it, Charlie. I'm talking to you as your friend now . . . not as your coach. I'd love to work with you for the next two years and see if we can't get you a college scholarship some-place—maybe even out East at one of the Ivy League schools. But it won't happen and I can't work with you unless you change your attitude."

Charlie was stunned. He didn't know what to say. His spine stiffened and instead of acquiescing as Warner had hoped, instead, he felt betrayed.

"Charlie. Listen to me, please? I knew your dad . . . quite well, actually. You probably didn't know that. Your dad wanted to keep our friendship quiet so you didn't think your making varsity would be anything but on your own merits." Warner waited. "Through another friend of your dad's, he arranged for a college hockey scout to come west and give me a look. I couldn't afford college and your dad knew that. Anyway, thanks to Frank Nash, I got my scholarship to Dartmouth, and I'll always be grateful to him. Believe me, son, he would not want you behaving as you are right now. He'd want you to work to your full potential . . . whatever that might be. Don't disappoint him, Charlie. Don't disappoint yourself."

Charlie's reaction was muted. "Is that all, Coach?" Charlie grabbed his books and flexed his knees—ready to stand.

Warner's head dropped. Saddened at the boy's response, he said, "Yes, Charlie. That's all. Think about what I just said. Okay?"

"Yes, sir," Charlie muttered as he spun away and left the classroom.

Friends don't treat friends that way, he mused as he stomped down the empty hall to his locker. Quill certainly wouldn't have spoken to him that way. *Or would he?* Charlie wondered.

Practice later that evening was uneventful. Charlie skated as if in a trance. Uninspired, resentful of the coach's words, the boy spoke little to his good friends and teammates. Morrie and Shelly were puzzled by Charlie's mood, but too involved with trying to make something happen on the ice. They didn't say anything.

Game day arrived. The city conference championship game with Southwest. The Minneapolis Arena was jammed with students from both schools. Coach Warner had little to say to his team before the big game. He knew the boys were fired up. Instead, as was his habit, he scribbled one of his favorite slogans on the chalkboard:

"BRICK WALLS ARE THERE TO STOP THOSE
WHO DON'T WANT IT BADLY ENOUGH."

Warner scanned the quiet room and glanced at Charlie as he finished. He was unable to detect what sort of mood the boy was in, or if what he had written had had any effect.

Assistant coach, Ben Addison went around the locker room and had a few words to say to each boy. His last stop was Charlie.

"You ready, Charlie?" He sat down next to the boy with his arm around his shoulders.

Charlie looked up and to the side. "I think so, Ben. Pretty nervous, ya know?"

"Yeah, I remember that feeling. That's good though, Charlie. It means you care and your body is telling you it's ready to perform. Just play your game, Charlie. If they try to take you out of your game with any rough, chippy stuff, just skate away, okay?"

Charlie considered the coach's words and nodded. "Sure, Ben. I'll do my best."

The Cowboys were awful for the first period. The score was 3 to 0 in favor or Southwest. At the intermission, Coach Warner waited until the boys had settled in the locker room, then stormed through the door.

"Here's the deal, boys. You've been playing worse and worse every day lately and now you're playing like it's already tomorrow!" He paused for maximum effect. "Get your heads up. Move your feet. Pass the damn puck to the open man, instead of hanging on to it like it's made of gold! It's a simple game, boys—not rocket science. Come on! Let's start playing hockey!" Warner left the room without another word.

After Coach's tirade and curious metaphor, the boys played the next two periods and finished with their best game of the year. Charlie scored two goals, assisted on one more, and only took one penalty. His friends and linemates were key to not only Charlie's great game, but to the team's success as well. Shelton also contributed with a goal, and Peyson added two assists.

Tied 4 to 4 at the end of regulation, the game went to overtime. At the nine-minute mark, Charlie picked up a loose puck, glanced to his right, and saw Peyson crossing the center ice red line. He knew he could thread the puck through one of the Southwest defenders so he flipped a gentle pass over the opponent's stick to Peyson and flew across the blue line into the offensive zone.

Charlie tapped his stick on the ice for the expected return pass. He knew he had a clear path to the goal as the defenseman was occupied at center ice. Peyson fed the puck to Shelton instead. He then tried to pass the puck to Charlie on his back hand—a weak move at best, and the puck slid off the heel of his stick directly to the opposing winger.

The Southwest player gathered in the puck and headed back the other way. As he neared the Cowboy's blue line, he was confronted by defender, Tim McInerny. The player tossed a desperation shot towards the West High goal tender that skittered through McInerny's legs.

The puck bounced twice, fluttered crazily, and flopped beneath the goalie's out-stretched glove. It was the winning goal. The game and season were over.

Nine

few weeks later, at the end of February, Charlie and Posey walked home from school. They had become quite good friends by now and chatted about hockey, specifically the winners of the recent state championship played in St Paul.

"Still can't believe Southwest won state," Charlie muttered.

"Yeah, I know. Just think: If you guys'd won that last game, you might be champions now instead of Southwest."

"Maybe, maybe not. Southwest was a really good team, Pose. I think we were lucky to play them as close as we did."

"I don't know. Anyway, hockey's a great game to watch," Posey offered. "I watched all your games, Charlie. You're really good."

"Huh. Not sure about that. But, for the most part, at least until that last game. We had a shitty year this winter. I didn't help much, either," Charlie replied thinking about his last conversation with Coach Warner.

"Nah. I thought you were the best kid on the ice in the Southwest game. You seemed different, somehow. Like you really cared and just wanted to play hockey. I don't know what happened, but for the first time, you looked like you were having fun . . . smiling even when some of those Southwest goons tried to run you into the boards." He kicked at an ice clod and continued. "Your goalie sucks, though. He's a sieve. Get a goalie that can stop something smaller than a basketball, and you guys would have been *really* good."

Nash smiled. Posey was right. They did have a lousy goalie. No matter what he and his teammates did offensively, Terrence "The Claw" Hornsby couldn't stop much of anything. "Yeah, maybe you're right."

"I know I'm right. Crap, that last game you scored two goals, and you guys still lost 5 to 4. It's the goalie. Trust me," Posey offered with a degree of finality.

A seldom-seen twinkle shone in Charlie's eye. "You ever play, Russ?"

"I was a pretty good skater, but there wasn't any organized hockey where I come from."

"Can you catch?" Charlie asked.

"Yeah . . . . Why?"

"You should try out for goalie next year."

"Hah! With my eyes? Look at these." Posey removed his glasses and waved them at Charlie. The glasses flashed from the overhead lights. He carefully settled them back on his face. "I'd have to buy a pair of contact lenses—course that'll never happen—too much dough, ya know? So, I don't think I'm your guy, Charlie, but thanks for thinking I might have a chance."

"Well, let's talk about it. I want to try something with you later on. We'll go down to the rink. Ice's still solid. The boards are still up. I've got a baseball glove so I'll shoot some tennis balls at you. Think the nets are still on the rink too. It'll be fun."

"Okay." Posey looked doubtful. He was inclined to change the subject as he knew the chances of ever playing hockey were slim to none. "Hey, tell me about your date with Sally Stensrud."

The comment caught Charlie by surprise. "Huh. What? What about it?"

"Tell me what happened?"

"Nothing," Charlie stated, then relented. "Well, almost nothing." Having received a varsity letter the previous year as a sophomore, Charlie attracted the attention of a very popular cheerleader named Sally Stensrud.

"She invited you to the sock hop last Saturday. And . . . ?"

Charlie remembered every detail of the night, quite vividly. Sally and he had danced all the "slow" dances at her insistence. In spite of Charlie's lack of dancing prowess—and in spite of Miss Mayhew's dance class, he managed. The nubile and vibrant cheerleader pretty much led him around the floor and, before long, had pressed close into the front of his chinos. She draped both arms around his neck and breathed heavily into his ear. The scent of her perfume was intoxicating. Head spinning, unable to concentrate on what Sally was whispering, he simply mumbled, "Okay."

In point of fact, Sally had asked if they could drive to the "submarine races" with all the other kids. He apparently had concurred.

Sally bounced away and took his hand. "Good. Let's go." She tugged him off the gym floor.

"Sally, wait. What do you mean, 'submarine races'?"

"You'll see," she promised and gleefully led Charlie to his mom's Pontiac.

Charlie opened the door. Sally climbed in. As he walked to the driver's side, she slid across the seat. When Charlie got in, she was already close enough to nestle against his right leg. "This is going to be sooo much fun," she enthused.

He started the car. Then nervously put it in gear. Still uncertain about what was really going on, he asked, "Where to, Sally?"

She snuggled closer. "We have to drive to Lakewood Cemetery . . . you know, at the end of Lake Calhoun. There's a secret spot there and when we get to the end of this gravel road, turn your lights off and we park." She giggled and continued. "Then we sit and watch the lake for the submarines. They're out there . . . really." She batted her long eyelashes furiously and threw an arm behind him over the seat.

Charlie looked at Posey as he finished the telling. "I had no idea what she was talking about, Pose, but I was game for most anything at that point."

"Oh, boy! I'll bet you were," he countered. "Keep going, Charlie."

Charlie tried to describe a brand new and exciting thrill. "It was like a jolt of electricity, Pose."

"When? What do you mean?"

"When she put her hand on my thigh."

"What? Did she really? Oh, this is getting really good. Continue."

"Hmmm. Well, I really thought she was serious, Pose."

"About what?"

"The submarine races."

"What submarine races? Are you that naïve? You really are a dork, ya know? Submarine races is code for, 'let's make out,' dummy!"

"No. Really. I thought at first that maybe there was a new amusement park over there . . . hadn't been to that part of Calhoun for a while—kinda like Excelsior Park, ya know?"

"Holy Christmas!" Posey exclaimed.

"It might have been real? Right?" Charlie pleaded for understanding.

"No. No chance in hell. What happened next?"

"Well, we parked. I kept looking out the windshield. Kept waiting . . . couldn't see anything. Next thing I know, she kinda sighs real heavy like and pulls my head around. Then she's kissing me. Hard. Stuck her tongue in my mouth and started moaning."

"Oh, boy. Then what?"

"Well, we kissed some more, and I twisted around to face her, and, ah . . . well she took my left hand and put it on her sweater . . . right on her boob. Then she moaned some more and slid down in the corner, I guess . . ."

"You guess?" Posey was beside himself with envy at this point. Sally Stensrud was hot, and a date with her had to be something to remember. "Holy shit, Schmitt. You're on second base headed for third and didn't even know it!" Posey howled with laughter. "My, oh, my, Charlie. You are one simple-minded son-of-a-bitch."

Charlie smiled and was not at all angered by his friend's taunting. None of what he had felt that night was unpleasant, of course. All of it was new, exciting, and perhaps a taste of what the future held as he grew older. "Anyway, I'm not sure she'll want to go out with me again."

"Why? 'Cause you're such a dork?" then he grew wide-eyed. "Oh, no. Wait. You didn't take Taffy with you, did you?"

"Yeah. Why not? She loves to ride in the car."

Posey was incredulous. "You are such a dumb ass, Charlie. What do you think the lovely and lustful Sally was thinking about as she put the move on you while Taffy was panting in the back seat? Huh?"

"No, it wasn't that. I'm sure. It's 'cause I was such a jerk. 'Cause I didn't know what I was supposed to do. I just kinda sat there and let her do everything."

"Yeah? So what?" Posey offered. He wanted more details. "Go on. What else?"

"Well . . . I never did see a submarine." Charlie laughed.

Posey rolled his eyes. "So, you going to ask her out again?"

They had reached the corner of Oliver and Twenty-first Street. "No. I don't think Sally and I have much in common, ya know?"

"Why?"

"Hard to talk to. Besides, I heard she's dating Arnie Stenson now."

Stenson was a senior and captain of the football team. The somewhat horny, more experienced Sally had moved on. "Well, I bet Arnie doesn't take the family pet along on their dates," Posey offered.

Charlie laughed. "Probably not," and asked, "Wanna get a coke?"

"Sure." Posey replied, still hoping for more details.

They sauntered into the Kenwood Drugstore on the corner of Penn and Twenty-first.

Tabor Splinter had followed the boys from school. He lagged behind and entered the store shortly after they did. He wandered over to the magazine rack, picked up a copy of *Life Magazine*, and began flipping the pages—all the while observing the two boys.

Charlie spotted Penny at the lunch counter sipping a soda. He was actually quite happy to see her. It had been a long time and he missed her. The stool on her right was open, so he slid onto the red vinyl.

"Hi, Penn." He spun the seat toward her.

Posey sat next to Charlie.

Penny had seen the boys coming and pretended not to notice. She was not quite as tall as Charlie. With light-brown hair, athletically formed with long, slender legs. She had a wonderfully soft, clear complexion. If it weren't for her dark eyes, she and Charlie might have been mistaken for siblings. She lifted a stray strand of hair, and tucked it behind her ear, a slight maneuver that permitted her to glance at Charlie. The two had not spoken to each other for quite some time.

Penny couldn't carry on the ruse any longer. Nor, did she want to continue ignoring him. "Hey, hot shot. Great game last time out." She leaned over even further and said to Posey, "Hi, Russ. How are you?"

Posey was thrilled a girl as attractive as Penny remembered his name. "I'm good, Penny. What are you up to?"

"Needed a little ice cream before I headed home. Have to write a term paper for English."

"Ugh. Geez. That's right. I forgot about that," Posey said. "I better get home and start on that." He slid off the stool.

"Ah, sit down, Pose. We've got plenty of time. It's not due until Friday," Charlie said.

"You better pay more attention to your studies, Charlie," Penny said. "If your grades slip much more, they won't let you play hockey next year, you know." Concern for her friend filled her voice.

"Nah. No big deal. Besides, if I'm off the team, *you* can fill in for me."

"Oh, sure," she replied.

"I ever tell you about Penny? About her hockey, Pose?"

"No. Penny? You play hockey?" Posey asked and sat back down.

Penny lived three houses away from Charlie. As little kids, they spent almost all their time together. Their parents were very close friends. The families even vacationed together. Charlie and Penny and all the other boys in the neighborhood had played together since they were seven. The same bunch had been friends for many years: John Shelton, Jamie McCarthy, John Peyson, and Bob Andreason. They called themselves, the Kenwood Alley Gang as little kids; ran through the neighborhood chasing make-believe bad guys. Friendships between all were formed early and lasted for many years.

None of the bonds were any stronger than Charlie and Penny, however. The hockey players in the bunch included Peyson, Shelton, Charlie, and of course, Penny.

As the children grew, it became apparent to all the kids down at the Lake of the Isles hockey rink that Penny Tercel even on figure skates, was a better hockey player than any of the boys. "She was very, very good," Charlie reported.

As Charlie continued telling about Penny, Tabor Splinter stepped closer to listen in.

Charlie spoke glowingly of his friend. "Well, Penny could skate circles around most of us. The first teams we ever played on were just pickup games . . . nothing really organized until we were old enough for PeeWee's. "What, eleven or twelve, Penny?"

"Yes, I think so, Charlie," she replied.

"Anyway, Penny found an old pair of shin pads from her older brother, Bill, but instead of hockey gloves, she played with a pair of those bulky, leather choppers. Didn't matter much to Penny, though. She was so good, Pose. Still is, right, Penn?" Charlie nudged her gently.

Penny sipped her soda and smiled. Many times, talk of her athletic prowess compared to boys her age embarrassed her. She felt comfortable talking to Charlie and Posey, however.

"Didn't they let you play on the PeeWee team, Penny?" Posey asked.

68

"I could have . . . maybe," she said. "Don't think there were any rules about girls playing. But, my dad just didn't think I should. Too rough, he thought, after watching my brother play for a couple of years."

Posey made a mental note to ask Charlie about why he wasn't dating Penny, or more specifically, if he, Russell might have a chance with her. But for now, he rose and said, "Too bad. Might have been a hoot to see you playing on a line with Charlie." He finished with, "I gotta go. See ya in the morning, Charlie?"

"Sure. Seven fifteen?"

"Yep."

"Okay. Bye, Penny."

"Bye, Russ," she replied, and turned toward Charlie as Posey left the store. "Well, stranger? Haven't seen you for quite a while. What happened?" Her voice was full of hurt.

"Huh? Nothing happened. Why?"

"What do you mean nothing? I know you pretty well. Something's been bugging you. You've been trying to avoid me ever since . . . since your dad's funeral. Did I do something or say anything you didn't like?" Penny was on the verge of tears and had to take a sip of her soda to hold in the flood.

Splinter took a stool on the far end of the counter, his curiosity growing about the relationship between the Nash kid and the girl. He was still within earshot.

"No, Penn. I'm sorry." Charlie gently touched her arm. "It was nothing you did, honest. I . . . uh, just . . . I don't know. Just feel crappy all the time, is all."

"Is it your dad?"

"No. Yes. I don't know, Penn. Maybe. The funeral brought everything to the surface, I guess. Everyone wants me to be cheerful and happy and stuff, and I just don't feel like it. And, it's like there's a road map of my life all laid out by someone else, and I just seem to want to do the opposite and go in a different direction. And, now that hockey's over I don't have much to look forward to, ya know?"

"Does that include me, Charlie? Was I ever on that map?" Penny asked.

He considered her question, matched her gaze, and answered honesty, "Maybe. You know how our parents have always kinda pushed us together?"

She studied his face. "Hmmm. Yeah, now that you mention it. Guess I do. My mom kinda kids me about you and me once in a while, so yeah, I think that's something they probably have talked about." She leaned over and looked at him closely. "But? So what, though? Let them think what they want. No one knows what's in anyone's future, anyway, so why get all undone about it?"

Charlie laid both forearms on the counter, breathed out, and visibly relaxed. He experienced a sudden, huge sense of relief. *Leave it to Penny*, he thought. He smiled knowingly at her and said, "Thanks, Penn. I knew you'd understand."

"So. What're you going to do for a spring sport, then? Play tennis?" Penny asked, her question full of hope as she loved practicing with her friend. "Won't be long before the snow'll be gone, and you and I can play, right?" Her dark eyes sparkled as she spoke. "You were getting to be pretty good at tennis, you know. Maybe try out for the varsity?"

"Naw, tennis's your game, Penny. Not mine. You're really good. You'll make varsity again, easy. It's not as important to me like it is for you."

"Well, what are you going to do? You can't just mope around all the time."

"I don't know. Spring break's coming up in a few weeks . . . maybe I'll go up to the cabin. Got something I want to do up there."

"That's a great idea, Charlie," Penny enthused. Secretly she wished she could go with him. Penny loved being at the Nash cabin. "Will your mom let you go? Would she go with?" She was confident her parents would let her go if Mrs. Nash went along.

"No. She's too busy. She's hanging out with this family financial guy. Did you meet him last week at your parent's party?"

Penny kept her disappointment about the cabin to herself. "Yeah, I met him. Yuck! He's creepy. He kept leering at *my* mom . . ." She shuddered as she spoke the words. "Anyway, where were you? Mom was hoping you'd come. I did too," she added.

Charlie noted her disappointment. "Yeah. Probably should have. It's that guy. Silk. Duane Silk." He spit out the name.

Penny wanted to hear more about the trip north. "So, if your mom isn't going to go with you up north, who is?" She was already envisioning lots of time alone with Charlie and that felt thrilling . . . romantic, even though she knew her parents would never let her go.

"Maybe Morrie. Or Shelly. Posey could probably go."

Penny's voice dropped. "Oh, I see." Charlie clearly missed her hopeful tone.

"Yeah. Maybe Posey. The other guys don't have the same freedom Russ, does. I think most of the parents think I'm a bad influence now, or something," he added.

Penny wasn't bold enough to invite herself, so she decided to let the cabin topic lie for now. She wanted to find out more about his attitude. "Well, are you?" She asked and leaned forward to study his face. "A bad influence?"

Charlie leaned close, looked directly in her brown eyes, and said, "No, I'm not. At least I don't think so." He smiled and waved the loose strand of hair from her face. "Am I a bad influence on you?"

Penny laughed. "Probably." She bumped him with her shoulder. "But my parents always liked you Charlie, so that's never going to be an issue." She took a sip through the straw and swallowed. "Except for the time you hit me in the head with the baseball."

She laughed at the memory. She and Charlie had been playing catch in her backyard as her dad worked in the garden. Just as Charlie threw a wicked fastball at Penny, her father called out to her. She took her eyes off the ball, and it hit her smack in the forehead. Charlie was afraid he'd killed her. Mr. Tercel was livid. 'You Goddamned Dutchman,' he shouted and chased him out of the yard and down the alley.

"Oh, boy. You had to bring that up, didn't you?" Charlie said.

"Sorry. He forgave you. But not until the knot on my forehead went down."

"Yeah, three days later. I thought he was going to strangle me," he added.

"You know, people do wonder about you and some of your friends, though," Penny said sincerely.

"What do you mean?" Charlie asked.

"Hmmm. Your attitude. It's what you just said, Charlie. They wonder why you don't smile much anymore. You used to smile all the time. You used to be so happy. Now, you're so angry all the time."

He reacted quickly. "Like who? Who do you mean, Penn?" Charlie flared. "Morrie? Shelly? Posey?" Charlie softened.

"No, not them . . ." Her voice trailed off. "Some of the Bryn Marr bunch . . . the guys you play cards with."

He was a little surprised she knew about the clandestine card game. "How's you know about that?"

"It's no big secret, Charlie. Lots of people know about the card game."

"Hmmm. Well, for the most part, those guys're all okay, Penny. A couple play hockey. They just like to gamble. Poker's a big deal to them."

Penny still had one more piece of business to deal with. "Okay. Then what about you and Sally Stensrud?"

"What?" Charlie did not want to talk about Sally. Not to Penny. "What about her?"

72

"I heard you two were dating." She waited for Charlie's reaction and added, "She has a reputation, is all . . ."

Charlie noted the disappointment in her voice. "Ahhh. Jeez. She asked me to that stupid sock hop. One time, Penn. I took her out *one* time. That's it." Charlie did have strong feelings for Penny, and he certainly didn't want her thinking he was interested in Sally Stensrud. He also didn't want to talk to her about where they went.

She held up her hands. "None of my business, Charlie. I'm sorry. I shouldn't have said anything." She was pleased he hadn't gone out with the cheerleader more than the one time. "Come on. You can walk home with me." She grabbed her books and slid from the stool.

It felt good to be with Penny, and Charlie had a brainstorm. "Hey! Why don't you come up to the cabin with me over spring break, Penny?" Charlie asked. That week-long vacation was not too far away.

"Oh, sure." Penny was thrilled he even asked. "Without your mother? That'd look good, wouldn't it?" She gave his bicep a punch. *There's hope for Charlie yet,* she thought.

"Ow!" Charlie feigned real pain. "Will you think about it, Penn?"

"The cabin?"

"Yeah. Really, it'd be a blast, and you could help us look for that box I told you about."

"The one . . . the one your dad found and buried?"

"Yeah. I really want to find it. That little piece my dad found is valuable. I'd like to see how much more there is. Will you think about it, Penn? Please?"

"Oh, Charlie. My parents would never let me go without an adult along. Jeez, I'd have to make up a story or something. You trying to get me in trouble now, you big nut?" She stepped in front of him, planted both feet firmly on the wet concrete, and leaned close. "If I said yes, you'd have to promise me one thing."

Charlie was growing excited at the thought of spending days with Penny at the cabin. "Anything, Penn."

"You have to find one more person to go along. It can't just be you and me alone together, Charlie. Okay?" She stared into his blue eyes. "And, remember . . . I'm not Sally Stensrud."

"I understand, Penn, and for the record, nothing happened that night. We made out a little, and that was all. Besides, I was too busy looking for submarines . . . " He smiled and leaned down.

Penny tilted her head, laid four fingers gently on his cheek, and looked him squarely in the eye. They were close enough to kiss but didn't. Finally, Penny took a breath and said, "Okay. I know you pretty well. I trust you." She brushed his lips with hers, and stepped back. "Submarine races? Really, Charlie?"

"Yeah, I know." His face flushed.

"I think that's why I like you so much, Nash. Sometimes you just don't have a clue . . . Now, if we are really going to do this . . . God, I can't believe I'm even considering it . . . you have to help me invent a very believable story for my parents."

"Okay. No problem." Charlie's blood was surging through every vein in his body. His heart felt like it would burst from his chest. He'd take good care of Penny and make sure nothing happened she'd later regret.

"Boy, oh boy, Charlie Nash," she replied. "I've been tagging along with you for too many years, I think. Nothing's changed, I guess. C'mon. Let's go." She took hold of his hand. They walked up Oliver together.

Splinter had followed the pair out of the drug store and kept an eye on them in the rearview mirror of his car. Charlie and Penny walked down Twenty-First and turned right on to Oliver. He turned the car around, and slowly followed at a safe distance.

Been tailing this kid long enough, Splinter thought. *Time to force the issue. Kid's got good taste in girls though . . . that one's a real cutey. Could be valuable at some point. Might be able to use her for leverage,* he considered.

Splinter was growing impatient. He believed it was necessary to pressure his employer to speed things up, knowing the man would not give the go-ahead on any action against the kid or his girlfriend until he was ready. He noted which house the girl entered, then drove slowly past and eyeballed Charlie as he turned into his home.

One of these days, young fella, you and I are gonna to have a little chat. You're going to tell me everything I need to know. One way or another. Splinter smiled as he ducked to watch Charlie enter the house at 2300 Oliver. *See ya soon, young Buck.* Splinter sped away . . .

* * * * *

WEST HIGH'S SPRING BREAK was scheduled for the last week of March. Charlie and Posey were spending more and more time together, and Charlie had been taking Penny out almost every weekend for the past month. She was very happy to spend the time with him, and considered their time at the movies or having ice cream at Bridgeman's, to be the real dates she'd dreamed of. They still hadn't figured out a plan for their trip to the cabin.

Charlie never actually admitted to "dating" Penny Tercel, but endured teasing from his friends, nonetheless. Being with Penny felt good . . . it felt right. They could be together without even talking sometimes, and not feel awkward. They knew each other that well.

After a couple of dates, Charlie even boldly gave Penny a kiss at her front door. It was late, and they had just returned from seeing *The Sting* with Paul Newman at the Uptown Movie Theater. Charlie began to pull away, but Penny held him close and returned the kiss with enthusiasm. She opened her lips and tentatively explored his mouth with her tongue. Charlie responded by touching her tongue with his own. This time, unlike the last time with Sally, the kiss felt completely natural . . . it was exciting—warm and electric.

The overhead light suddenly flashed. Dave Tercel had been waiting up for his daughter's return. Against his wife's wishes, he was compelled to break up the young couple.

Charlie relaxed his arms and stepped back. "Oops. Guess I better go."

"Yeah. Dad's not used to me dating."

"Me either," Charlie laughed.

"Oh, right. And what about your date with Sally?" she teased.

Very seriously, Charlie put both hands on Penny's shoulders, leaned close, and said, "That was nothing like tonight, Penn. This was really neat." He tilted his head, and gave her another kiss . . . this time with much greater emphasis.

She gasped and threw her arms around his neck. The kiss ended. "Oh, Charlie. I wish we . . ." She never finished as the door flew open. Dave Tercel stood glaring at the two teens.

"All right, you two. Time to say, 'Goodnight.' Take off, Charlie." He wasn't angry, exactly, being very fond of Nash. "There's always tomorrow, son."

"Nite, Penn. Good night, Mr. Tercel."

"Bye, Charlie," Penny said. "Call me tomorrow?"

"Okay. See ya."

His time with Penny was exactly what Charlie needed. It was a start back to a normal life. Slowly, he had begun to shake loose his depression. He smiled to himself as he ran down the walk to the Pontiac. He opened the door and noticed Penny watching him. He waved. Penny waved back and closed the door.

Charlie started the car and pulled away. Taffy, in the back seat, stretched and licked the back of his head. "Time to go home, girl."

As he drove off, the dark Plymouth driven by Tabor Splinter fired up and left the curb a half a block away. My, my, this is going to be fun, Splinter thought.

* * * * *

HOCKEY SEASON WAS LONG OVER. The ice at Lake of the Isles hadn't melted yet though, and Charlie and Penny managed to lure Posey onto the ice. They slid around in sneakers. Charlie dropped a couple of pucks and stickhandled around Penny.

"Show off," she teased.

Charlie laughed and said to Posey, "Okay, Pose. Stand in the net." He handed his friend a stick. "Here. Put the baseball glove on."

"Whoa, baby! You two aren't going to shoot pucks at me, are ya?"

"Sure," Penny said. "Why not?"

"No way," he replied.

Penny faked a shot with a puck, laughed, and pulled a couple of tennis balls from her pocket. She passed one over to Charlie, and called out, "Get ready, Russ." She stickhandled the ball a bit, looked up to be sure Posey was ready, and fired the ball at him.

He caught the ball with ease, dropped it from the glove, and kicked it back to her. "That your best shot, Penny?"

After an hour of shooting, and playing two on none, all three were exhausted. Charlie and Penny agreed that Russell had real potential as a goalie. He was tall and rangy, had great hand-eye coordination and was very quick. Charlie encouraged Posey at least to think about going out for the team the following fall.

"We'll see. Have to convince my parents I won't get killed, first. Maybe I can save enough money for a pair of contacts over the summer by mowing lawns. By the way, you didn't run into the Slocum's again, did you, Charlie?"

"No. Why?"

"Well, the younger one, Louis? He's in my shop class and had to be excused 'cause someone broke his arm. In two places."

"No kiddin'?"

"Yeah. Poor kid has to take Creative Homemaking, instead of shop."

Penny joined the conversation. She looked worried. "Charlie? You didn't tell me you had a fight with those two. When was this?"

"Last winter. No big deal," he said. "What about Vernon? Those two are usually inseparable."

"Apparently, Vernon should have stayed home that night instead of going downtown with his brother. He's still in the hospital. The way I heard it, they stepped off the bus on Nicollet, turned into an alley to take a shortcut to Dayton's, and some guy jumped 'em. Guy snapped Louis's arm like a twig, then took a chunk of concrete and smashed the fingers on both of Vernon's hands. Guess those two dipshits won't be bothering anyone for a while. Maybe the two of them finally got what they deserved, ya' know."

"Let's hope . . . that's a pretty brutal beating, though," Charlie offered.

Penny was silent. She knew the Slocum's were trouble and worried that at some point, they'd want to finish things with Charlie. She decided to wait until later to talk more about this incident with Charlie.

* * * * *

WITHOUT HOCKEY, the boys—Charlie, Posey, and the other neighborhood group, were pretty much without direction that spring. Penny's time was occupied practicing for tennis tryouts. Every afternoon, she'd head down the block to Kenwood School and pound balls against the large brick wall on the north side of the elementary school. Her focus and dedication left little room for Charlie for a couple of weeks.

So, Charlie and his buddies spent weekday afternoons watching, *Dick Clark's American Bandstand*, poking fun at the boys on the show but, in truth, envied them as the girls they danced with were really good looking.

"Look at the ducktail on that kid," Morrie said.

"You're just jealous, Morrie. You'd have a doo like that if your mom didn't cut your hair for you," Shelly offered.

"Does she really cut your hair, Morrie?" Posey asked.

"Yeah," Peyson replied rather meekly.

"She cuts your hair?" Posey asked. "Why?" He leaned closer to inspect Peyson's hair.

"'Cause she won't spend a buck to get him a decent haircut is why," Bobbo exclaimed.

"Ha, ha! That's so funny I forgot to laugh," Peyson said. "Just shut up for a while. Okay?" The Peysons were notoriously frugal as John's father, Morrow, was a banker. All the boys loved to tease Morrie about how cheap he was.

Actually, the Kenwood group was slightly jealous of the Bandstand boy's prowess on the dance floor. As a group, they themselves had suffered through Miss Mayhew's Dance class at Woodhill Country Club for one entire month of Friday nights in the eighth grade.

Forced to attend by their parents, they hated every dippy moment and resisted every attempt to learn the rudiments of the Fox Trot, Mambo, and Waltz Now, however, they all secretly wished they were whipping around the bandstand floor with either Sandy, Marnie, Sharon, or, perhaps Annette—a few of the really cool girls on the show.

As interest in *Bandstand* waned, they invented a game called knee hockey in Charlie's basement. Instead of a puck, they taped over a tennis ball, cut down old hockey sticks and played the game on their knees. Posey excelled in goal, just as Charlie knew he might. Before long, the other boys grew frustrated at their collective lack of scoring skill when Russell was in the doorway-goal. He was that good.

Interest in knee hockey, lessened. Without other organized activity to hold their interest, they spent afternoons at their homes watching television. Some even managed to study. All but Charlie.

Ten

PENNY BECAME INVOLVED with the school paper. She was editor, and the work took much of her time. Because Charlie was bored and lacked sufficient motivation to study, he would sneak out of the house at night. His mother was spending more time with Duane Silk, so Charlie had no trouble leaving. It was quite simple to grab the extra set of car keys, and take his mother's Pontiac down to Bryn Marr, a neighborhood on the other side of Kenwood Parkway.

A few of the seniors from the hockey team had started a poker game on weekday nights, held in the Bryn Marr Park boys' restroom. These were some of the same boys Penny had warned Charlie about.

Most of the players were good kids. Other than one or two older boys who wandered in and out of the game, Charlie felt comfortable with the bunch. Much like Charlie himself lately, these boys had little parental control. Leaving the house on a weeknight was no big deal.

Timmy Moe, Jack Dooley, Jerry Townsend, and Bobbie St Clair were regulars in the game. Good guys, all. It was nickel-dime stuff . . . pretty harmless, but serious nonetheless. All were very competitive. They hated to lose. Especially money.

While Charlie's bitterness had tempered to some degree, he still harbored very deep disappointment at the world in general. The chip on his shoulder was still perched. Charlie did enjoy the company of his friends—especially Penny and Posey—but he had slipped lately. He'd retreated back into the former, darker world of depression. He couldn't identify exactly why he felt so bored and depressed. He just knew he needed diversion. Poker was the perfect outlet. Much like hockey had been.

Losing, at anything, however, seemed to bring out the worst in Charlie. When losing at poker became a regular event, he just couldn't handle the negativity in any other way but to strike out.

"You're so lucky, Moe," Charlie said after a particularly bad evening on the bathroom floor. "If you ever developed any real skill at seven stud, you'd be dangerous."

"Oh, I see," Timmy said. "We're all a bunch of lucky bastards 'cause we take your money every night, right?"

"Pretty much," Charlie said. He knew it wasn't the money; he had plenty of that. It was just, so . . . *humiliating*, he thought.

Dooley jumped in, "Ya know what, Charlie? You're such a sore loser, you really oughta stay home. Go back over to Kenwood."

At that moment, one of the older boys Charlie didn't know very well, had just entered the restroom. He managed to squeeze in next to Charlie . . . after a not so gentle nudge.

Charlie nudged back.

"Hey! Watch it Nash."

"Take it easy, Nolan," Moe said.

"Aw, I'm sick of this guy crying all the time," Nolan said. He looked at Charlie. "Know what, Nash? Why don't you pick up your nickels and go home. No one wants you around here, anyway. Get the hell out of here before I knock the snot out of you." Nolan stood, grabbed Charlie by the back of his jacket, hauled him to his feet, and threw him toward the door.

Charlie charged back and threw a punch. Nolan blocked it with his arm and slammed a fist into Charlie's cheek. Seeing stars of every color, Charlie barreled into the other boy blindly. Nolan's breath left his chest with a loud, "whoosh," as the smaller boy slammed a forearm into his chest.

Nolan fell back into one of the stalls and landed on the toilet. Gasping for breath, he looked up in time to see Charlie punch him in the stomach. The older boy's head slammed against the porcelain, and he drooped to the floor.

Charlie was panting with fury as he stood over Nolan. He took a deep breath and backed away.

"You better get the hell out of here, Charlie," Jerry said. "Nolan's friends'll be here in a minute. They'll pound the crap out of you."

Charlie felt strangely unafraid. He really didn't care much anymore. He left that night and never went back to Bryn Marr.

Penny heard about the fight at Bryn Marr and tried to talk to Charlie about it. He avoided her. She hadn't been around when he needed her, so he wasn't going to be around for her now.

During this period, Charlie drifted apart from his mother. He still maintained a meaningful relationship with Grandmother Nichols, but his mother's new friend left the boy feeling uneasy. The man was bad news. *Slime ball*, Charlie thought. *Name should be Slick . . . not Silk.*

Charlie disliked Silk intensely, didn't trust the man and knew his father would never have done business with him. His mother, however, openly touted Silk's financial acumen and had no problem confiding in him. In fact, she was considering turning over all their financial affairs to Silk.

Increasingly more comfortable with Russell Posey—and much like his old friend, Quill Purdue back in South Dakota—Charlie was able to discuss his feelings openly with his new friend.

"No, it's not just because he likes my mother, Russ. It's something else. The guy's sleazy."

"What do you mean, Charlie?"

"I don't know. He's always hanging around. Whenever I'm there, he puts his arm around me and tries to buddy-up. I think he wants to marry Mom or something. He's creepy. Just because he worked for

Dad's accountant, Earl Foster, he seems to think he's the right guy to handle our family finances. I don't trust him one bit."

Posey wasn't convinced. "You sure you're not just jealous?"

Charlie flared at that. "No. It's something else, Russ. He's even been trying to get close to Gramma, but I think she's too smart and sees right through him." He proceeded to tell Posey about a meeting Silk called awhile back that involved his mother, grandmother, and himself. They had met in the Nash living room.

Duane Silk, showing up shortly after Frank Nash died, introduced himself to Marsha Nash and Charlie as the accountant-partner of Earl Foster. After expressing condolences, he wasted no time working on Marsha and very soon, managed to convince her that she needed his competent financial advice to manage things now that her husband was gone. Charlie had listened carefully to his initial pitch without comment.

Before long, Duane Silk brought the Nash family together for a meeting. He was quite eloquent in his presentation. "Before Frank and Earl's, ah . . . tragic accident, the three of us met and discussed what to do about the family's investments. It was Frank's wish to diversify. Being respectful of his wishes, I've taken steps to move much of your investments into something with, ah . . . far greater returns. I have a good friend who's created a spectacular new investment product and granted us an exception . . . ah, an exception to their normal rule of entry into this fund. He's facilitating our early participation into something called, a 'Hedge Fund.' They've named it, the Blackwell Fund, and they guarantee a fifteen to twenty percent monthly return: *Guaranteed.* Pretty impressive, right, Marsha? Mrs. Nichols?" Silk's dark eyes darted from one to the other of the women.

Marsha Nash seemed impressed, as did Grandma Nichols. "Oh, my, yes, Duane. Those are remarkable returns, right, Mother?"

"Well, I certainly have never seen anything close to that with any of *my* stocks," Grandma Nichols huffed. She cast a glance at Charlie who simply rolled his eyes in disbelief and looked down at Taffy.

"Seems maybe . . . uh, too good to be true, Mom?" Charlie boldly proffered. "Quill's been making some inquiries for us about all this. Thinks we should hold off for now. Says he can't find much information about this Blackwell Fund." He shot a look at Silk.

Silk's face reddened. "And, who might this Quill be, young man?"

"Oh, Quill Purdue befriended Charlie on his odyssey a few years ago. He lives in South Dakota," Marsha stated. "He and Charlie are very close. Quill really is a dear friend of ours."

"Perhaps Quill's right, Marsha," her mother said. "Maybe you should wait and see what he finds out."

Charlie smiled and shot a challenging glance at Silk.

The man tugged at both shirt sleeves, coughed, straightened his tie, and said, "Well, of course it's your decision, Marsha. But, this fund is a beautiful instrument." He turned toward Charlie. "Not surprised your friend didn't find out much, Charlie. It's a very closely held product . . . very new on the market. Not many people know about it."

He cleared his throat, lit a Chesterfield, and continued. "Let me try and make you understand how this works: The fund managers have actually managed to mathematically account for both the upside and downside of something called, 'an annuity float.' It's all accomplished with algorithms. Not sure even *I* understand what those are." Silk laughed nervously. A tiny line of sweat appeared on his forehead. He stroked his thin mustache and exhaled a thick stream of smoke, and continued, "Anyway, of course it's all very complicated . . . very hard for the average person to understand all the ramifications. I doubt your South Dakota friend will grasp it either, young man. The important thing here is that Blackwell's going to let us come in on the second offering. Matter of fact, I plan on investing a sizable sum of my own. Doesn't this sound great, Marsha?"

"Why, yes, Duane, I believe so. It's a wonderful return, for sure. Did you hear that, Charlie?" She turned to her son, hoping for some indication of his willingness to go along with Silk's proposal.

Charlie declined to answer. Instead, he merely stretched, looked down at Taffy, who was parked under the table, and scratched her ears. Finally, he muttered, "Quill always said, 'If it sounds too good to be true, it probably is." Privately he thought, *Quill also said, never trust a man with a mustache or a beard: 'They've something to hide, Charlie.'*

Silk flared. "What the hell could this Quill possibly know about such a complicated investment? Pardon my French, Marsha, but, good Lord, at some point you have to sit back and let more knowledgeable people guide your decisions."

Charlie fired back, "No one ever said a decision had to be made about *anything* right now." He stood and faced Silk, ready to leave the room. He would have but didn't want to leave his mother and grandmother to deal with the slimy man. "Mother, please remind your friend that this is our money. Money from the pennies Uncle Nat gave me."

Silk was undeterred. He forged ahead, sensing a weakening in Marsha. "Yes, yes, of course, Charlie. I know all that. But, I've been charged with seeing that the money is invested intelligently, and I take my responsibility very seriously."

He paused to collect himself, stubbed the butt in a standing ashtray, and continued. "All right, let's move on." He focused his attention on Marsha. "I've run a tabulation of the family's finances. Of the original $723,000 from the sale of Charlie's pennies, and after the purchase of the property up north, building the cabin, and miscellaneous other purchases, much of the original amount remains. I must say with some humility, Earl and I took very good care to maintain the principal, even with the meagre returns from passbook savings." Silk beamed, daring the boy to challenge him on that bit of news.

"That being said, at our last meeting, Frank agreed it was time to take advantage of the growth of equities in this new, booming, post-war economy." Silk smiled broadly, looking from mother to son and back, pleased with his presentation, Charlie's resistant attitude notwithstanding.

85

"Furthermore, if the mineral Frank discovered proves to be as valuable as Earl *thought* it might, you'll have much, much more to invest in the Blackwell Fund. The principles of the fund will hold it open for you—as a favor to me—for a limited time, Marsha. But, once the door closes, we can't get in, and we are back to a meager five percent bank interest." Silk rubbed his hands multiple times and grinned at the two women.

Time for the close, Silk thought. "We need to get an official assay of that piece of metal, however." Silk looked at Charlie. "The sooner we know its purity, value, and specific analysis, along with the total amount of what Frank found, we can get it sold and invested in Blackwell." Silk sat back and looked at the two women.

Charlie bristled. Face red with anger, he exploded. "Mom, why did you tell him about what Dad found? We agreed . . . with Dad, remember? To keep it a secret, Mom. Not blab it to anybody . . . much less this guy." Charlie pointed a finger at Silk for emphasis.

"Charlie, don't be rude. Mr. Silk has been so helpful as we struggled through all this. We should be grateful for his input."

"Yeah, right. Like we wouldn't know how to wipe our . . . uh, nose . . . without, *Duane's* help."

"Charlie! That's enough. You know I can't deal with these things myself and, well, he was Earl's partner, after all . . ."

Charlie had serious doubts about Silk's true position in Foster's firm. His father never once mentioned the man's name. Actually, before the accident, Nash had begun making his own inquiries regarding Silk.

Charlie saw Silk as a mere flunky recently hired to perform nothing more than menial tasks. A file clerk, perhaps. He had no proof, of course. Charlie stood up. "I've heard enough. Remember what Dad said, Mother: 'This is only one small, wafer-sized chunk. There is no guarantee there's any more than the one piece.' Remember?"

The boy visually pleaded for her to go along with him and not reveal any more of Frank Nash's secret. "Don't let him get involved with this, Mother. Please." With that, he pushed away from the table, stomped out of the kitchen and slammed the door on the way out of the house. Taffy followed close behind.

Silk looked to Marsha with a sympathetic nod. "The boy's been through a great deal, Marsha. I'm sure the recent defeat in that hockey tournament doesn't help his mood. He's just a young boy, remember. You need to take charge . . . need to consider what's best for the both of you. Right now, we can maximize the value of everything, by cashing out the material Frank found and putting that money to work. Now." He finished with, "Next week, or next month might be too late. I don't think Blackwell will hold their fund open very long."

"I don't know what to do, Duane. Frank was quite insistent that the wafer remain a secret until Earl could have it analyzed. He had a friend who worked for 3M, an engineer or chemist, I think. Frank felt confident that fellow could examine the material and put a value on it." Marsha fiddled with her kerchief and sat back. "We're still waiting to hear what he has to say."

Silk lit up like a candle, absolutely convinced there was more than just one, small wafer. Whatever the mineral was, he knew it was valuable. He had to get his hands on it and follow the trail to the rest of the stash. "You, mean, ah . . . that this 3M fellow has the sample in his possession?"

"Well, I believe so, yes. Frank originally put in our safe deposit box, but he took it out to show this man. I guess I'd have to open the safe deposit box to see."

Silk was losing patience with Marsha's scatter-brained approach to life. He opened his notebook and scanned his notes. "I couldn't find the man's name among Earl's files. Surely you have his name . . . a phone number, someplace? We should really call him, Marsha." Silk reached across the table and laid his well-manicured fingers on her arm. "Marsha? Look at me, dear. Do the right thing and soon all of this confusion and distress will be in the past."

"Oh, dear. I'm not sure, Duane. Frank kept all that sort of thing to himself. I'm not certain where to start looking," Marsha said. "Maybe Charlie should talk to Quill first."

"Time is of the essence, my dear. I think the most important question right now is: Where would the rest of the, 'whatever it is' he found, be? Certainly there's more, right?" Silk gazed intently at the diminutive, Mrs. Nash.

Marsha hesitated, then answered, "I don't know, Duane. I never thought to ask Frank that question, you know?"

"Would Charlie know?" Silk asked with great anticipation.

"Yes, probably. He and Frank were very close. They shared everything. If he told anyone, it would've been Charlie."

And, if they were that close, Silk thought, *then maybe the kid knows where the wafer is too . . .*

* * * * *

WHEN CHARLIE FINISHED telling his friend about the meeting, Posey said, "Yeah. I see what you mean. I wouldn't trust that guy either. Tell me about Quill, Charlie. He sounds like a real good friend."

Charlie described the events that led to his meeting Quill Purdue. How everything that happened that fall involved the three 1943 pennies gifted by his uncle. The telling took quite a while. They were in Charlie's room, sprawled on the floor. A half-eaten bag of Oreos was tempting Taffy, but she patiently waited for an offer.

"Here, Taff." Posey handed her a cookie. When Charlie had finished, Posey exclaimed, "Holy shit! You're lucky to be alive."

Charlie was tired by now. "Yeah, I guess." Describing the events left the boy feeling depressed and incredibly sad. He was uncomfortable talking about anything that tended to touch on his feelings. He was growing away from his mother, and that hurt. Some of the separation was natural and inevitable, but much was not. Their estrangement was a function of Frank Nash's death and Marsha's involvement with Silk.

"Anyway, this Silk guy's a phony, and I don't want any part of him," Charlie offered.

"You may be right," Posey offered. "Sooner or later, then, he'll show his true colors, Charlie."

"Well, I just hope my mom is around to see that side of him, before it's too late." Charlie offered. "Come on. Let's go watch television."

Eleven

FTER THAT, CHARLIE AND POSEY pretty much hung out together all the time. The other boys Charlie had grown up with had all been good friends and readily accepted Posey into their circle.

Together, however, it seemed the boys couldn't avoid trouble. Never anything too serious: pitching snowballs at passing cars, taking Charlie's mom's car out late at night without permission. Cruising Lake Street in futile and feeble attempts to pick up girls. More than once, one of the boys managed to sneak liquor from the house. The boys thought the whiskey and gin they tasted was pretty awful but gagged it down anyway. Their respective, "buzzes" created all sorts of harmless fun.

Their activities were pretty typical teenage stuff, but they always seemed to get caught . . . mostly by one or another of the boys' parents. And mostly, the blame fell on Charlie as the ringleader.

Before long, most of the mothers refused to let their boys spend too much time with Charlie, as word had traveled that Marsha Nash wasn't around much to supervise her son.

While the boys' prime motivator was to derive a good laugh from whatever situation they found themselves in, that desire for a good time could, and often did, lead them astray. Charlie in fact, did seem to seek trouble and frequently rebelled against authority of all types.

Trouble seemed to follow the Nash boy during this period of his life, and he did little to stop it. It seemed as if he was out to prove something to the other boys . . . what a risk taker he could be. He really didn't care much about the consequences of his behavior. Confrontations with other cruising carloads of teens inevitably led to shouts and challenges. Generally, these episodes were harmless and led to nothing, but whenever Charlie was involved, the challenges grew ugly.

On one such night, the boys were returning from Excelsior after watching and listening to a new band called, the Beach Boys, at Big Reggie's Danceland on Lake Minnetonka. They'd managed to avoid trouble at the dance hall, but ran into a carload of boys while cruising Lake Street. Shouts were exchanged. Charlie was driving his mother's Pontiac. Before long, one of the other boys made a crack about Charlie driving his parents' "wimpy car." Jamie McCarthy wondered if the boy's chopped Chevy would make it back to north Minneapolis.

"Nice pimp-mobile, Butt-head," Paddy O'Rourke yelled. That proved too much for the other gang of four. The driver challenged the Kenwood boys to a fight. Charlie shouted, "Any time, jerk-off," and waved for the other bunch to follow his car around a corner.

"Charlie, don't stop!" Bobbo Andreason pleaded.

"Yeah, no shit, Charlie. Just keep driving," Jamie McCarthy begged.

Charlie refused to back down. He pulled over to the curb on a quiet street in St Louis Park.

The other car stopped a hundred feet behind. Four boys poured from a bright red, 1955 Chevy Bel Air.

"Oh, crap," Morrie exclaimed as he looked over his shoulder. The Kenwood crew were not fighters. They all, without exception, prided themselves on getting through their difficult teenage years with wit and wile. They were in serious danger of getting the crap kicked out of each of them, thanks to Charlie's crazy behavior.

As the four approached the Pontiac, one of the boys swung a chain menacingly. Another slapped a tire iron against his open hand, beckoning for the Kenwood boys to come out. The four strolled forward shouting insults and taunts. "Come on, you wimps! Let's see how tough you are!" the boy with the chain shouted.

"Charlie! For God's sake, put it in gear," Bobbo shouted.

None of the Kenwood boys were interested in fighting. Certainly not against a gang with chains and who knew what else. But, Charlie had been behaving so strangely lately, his friends wondered if he was seriously thinking of fighting this bunch.

Charlie opened his door, left the car running, and stepped out. "Okay, pin-head, let's go!" He felt confident in what he was doing.

The boy with the chain separated from the others and angled toward Charlie's side of the car.

"If we live through this, I'm going to personally kill you, Charlie," Morrie declared and opened the passenger door.

At the very last moment, Charlie ducked back inside, and yelled, "Come on, Morrie! We're leaving!" He threw the gear shift into drive, and stepped on the gas.

The boy with the chain swung and barely missed hitting the car.

Charlie laughed and shouted back, "Later, boys. We've got to run now . . ."

After that night, Charlie's friends decided he was a bit too reckless for their own good. They were of one mind to be careful around Charlie, but their parents also pressured their sons to separate from him.

All, but Posey. Posey's parents were pretty much out of touch with his comings and goings. Before long, it was mostly just the two of them hanging out together. Charlie had not forgotten his plan for the cabin. With spring break rapidly approaching, he needed to find one of his friend's to go along. Based on the way things had been going recently, he was certain Posey was his best shot.

"I've got an idea," Charlie said one Saturday. "I can get my mom's car over spring break. Do you want to go up to the cabin, Pose?"

"Cool," Posey replied. "Bet I can go."

"I've asked Penny to go along, too. We'll have a blast, Pose. Penny said she'd go but only if someone else came along. Wanna be our chaperone?"

"Sure, but are her parents going to be okay with this?"

"Hmmm. No. She has to cook up some story so they don't find out. Anyway, I've got that new .22 that Silk guy gave me. He keeps trying to be my buddy and all. So anyway, the three of us can go across the lake . . . poke around all those old buildings over there. Still think we might find something."

"Like what?" Russell asked.

"I don't know. Something's funny about that side of the lake. Dad always thought there was some sort of secret experiment or something going on during the war. The whole area, including Shepherd Lake was closed off then and for ten years after. Never did hear what was going on. I've been over there a couple of times. There's some old buildings and stuff I'd like to look at." Charlie knew exactly why he wanted to go back across the lake: To find the box his father told him about.

"Will the ice still be on the lake?" Posey asked?

"Probably. We'll take a toboggan . . . just in case we find something over there," Charlie offered.

That night, Charlie received a phone call from Penny. "Hey, Penn. What's up?"

"Guess what?"

"Ah, you got an 'F' on the English term paper."

"Nooo. Be serious. Try again."

"Okay, you decided to tell your parents the truth . . . that you and I are going to the cabin alone next week."

She paused, bewildered by his reply. "How'd you know?"

"Huh? I didn't. Did you really tell them?"

"Yes. I had to, Charlie. It just didn't feel right. Besides, I'm almost seventeen, and as I told my mom I'll be going off to college in a year or so, and they have to turn me loose sometime."

"And, so . . . what did they say?"

She smiled sheepishly. "Well, Mom said, 'yes' and Dad said, 'no.' No surprise there. Mom won. Dad said if you, 'weren't a complete gentleman, he'd, kill you!"

"I can't believe it, Penn. That's great!"

"I think it helps that Mom and Dad are going out to Colorado Springs to watch Bill play hockey that weekend. CC is playing in the NCAA Regionals, and they want to watch. I said I didn't want to go."

"Well, then we're all set, Penn."

"Yeah, but what about your part of the deal?"

"Done. Posey said he'd go and would be happy to be our, 'chaperone.'"

A week later, the last Saturday in March, Charlie, Penny, and Russell Posey drove north to Shepherd Lake in Charlie's mom's car, the 1957 Pontiac convertible. Posey lied to his parents and told them that Mrs. Nash and her friend would be going along. Penny's parents left for Colorado a day early, so all Charlie had to do was stop at Penny's on his way to Posey's, and pick her up.

In truth, Marsha Nash was glad to have the freedom to be alone for the week, without Charlie glowering around the house. Charlie had been lobbying long and hard for the Pontiac to become his, and he could sense his mother slowly relenting. His primary argument was a simple one: "You don't want to have to drive me all over the place, do you?" She loved Penny, and after talking to Penny's mother, they agreed to let the kids go. It helped that Russell was going along.

Marsha Nash had a difficult time arguing with her son. Distracted lately by an almost constant companion in Duane Silk—who by now had officially become the family's financial planner, she thought Charlie's going to the cabin a wonderful idea.

Papers giving Silk the authority to conduct business on the Nash's behalf had been filed the previous week. Silk was relentless and managed to find more reasons to spend time with Marsha Nash. Ultimately, he managed to convince her to turn over all the family's financial interests to himself, against her son's wishes.

Silk's latest argument had been for Marsha to give him full power of attorney so he could make important, fast moving decisions with their investments. Marsha wasn't too sure about that. She resisted and questioned whether her husband ever would have consented. Nonetheless, Silk was very convincing. He was slowly winning her over.

Charlie had stormed out of the house when told of Silk's control over the family's business affairs. He could barely be civil to his mother, he was so angry. "Dad would not have agreed to this, Mom. You're trusting a guy you hardly know!"

"But, he was Earl's partner, wasn't he?"

"Not his partner, no. And, not for very long, Gramma said. He'd just gone to work for Earl a few months before . . . before the accident, Mom."

"But, he's been so nice to us, Charlie. I'm a pretty good judge of character, and I think he is truly well intended. Besides, it's still our money and nothing can be done without our approval."

Charlie wasn't convinced. He felt Silk was just sly enough to convince his mother of just about anything he wanted . . . for a reason. He began to wonder about Silk's intense interest in the silver-colored metal wafer his dad had found. "You didn't give him access to the safe deposit, did you, Mom?" His heart skipped a beat as he waited for his mother to answer. "Or, tell him that there might be more? Mom?" He stared at his mother waiting for an answer.

Marsha dodged his question. Instead, she said, "Charlie, you're worrying about nothing. Now you and your friends go and have a good time at the cabin. Call me when you get there so I know you've arrived safely." She attempted a fly-by hug and kiss but was too late. Charlie was already out the door with Taffy close behind.

Charlie had been given a key to the safe deposit by his father, and added his name to the signature card. He raced downtown to Midland Bank, hurried downstairs to the vault room, and promptly had the family box before him.

With relief, he discovered the wafer inside the box. He removed it, stuck it in his jeans, returned the box to the attendant, and headed home. *There, Silk—you jackass. You're not as smart as you think,* Charlie thought to himself as he left the bank.

Twelve

THINGS ARE GETTING COMPLICATED, boss man," Splinter said, calling from a phone booth across from the drug store.

"Why's that?" Silk replied.

"Because the kid, his four-eyed buddy, and the girlfriend just left town."

"I knew the Nash kid was going up to the family cabin with the boy, but not the Tercel girl. Shit!"

"What do you want me to do?"

"I think the kid has the sample. And, if he's going to their cabin, there might be a good reason for it. That's where the old man found the wafer. That's got to be where the rest of it is." Silk's voice rose with excitement. "I'll give you directions. You head up to Hackensack. Stay close, Victor. The kid's the key."

"You forget, I've been up there before."

"Oh, yeah, right. Forgot."

"I haven't. You still owe me, remember? And, if the other two get in the way?"

"Lose either or both as you deem fit. I could care less." Silk hung up.

Hmmm. Okay, boss man, you've just given me a green light. This could be fun. Splinter whistled a gay tune as he left the phone booth.

* * * * *

The three teens stopped off in Brainerd on the way north at an A&W Root Beer drive-in. It was warm for late March in Minnesota . . . almost fifty degrees, actually. Charlie toyed with lowering the top on the Pontiac but decided not to.

"What do you guys want," Charlie asked as he reached for the speaker. Posey was in the passenger seat, Penny in back with Taffy.

Posey was quick to answer. "Hmm, maybe a cheeseburger—loaded. And fries? Large root beer, too."

Penny leaned forward. "Just a burger and coke, Charlie. No, make it two burgers. Taffy's hungry, aren't you girl?" Taffy had her head in Penny's lap, eyes cast to the back of Charlie's head.

Charlie pushed the button on the heavy, metal speaker. "Hello? Anybody home?"

Static followed, then: "Welcome to A&W. May I take your order?" The voice coming through the device was young . . . definitely female.

Charlie gave the girl the order. Before he replaced the speaker, Posey grabbed it from his hand, punched the button, and asked, "Say, what are you doing after work?" He chuckled to himself.

More static, then, "Sorry, my boyfriend's picking me up at 3:00. Oh, and by the way, he's the captain of our wrestling team."

"That's okay, sweetie. I don't care," he added with a smirk.

"Worth a try, Pose, but not worth a fat lip," Charlie said.

Before long a slender girl with a blonde ponytail slipped out the door on roller skates, and glided over to the Pontiac. Charlie rolled the window up half-way to accept the tray of food.

"Here ya go, guys," the girl said. Her name tag read, Tammy. "That'll be 5.75 with tax."

Charlie said, "Thanks," and handed her seven dollars. "You can keep the change."

"That's swell," he said. "If you want anything else, just press the red button, okay?"

Posey leaned over, and asked, "How about later on, Tammy? You busy tonight? My friend here has a date, but I'm all alone," he pleaded, then added, "We're visiting from the Cities." Posey had always heard that any reference to the Twin Cities was a certain ice-breaker with girls up north. He had slipped off his glasses hoping to look slightly more attractive to young Tammy, and was squinting rather fiercely.

Tammy leaned down to speak to Posey. "I don't think my dad will let me. Sorry. Say, you got something in your eye there?" she asked Posey.

"Little allergy thing is all," Posey replied.

"Well, I better go. Love your dog . . ." She reached inside to give Taffy a gentle rub on her nose. With that she skated back to the restaurant.

"Well, you don't give up easy, do you, Pose," Penny said.

He took a bite of his burger and said, "Can't hurt to try. Worst case? I get a, 'no.' Good burger, though . . . Oh, oh." Posey caught sight of a couple of tough looking guys coming out of the restaurant. Their waitress, Tammy, had skidded to a stop in front of the boys, listened briefly to their questions, and pointed at the Pontiac.

"What's wrong?" Charlie asked.

"I, ah . . . think we have a problem." Posey replied. He dropped the burger and wrapper back into the plastic basket, wiped his mouth, and reached for the window crank.

The three watched as the two boys crossed the pavement, and separated at the hood of the Pontiac, one going to either side and stopped. The husky guy on the driver's side, leaned down and asked Charlie, "Which one of you clowns was giving my girl a hard time?" He cracked the knuckles on both hands as he spoke.

Charlie started to reply, but Russell quickly answered, "I did. No harm intended, bud." A noticeably hopeful lilt filled his voice.

The driver's side guy came around to Posey's side. The other boy stepped back. "Get out, asshole," the boy demanded as he widened his stance.

Posey looked at Charlie, sighed, removed his glasses, and carefully placed them on the seat. He shrugged at Charlie, opened the door, and stepped out. Tension and apprehension filled the air.

Penny said, "Charlie? Can you do something?"

"I'm going to mess up your face, kid," the boy said to Posey. "And Gordi here is going to do the same to your buddy."

Now, Posey had what remained of a pretty good shiner from when he was playing goalie for Charlie and Penny. Although quite quick and adept at stopping the tennis balls, one slipped past the baseball glove he was using and smacked him in the eye. The blow knocked his glasses off at the impact. Posey actually looked pretty mean with a black eye and no glasses. He'd gained a few pounds over the winter, and was quite a bit taller than the Brainerd kid—but not nearly as broad.

As Posey prepared to defend himself by raising his fists, Charlie left the car, whipped around to the other side, and stepped between the two. "Hang on a minute, pal. I think you should know something about my friend . . . uh, *Rocky*, here." Charlie gave a nod to Posey and winked.

"Yeah? What?" the guy snarled.

"Well, it's just this. Rocky here just finished taking second in the Upper Midwest Golden Glove finals down in Minneapolis. Thus, the black eye." He motioned to Posey's face. "Anyway, he needed a break from his training before heading to Kansas City . . . the Nationals, ya know? So we came up here to spend a week at our cabin. Fair warning, chief. I'm not so sure about whose face is going to be messed up here."

Charlie shrugged as if to say it was the other kid's call, and turned to Posey. "You really want to fight this guy, Rock?" Charlie asked his friend.

By now, Russell was well into the scam . . . especially as it concerned his immediate physical being. He was pretty sure he had no chance against this guy, but if he could just convince him he was exactly who Charlie said he was . . . "Nah, I really don't, Charlie. Coach keeps telling me my fists are, 'lethal weapons' and all . . . and I do need to be ready for the Nationals, but if this guy really wants to go, then I guess we've given him plenty of warning," Posey made a feeble attempt to crack his knuckles, rotated his head in an intimidating sort of gesture, blew snot at the other boys' feet from one nostril and raised both fists. As if that wasn't enough, he began a little bob and weave dance—actually started bouncing on his toes . . . purely for effect.

Penny observed the entire charade from the back of the Pontiac. She could barely restrain her laughter. Taffy sensed trouble and growled. "Shh, Taff. It's okay, girl."

The other two boys looked at each other with questioning faces.

"Okay. I guess we gave him fair warning, Rock." Charlie turned to the other boy and said, "Let's you and I step over here, pal, while Rocky takes care of business. Be careful with your knuckles, Rock. Maybe use your elbows like you did to that guy last month? It was only that one tooth that fell out."

By now tough guy number one clearly had doubts about whether or not defending his girlfriend's honor was worth getting his lights punched out. He looked at tough guy number two for support—for an easy out of what had become a bad beat, for sure. "Uh, well, I sure don't want to mess up your chances at the Nationals, uh, *Rocky*. What say we call a truce and you fellas go on up to your cabin. That okay with you, Gordi?" he asked his friend, hopefully.

By this time, Gordi had lost all interest in mixing it up with any friend of Rocky, the Golden Gloves Kid. He had already stepped back a good ten feet from the gathering and any possible mistaken intention on his part. He wanted no part of trouble from either occupant of the Pontiac. "Yeah, you bet. Let's let these guys get on their way, for sure," Gordi said.

Charlie smiled. Gordi was folding like a cheap suit in a heavy rain.

"Okay, then." Tough guy number one said. "Let's shake, okay? And stuck out his hand as a gesture of good will to his new friend, *Rocky*.

Posey wasn't done yet, though. He chose to milk the situation a bit longer. He blew his other nostril onto the pavement, rolled his shoulders, and turned his back on the guy's proffered hand. "Guess you guys better get on out of here before I decide I need to get a little training in before next week," he said. "Beat it."

The two Brainerd boys backed away with their hands raised in compliance, hustled to the front door, and bumped against each other as they hurried back inside.

Charlie started laughing, and once they were back inside the Pontiac, all three were hysterical. "Oh my, Charlie. You have the balls of a brass monkey to come up with that pile of crapola. Golden Gloves? Do I look like a boxer?" Posey said.

Charlie caught his breath, and said, "I had to come up with something, and with that shiner of yours, you do look kind of mean . . . Rocky. I think we just found you a new nickname, tough guy." He chuckled more.

Penny offered, "You were piling it on pretty thick at the end there, weren't you?"

"Probably, but I don't get opportunities like that very often. I couldn't resist. Besides, I had Charlie to back me up."

"Yeah, right. Like Charlie is some kind of hard case," Penny said. "That guy looked like he was all muscle, Russ."

"Ah, Charlie coulda taken him," Posey said, remembering what happened to the Slocum brothers.

"Well, let's get out of here before those guys get a brain and really think about the all the bull crap we just slung," Charlie said.

"Good idea."

Charlie honked for Tammy to come and pick up their window tray.

She had been leaning against the order window and glided over rather quickly. "Say, what just happened there?" she asked. "Bryon and his jerk buddy, Gordi came hightailing it back inside like a couple scalded cats. I thought they were going to mop the lot with you two for a minute there. What happened?"

"Oh, we just convinced them it was in their best interest to leave us alone . . . once they found out that, my friend, Rocky here, was a golden glove boxer," Charlie replied.

Tammy leaned over with a sudden, renewed interest in the blond-haired, lanky kid from the Cities. "No kidding, huh? That how you got the black eye?" she asked. Posey had yet to replace his glasses.

"Maybe," Posey said. "Tell ya what, if you can convince your folks to let you out tonight, I'll tell you all about it." He smiled coyly.

"Aw, Gee, I'd really like to, but no way tonight," Tammy said. "But, I'll give you my phone number. Next time you guys are in town, will you call me?" She winked at Posey, scribbled her number on a napkin, and handed it over.

Russell covered up his glasses, smiled, and said, "Thanks, Tammy. Just might do that. Maybe even later this week?"

"Yeah, for sure," Tammy squealed. "I'll see you again . . . real soon, right?" She cracked her chewing gum for effect and whizzed off with the tray.

"You bet. Bye, bye," Posey called.

Penny handed the last bite of burger to Taffy. "Let's go," she said. "Boy, you two guys are a thrill a minute. Is this any indication of what the rest of the week will be like?"

Charlie started the car, put it in gear, and pulled out of the lot. "Let's hope not. That could have been ugly back there. C'mon. We need to get *Rocky* here up to training camp. We're burning daylight . . ."

Posey turned up the volume on the AM radio. Frankie Valli and the Four Seasons were cranking out their latest hit, "Shari Baby!" "My favorite song," Posey declared and began singing along.

Soon, both Charlie and Penny joined Posey, and the three teens sang their way north . . .

Thirteen

N HOUR AND A HALF LATER, they reached Hackensack. Charlie stopped at the local IGA for groceries. Once the bags were in the car, they headed west out of town for the Nash cabin at Shepherd Lake.

Just before they came to the Y where the road branched off toward the other side of Shepherd Lake, Charlie stopped the car. The original gate that guarded the road to the south side of the lake during the war, was gone. Heavy timbers on either side, remained, however. Charlie climbed out. Taffy slipped through the open door. "This road leads to that area I was telling you guys about . . . on the other side of our lake. We'll go over there tomorrow. I want to see what my dad might have found over there."

Charlie turned back toward the car, looked over the hood, and studied the only home on the road. A wooden structure, well-kept, the Nash's had never managed to meet the owner, a local logger who had been in the area for many years. Charlie felt as if someone was watching them. He shivered and called, "Taffy, let's go."

The dog's nose was into the wind, pointed the same direction as her master's gaze . . . directly at the dark, green-clad home across the road. She bristled as a fresh scent wafted on the breeze.

"Taffy! Come on," Charlie commanded.

"Who lives there?" Penny asked.

Charlie craned to read a name on the mailbox, but only saw a rural number. "Not sure. Hermit, maybe. Never met him."

"Then he's a hermit living pretty darn well," Posey said. "That's a nice house, Charlie."

Charlie put the Pontiac in gear and stayed right at the fork. They still had a couple of miles to go on the dirt road before their turn-off. Most of the snow had melted except in shady areas, and north facing slopes. All three were quiet for a short while.

Then Russell, blurted, "Charlie. I gotta ask you a question, but don't get mad, okay?"

Charlie turned briefly toward Posey, and said, "Sure. It's okay. I won't get mad."

"Okay. Well, what I'm wondering is this: If your dad died up here . . . uh, if you and he and this other guy had this accident, and, uh, well, what I don't get is how you can come back up here now? I mean, doesn't this just bring back some really horrible memories?"

Penny leaned forward to hear Charlie's answer. She too, had wondered the same thing.

Charlie considered his friend's question and was about to reply when they arrived at the gate to the Nash property. "Hang on. I have to open the gate." Charlie stepped out of the car, keyed the lock, and swung the gate wide.

Once again, Taffy jumped out. This time she ran on down the two-lane path, full of energy after the long drive. Charlie let her go. He climbed back in, put the car in gear, and said, "Hope to hell she doesn't run into a porcupine."

A hand-carved sign reading, *Nash's Ache-less Acres*, caught Posey's eye. "This is a really cool spot, Charlie." Posey marveled at the tall pine trees and patches of poplar, alder, and birch as they glided down the path. Most of the snow had melted and the road was easily drivable. "I can see why your dad bought this place."

"Yes, I agree. It really is kind of magical, isn't it?" Penny added, having been to the cabin on other occasions.

"It is, and that's part of why I had to come back. I try not to think about what happened, Pose, but some things I still can't quite understand about the accident. I'm drawn here. Don't know why. Don't know if I can really explain it to you guys." He parked the Pontiac behind the cabin.

"Like what?" Penny asked.

"Uh, I'll tell you later, okay? Let's get unloaded and get inside."

* * * * *

CHARLIE AND RUSSELL SAT back after dinner Saturday night and looked out the wide set of windows fronting the cabin. Penny was in the kitchen doing dishes. It wasn't a big place, but with a small guest house in the back, there was room for quite a few people. The main cabin had two good-sized bedrooms, a smaller room with bunk beds, a bathroom, and the kitchen that opened to the dining-family room. Windows wrapped around three sides of the main room of the cabin. A well-used, brick fireplace took up the far corner of the living room.

"This is really neat, Charlie. Thanks for inviting me," Posey said. "You keep it heated all winter?" Posey had noticed that the cabin didn't feel very cold when they came in.

"No. Not normally. Dad had the cabin fully insulated and winterized so we could come up here during the snow months, and . . . uh, I guess after the accident, someone just locked the door and left the heat on. Never gave it much thought, ya know?" He looked around the cabin and for the first time, realized it was pretty much the way they left it last October. *Still looks lived in,* Charlie thought.

Posey said, "You were going to tell us about your dad."

"Yeah, I know." Charlie went to the kitchen and poured himself another cup of coffee. He settled back down at the head of the large, round dining table, and spooned in a generous quantity of sugar. Penny sat close on his right, Posey on the left. "My dad found something on the other side of the lake. He was up here with Taffy a month before the accident . . . wanted to do some fishing, and the grouse hunting season had just opened. Dad loved hunting grouse . . ." Charlie's voice drifted off as he considered his words.

"Why weren't you here?" Posey asked.

"Hockey tryouts. Couldn't miss that . . ."

"Yeah, right. Go on."

"Well, anyway, like I said, he was over there on the other side, hunting a patch of poplar on Saturday morning. Taffy began rootin' around something she came across. He tried calling her off, but she just kept digging away . . . don't know why."

"And?" Posey was getting real interested now. So was Penny.

"What I'm going to tell you guys has to be a secret, okay?"

"Sure, Charlie. No problem." Posey said.

"Of, course, Charlie. We're your friends, remember?" Penny replied.

Her warm answer reminded Charlie why he asked both to come along. "Anyway, Dad thought Taffy's interest was unusual. She's usually off in the brush looking for birds. He laid down his shotgun, knelt down where she was digging, and found a board near the hole Taffy had dug. He reached into the hole, dug around the edges, and felt a box. He pulled it out. Made of heavy wood, painted green, and stenciled 'US ARMY.'"

"No shit?" Posey declared.

"No shit. We had heard from some of the locals that this whole area was off-limits during the war and for ten years afterward. No one could ever say what was going on over there . . . something about secret experiments with sawdust or some crap like that. But the people we talked to remember seeing quite a few men in uniform around town, so it had to be a military installation of some sort." Charlie took a sip of his coffee, anticipating the follow-up question.

"And . . . ? What was in the box?" Penny asked as she leaned close.

"Well, he dragged the box out. 'Bout the size of a small chest, Dad said. Had a big padlock on it but the wood had been painted army green so it was still plenty solid. Tried smashing the lock with a rock but it wouldn't open. He said it was heavy as hell and no way he'd be able to drag it all the way to the boat. The place he described sounded like it was quite a ways back in the woods—away from all the other old buildings, kinda on the edge of a clearing, I guess."

"Dad figured he might as well leave it in the hole and cover it up a little better until he could get back with some heavy tools. As he started to cover it with dirt, this flat piece of silver metal caught his eye. Musta been loose in the dirt around the box, I guess. Anyway, Dad thought the box might be full of these silver squares . . . wafers he called 'em. Who knows, Dad always got pretty excited about stuff, ya know?" Charlie built a fire and waited for the kindling to catch.

"What'd he do with the, uh . . . wafer?" Posey asked, clearly into the excitement of the find.

"Put it in his pocket, filled the hole in with dirt, covered the spot with branches and leaves, and marked it so he could find it again."

"He told you where the spot was, right, Charlie?" Penny asked.

"No. Never did. Dad thought we'd both come back that weekend, probably with Mr. Foster. So there was no need to tell me, uh . . . and I never asked."

Posey asked, "Then what?"

"He and Taffy went back to the cabin. Not sure if he intended to go back alone and open it, but I doubt it. Dad wasn't the handiest guy in the world, so we never had many tools around the house . . . or the cabin. Maybe a hammer, screwdriver, you know . . . an axe for splitting wood. What he really needed was a bolt cutter for the lock, but then he realized that because it was so heavy, he'd never be able to move it himself, anyway."

"Yeah? So?" Posey again.

"One of the main reasons Earl Foster was with us that weekend last October was so we could drag that box to the boat and back to the cabin. Earl was like a brother to Dad, someone he really trusted . . . " Charlie's voice trailed off.

Posey waited a bit, then asked, "What about the piece of silver? You saw it right? What'd it look like?" Charlie had drifted off. "Charlie? You don't have to continue if you don't want to," Penny said and laid her hand on his arm.

"I'm okay, Penn." He reached into his jean pocket, and withdrew his hand. He held out a closed fist and slowly opened it exposing a piece of metal. "This is what he found." He let it slip from his palm onto the wooden table. It rocked on two edges, then settled with a gentle rattle. Its bright silver color sparkled from the overhead Tiffany lamp.

"Oh, my God," Penny exclaimed.

Posey reached for it, then paused. "Can I touch it, Charlie?"

"Sure you can, Pose. It won't bite." He chuckled softly.

Posey hefted it, and raised his eyebrows as if questioning its authenticity. "Is it silver?"

"Don't know. That's where it gets interesting. Earl and my dad took it to some guy they knew from 3M to have it analyzed."

"Why?" Posey handed it to Penny.

"Earl didn't think it was silver. Too shiny. Not heavy enough and too brittle, he thought. Color wasn't quite right for silver, either, he said." Charlie stood and went to the kitchen. He opened a drawer and came back with a fork. "Look at this."

"What?" Penny asked.

"Here, give me the wafer." He took the silver piece from her. "This fork is sterling silver. Earl brought it up here to show my dad the difference. See how dull the fork is compared to the wafer? Earl never thought it was silver."

"Well, then what is it? What'd the 3M guy say?"

"You're not going to believe this . . . "

Fourteen

TAMBOR SPLINTER WAS IRATE. The last thing he wanted was to return to Shepherd Lake. But, his instructions were clear: stay with the kid no matter what. So here he was, parked out on a gravel road down a ways from the Nash entrance, trudging through half-melted snow—in the dark. Small saplings thrashed his face as he felt his way through the brush. *What the hell are these three doing up here,* he wondered. As he neared the cabin, yellow light spilled from the front windows.

Have to be careful . . . remember that damn dog. Maybe should get rid of the mutt . . . make watching these three a whole lot easier. Splinter crept close and dropped to his knees right below the dining room window.

Too cold for windows to be open, Splinter could barely hear the teens' conversation. He only caught bits and pieces, but enough to know that the following day they were going across the still-frozen lake for some damned reason. Splinter hated the thought of going back through the woods on the other side.

Suddenly, he heard the dog bark. *Shit. I gotta get the hell out of here . . . now. If they let that damned dog out . . .* Splinter hurriedly followed his tracks back to the road and the safety of his car. He could still hear the dog barking in the distance. His feet were wet and he was shivering.

Okay. Find a place to stay the night and call the boss man, Splinter thought. *See what he says about tomorrow . . . Figure out how to get rid of the dog.* "And buy some damn boots," he said out loud.

* * * * *

CHARLIE AND HIS TWO FRIENDS were tired. It had been a long day.

Decision made about what they wanted to do the following day, Sunday, they pushed away from the table just as Taffy gave two, sharp barks. The hair on her neck rose. She rushed to the door.

"What's the matter, girl?"

"What is it?" Posey asked.

"Don't know. Probably some critter outside. If it's a skunk, I'm not letting her out right now. Come on, Taff. Let's get you fed."

Charlie filled her bowl and set it on the floor along with a dish of water. Taffy ignored both and headed for the door. "All right, let's see what's out there." He grabbed a flashlight from the counter, snapped on her leash, and they went outside.

Taffy immediately began barking and pulling on the leash. She half-dragged Charlie to the back of the house and headed into the woods. "Oh, no. We aren't chasing anything tonight, girl. Come on, do your business and let's get to bed."

Charlie walked her around a bit until she squatted, then went back inside. He closed the door as Russell asked, "Where should I sleep, Charlie?"

"Why don't you take the lower bunk in there, Pose. If you need another blanket, take it from the top."

Penny had earlier placed her suitcase in the Nash's bedroom. She waited for direction from Charlie.

"You two going to stay up?" Posey asked with a slight smile on his face.

Charlie answered for both. "Maybe for a little while, Pose. I . . . uh, want to talk to Penny for a while." He took her hand and led her into the living area. They sat down on the couch, Taffy at their feet. "Oh, crap. I forgot."

"What?" Penny asked.

"Forgot to call my Mom. Promised her I would." He reached for the phone on the side table and lifted the receiver to see if anyone was on the line. The cabin was on a party line, and occasionally the Nashes had to wait for the line to clear before making a call. Charlie recited the number to the operator, and waited.

"Hello?" Marsha Nash said.

"Hi, Mom. It's me. We made it okay. Sorry I didn't call sooner."

"Oh, Charlie. I'm so glad it's you. We were beginning to worry. You were supposed to call right away, dear."

"I know. Forgot. Who's we?" Charlie's pulse pounded as he envisioned the slimy, Silk with his mother.

"Oh, Gramma Nichols's spending the night. We watched the Ed Sullivan Show, had popcorn and milk, and were getting ready for bed."

"Say hi to Gramma, okay?"

"Of course. Everything all right, Charlie?"

"Yeah. Sure." Charlie took Penny's hand and squeezed it gently. "We're going across the lake tomorrow to that spot Dad told us about."

"Looking for that box of Dad's?"

"Yes." Charlie was reluctant to say more.

A voice interrupted their call. "You folks going to be much longer?"

"I better go, Mom. Will you call Mrs. Tercel and let her know we got here okay?"

"Yes, of course."

"Thanks, Mom. Tell you more later."

"Oh, all right, Charlie. I'm anxious to hear more about this. Be careful, dear. Good night."

"'Night, Mom."

Charlie hung up. He rose and turned off all the lights except for a small lamp in the dining room. He sat back down with Penny, put his arm around her, and pulled her close. She had curled beneath an afghan

Gramma Nichols had knitted. Her legs tucked beneath her so she snuggled against Charlie's side.

They were quiet for a long time. The fire had died down to a few flickering embers. Penny looked up. Charlie stared into the fire. "What? What's wrong?" she asked.

"Huh? Oh, nothing, Penn. Just thinking how good this feels to be here with you. Thanks for coming. I know this is not the sort of thing you normally do."

"What, you mean run off with my boyfriend to a north woods cabin for a week?" She giggled and nestled closer.

"Yeah. Kinda out of character for you, Penn."

"Maybe. Maybe not. Maybe you don't really know me as well as you think you do. You think I'm a real, 'goodie-two-shoes,' don't you?"

He chuckled. "No. Actually I know that you're really a bad girl lookin' for trouble. I've just never seen that side of you."

Penny grew serious. "No, not that. You do have an influence on me, though. Sometimes I feel like . . . like I'd pretty much do whatever you wanted me to. I care about you that much, Charlie." She twisted and put both hands on either side of his head. She drew him to her.

Charlie didn't know what to say. Penny's words echoed in his head. He had known for a long time that their relationship could be something very special, he just never knew what to do about it. His heart thrummed as he kissed her.

They pulled apart. "Penny, I'll always remember this time with you. I'll never do anything to hurt you." He kissed her again, this time it lasted much longer. The pair leaned back and slid lower on the couch.

Just then, a bright kitchen light flashed. "Charlie? Penny? Uh . . . time for bed, ya think?" Posey was taking his job very seriously.

The two on the couch laughed, shrugged, and stood. "Thanks, Pose. We're coming," Charlie called. "Come on, Penn." He pulled her close for one last kiss.

Charlie checked the thermostat, and walked with Penny to her room. "'Night, Penn."

"'Night, Charlie." She gave his hand a squeeze. "Thank you."

"For what?"

"For honoring your promise."

"Hmmm. It's a long week, Penn." He smiled coyly and winked.

"Go to bed," she said and closed her door.

Charlie went into his bedroom. He left the door open for Taffy to access her water and food, and rolled into bed. For the longest time, sleep alluded him. He tossed and turned. Readjusted his pillow. Went to get a glass of water. Still could not sleep. Something was wrong . . . something he forgot?

He gave up finally, rose, threw on a sweatshirt, and went out to the family room. Posey's room was dark and he could hear rhythmic, gentle snoring coming from his newest friend. He looked in on Penny. She was a curled up ball beneath the quilt. He quietly closed the door.

Charlie smiled. *I'm pretty lucky, I guess. Posey's a good guy. Reminds me of Quill somehow. And Penny? God, I love being with her . . .*

Charlie poured a glass of milk. He opened a bag of Oreos, grabbed a couple, and sat at the dining table. He left the lights out. As he bit into the cookie, he thought about the last time he was at the cabin. Suddenly it all came flooding back. He felt very sad. Tears formed and slowly rolled down his cheek. He gagged on the cookie and spit it into a napkin. Taffy came close. Put her head on his knee as if understanding completely the sadness her master was feeling.

Charlie didn't hear the bedroom door open. Penny slipped across the linoleum. She put both arms around his neck from the back and laid her head on his shoulder. "Charlie? What's wrong?"

He couldn't answer. He was glad Penny came to him but embarrassed by the tears. "I don't know, Penn. I just feel so sad being here, I guess."

"Come here," she commanded and pulled him over to the sofa. They lay down together and covered up with the blanket. "It's okay to cry, you know." She hugged him tightly and laid her head on his chest.

Taffy curled up at the far end of the sofa. The three would spend the rest of the night together.

In the adjacent room, Russell Posey rose and tiptoed out to the kitchen. He peered around the corner and noticed that both Penny and Charlie were on the couch. It was dark. Posey didn't feel he should intrude. Instead, he quietly went back to bed.

The teens slept through the night. Taffy stayed alert. The smell she detected outside the house brought the dog to full alert. Something was wrong with the odor . . . it was human, and not a friendly scent at all.

* * * * *

SPLINTER SPENT THAT SATURDAY NIGHT at a different motel than the one he used back in October. *No sense raising questions from the motel owner,* he reasoned. So he registered at the Pine Cone Inn on the other side of Highway 371. It was 9:00 p.m. Time to check in with his employer.

Splinter used a commercial pay phone on the corner. "Long distance, operator, collect." he said and gave her the number.

"Your name, sir?" the operator asked.

"Uh, Victor. Tell him it's from Victor."

The phone rang for a while and then was answered by the man.

"I have a collect call from a, Victor. Will you pay?" the operator asked.

"Yes, I will." He waited.

"It's me. Can you talk?"

"Yes. What have you to report?"

"I'm back in that same jerk-water town up north—Hackensuck."

"Yes, I know that. He's with his friends?"

"Yep. Four-eyes and cutey-pie."

"And? Don't drag this out, Victor. Bring me up to date."

"Well, they almost got their asses kicked by a couple of local yokels in Brainerd, but managed to talk their way out of it, I guess. Thought for a minute I might have to intercede somehow, but they got away clean."

"Any idea why they are up there?" the man asked.

"No, not really. Got close enough to hear snatches of conversation, but nothing more than they intend to wander across the lake tomorrow for some damn reason."

"Tell me, Victor. When you were up there last fall, did you notice anything over on that side of the lake? Anything unusual?" the man asked.

"Like what?"

"I don't know. Buildings? Machinery?"

"You forget, it was raining, I was wet. I was miserable. Guess I did stumble over some old timbers and log cabins. Never gave much thought to it. Why? What's going on?"

"Something the wife said about what her husband found and where he found it leads me to think the Nash boy knows quite a bit more than he's letting on. That's why he's back there now. If the rest of that silver-colored material is still up there, we have to get our hands on it, Victor."

Splinter's attention was at a very high level now, at the mention of a large quantity of whatever seemed to be so valuable. "You know, that's the second time you've mentioned the possibility of more than just the one piece. I think it's time to re-negotiate our contract, Mr. Silk."

"Huh? You, you know my name?"

"Of course I do, *Duane*. Who did you think you were doing business with? Some idiot from the sticks? I always do my homework. I find out all I can about my employer. It's called, leverage, Duane. So, now that we have that on the table, I want a cut of the prize."

"How much?" Silk asked.

"Thirty percent," Splinter replied.

"Too much."

"I'll even take care of any future dirty work as part of my thirty percent. How's that?"

Silk didn't reply right away. He knew Splinter was holding all the cards right now . . . especially if he managed to lay his hands on the treasured cache. *If* the boy managed to find it, of course. He relented. "Okay. Thirty percent."

"Good. Now I don't mind being up in this ratty berg quite as much. One thing more."

"Yeah?"

"The dog. It's proving to be a problem."

Silk never hesitated. Taffy had clearly shown a strong dislike for his own self. "Take care of it . . . "

"Done. I'll call tomorrow," Splinter replied.

* * * * *

ANOTHER PAIR OF EYES besides Splinter had been watching the teens at Shepherd Lake. This second pair belonged to a man with long white hair, a thick, gray beard and eyes blue as the sky. He studied the teens' activities from a distance—with extreme interest. Surprised by their sudden appearance at the cabin, the watcher was a squatter and had to relocate from what he had claimed as his all winter: Namely the Nash cabin. He'd have to adjust. The forest was getting crowded. Their presence would complicate things . . . or, *would they?* He wondered.

Fifteen

THE NEXT MORNING, Sunday, Charlie let Taffy out of the cabin. She immediately bounded away in into the woods north of the cabin. Charlie was pre-occupied getting things ready for their trek across the lake and lost track of her whereabouts. He was unconcerned, however, as she always came back to check in. A trait of most bird dogs, they ranged ahead and to either side, then almost always checked back to re-establish contact. This maneuver had always been true of Taffy.

"Come on, Pose. Let's go." Penny had elected to stay behind. She was tired, and unlike the boys, wanted to eat breakfast and nap a while.

"I'm coming. Don't get your underwear in a bunch," Posey said as he buckled his jeans. He threaded a sheath knife through his belt. "Gotta make sure I'm armed, ya know. Might run into a sasquatch or something . . ." The knife had been a treasured gift from an uncle.

"Don't worry. I've got this crappy .22 Silk gave me. I'll protect you." Charlie loaded a bullet into the breach, clicked the bolt closed, and aimed the rifle at a piece of cardboard he nailed to an oak tree. The crack of the rifle echoed through the woods.

"Lemme see if you're any good," Posey said. He ran to the tree. "Ha. You missed, Charlie."

"Told you the gun was a piece of crap. Sights must be cockeyed," Charlie offered in defense. Taffy came running at the sound of gunfire. She looked up at her master expectantly.

"Yeah. Right. Let me try, deadeye." Posey reached for the rifle.

"Know how to load it, Pose?" He handed his friend a .22 short.

"Pretty sure I do." Posey drew back the bolt, slipped the live round in the chamber, and closed the bolt. "No safety on this, Charlie?"

"No. Told you it was cheap. Once you throw the bolt, it's ready to fire."

Posey spotted the target, raised the gun to his shoulder, aimed, and fired. Once again, a fairly loud, "*crack!*" sounded, along with a simultaneous "*splat*" as the lead struck the cardboard. "Whoa, momma. Guess the sights are good after all, eh, Charlie?"

"Lucky shot, Pose. Come on. Let's get going." He waved at Penny who had been watching the boys through the window. She waved back and took a bite out of a piece of toast.

Posey handed Charlie the weapon, and they headed down to the shore. The wooden dock had never been removed the previous fall, and was beginning to show signs of a serious tilt. Damage from shifting ice. They stood on the end and surveyed the lake.

"Hey. What's that?" Posey shielded his eyes from the brilliant sun reflecting off the ice and pointed off to the right . . . to the west.

A small, wooden structure resembling an old outhouse sat on the ice, about forty yards from shore. "Huh. Someone must have dumped it there," Charlie said.

"Bet you a quarter I can hit that," Posey declared.

Charlie pulled another bullet from his pocket, loaded the rifle, and handed the weapon to his friend. "Go ahead, hotshot."

"Think I should?" Posey asked.

"Yeah, why not? Someone left it there . . . abandoned, I'll bet. Besides, technically, it's pretty much on our property. Anyway, what's one little hole going to matter on that old piece of crap."

With that, Posey raised the weapon, sighted down the lake at the wooden structure, and pulled the trigger. Once the echoes subsided from the rifle shot, there was dead silence. But only for a single moment.

Both boys watched in horror as the door to the fish house door flew open. A man stumbled out, ducking as he did, as if fearful of additional rounds heading his way. "Oh, shit!" Posey said.

"No! No! What was he doing in there?" Charlie muttered. He grabbed the rifle from Posey and laid it on the dock. If the water had been open, he would have immediately tossed it in the lake. Instead, it lay there as mute evidence of both boys' mistakes in judgement. The boys watched the man come storming up the lake, body language and flailing arms evidence of the man's anger.

By the time he reached the dock, Taffy re-appeared. Sensing a real threat from the man as he swore and spit out expletives, she stood in front of Charlie, hair on her neck, raised.

"What in God's name were you doing?" the man asked. "How could you be so damned stupid?" His wide eyes darted from one boy to the other. He picked up the rifle and held it out. "Which one? Huh? Who pulled the trigger?" Taffy began barking anew as he thrust the rifle in Charlie's face.

"Quiet, girl. It's my fault, sir. I shot the gun." He shot Posey a look that said, "Keep quiet." Resignedly, he was ready to take the verbal abuse. "But, honest, we had no idea what that thing was . . . or, that anyone would be in there. I thought it was abandoned . . ." Charlie pleaded.

"It's a dark house, moron," the man declared.

Charlie and Posey exchanged questioning looks. "Ah, we're from the Cities . . . what's a dark house?" Posey asked.

"What? A dark house—like a fish house except it's kept dark—for spearing pike. You city kids don't know squat all, do ya?"

"No, sir. Guess not," Posey said.

"You know how close that bullet came to my head?"

"No, sir," Charlie replied, afraid to hear the answer.

"This close," the man said, and held his thumb and forefinger about two inched apart. "Two inches lower and I'd be lying there dead." His anger flared again at the telling. He wiped the spittle from his mouth. "You got a handle on that dog, boy, or am I going to have to take control. She looks like she'd love to take a bite out of my leg."

"I've got her." Charlie reached for Taffy's collar and pulled her close. "Hush, Taff." She quieted down but remained in front of her master.

"It was an honest mistake," Posey offered.

"Honest mistake, my ass," the man said. "That was wanton and intentional destruction of my private property." He looked back up toward the cabin. "Where're your parents?" He nodded at the building. "They up there?"

"No. It's just me, Russell, our friend Penny, and Taffy. I, uh, my dad died last fall, and uh, the three of us came up," Charlie offered.

Then the man relaxed. He visibly softened when he realized who he was talking to. "Oh, yes. Of course. I heard all about it, son. Forgot for a moment who lived here. I'm very sorry for your loss." He removed his ball cap as a gesture of sympathy and respect.

"My name's, Early Ducet."

Sixteen

What's your name, son?" Ducet asked.

"Charlie. Charlie Nash. He turned to Russell and added, "And, this is my friend Russell Posey."

Ducet reached out to Russell and shook his hand. "Pleased to meet ya, Russell."

Posey let go and said, "Uh, me too."

"I was sure saddened to hear of your misfortune last fall, son. Terrible thing, that. Can't imagine how hard that must have been for you—and your mom."

"Yes, sir," Charlie answered.

Ducet replaced his hat and scratched his chin. Two-day's growth rasped in the still air. "Tell ya what, Charlie. Let's forget what just happened here and write it off to, uh . . . your mind being otherwise occupied. Understandable that you might not be thinking too clearly far as I can see. Guess a city kid could look at my old hut over there and think it abandoned . . . honest mistake, at that. Now that I look at it—does look like a pile of shit." Ducet chuckled, as did the boys.

Charlie was relieved at the man's forgiveness. "Thank you, Mr. Ducet. I'm normally very safety conscious around guns. What just happened was a mistake. I promise it won't happen again. If you'd like me to patch the hole or something?"

"Hell, boy. Hole's no bigger than a pea. That thing has cracks in it bigger'n that itty bitty hole. I'll stick a wad of chew in it," Ducet said.

He spit brown juice onto the ice and smiled. What teeth he had left were yellow-stained from tobacco. "What are you folks doing up here, anyway?" Ducet looked past the boys up toward the cabin.

"Oh, we're on spring break and decided to come up and just sort of fool around. I want to take Russell across the lake . . . over to, uh, well over there anyway." Charlie was reluctant to say too much.

Ducet looked across the lake. "What you think's over there, Charlie?"

"Don't know. My dad was over there with Taffy a few weeks before, before the accident and talked about how neat it was and all. Just kinda wanted to be over and be where he was, I guess."

"Understandable, that. Well, you fellas be careful over there. There were some holes and wells dug and what's left of them buildings is pretty rotten," Ducet offered.

Charlie was intrigued by Ducet's comment. "So, you know the area, Mr. Ducet?"

"Call me Early, son, and, yes, I know the area about as well as anyone. I worked over there during the war. Worked directly for General Abdelkader—the main man in charge of the whole shebang, actually."

"Really?" Charlie was impressed. A few tidbits his father had shared with him were starting to fall in place. "Well, maybe you could tell us what was going on over there?" Charlie asked hopefully.

"Not right now, no. Tell ya what, though. You two go on over there with your dog and poke around. What's her name?"

"Taffy."

"Think she'll let me pet her? Had an old dog died last year . . . sure miss old Blue."

"Oh, sure. She's checked you out now and knows you're a friend, right, Taff?" He steered her toward Ducet who had knelt down and clicked his tongue. "Hey, there, sweetheart. Aren't you the pretty one, though," Ducet said softly.

Taffy wagged her tail and stepped close. She looked into his face, sniffed his fingers, and permitted a scratch behind her ears. "Might have to get another dog one of these days, Charlie. Sure miss the company of a good dog, ya know?"

Charlie had noticed the missing fingers on Ducet's left hand. "Yes. I understand, Early."

The old man stood and said, "Be careful like I said. When you get back, come on over to my place later on and we'll talk about that project over there." He nodded in the direction of the far side of the lake. "Okay?"

"Sure. You bet. That all right with you, Pose?"

"Ah, yeah, I guess so." Posey was still processing the information Ducet had shared with them, and was very curious about what had been going on the other side of the lake.

"All right, then. I'll see you boys later." Ducet spit once more and headed down the lake—in the other direction. East.

"Say, where did you come in from, Early?" Charlie called after the old man.

"From Nelson's place on the east end of the lake," he replied over his shoulder.

"That's a pretty long walk, actually. I'm sure my dad, ah . . . my dad would have invited you to park on our property. Save you some walking and maybe you could keep an eye on the cabin once in a while?"

Ducet stopped and turned back. "That's real kind, Charlie. Might jest take you up on that next winter."

"Oh, and where do you live?" Charlie called.

"I'm the green house at the fork in the road, Charlie. The one with all the piles of lumber scattered around. Can't miss it."

* * * * *

THE WATCHER WITH THE WHITE HAIR relaxed. He stepped from behind the spruce tree and tracked the boys hike across the lake. He had not been close enough to hear the conversation between the boys and the angry fisherman. He had been concerned with the carelessness the boys showed with the rifle and alarmed when the man he'd been observing all winter popped out, but relieved no one was hurt. He wondered who the boys and girl were, but beyond that idle curiosity, couldn't waste time or energy thinking on it any more. He slipped back into the forest.

* * * * *

SPLINTER LEFT THE SUPERMARKET Sunday morning with a white package from the meat department, and angled toward the hardware store. Pleased with himself, he'd figured out the perfect way to take care of his four-legged problem back at Shepherd Lake. He would purchase the most potent rat poison he could find. Once the bait was set, he felt confident that no dog in the world was smart enough to resist a chunk of sirloin—even one laced with poison. Once the dog was out of the way, he'd be free to move in and find out what the boys were up to.

He opened the door of the mercantile and smiled at the proprietor. "Morning. Say, we've got some real big rats out at our place. I need to get rid of 'em . . ."

* * * * *

"BOY, THAT WAS REALLY SCARY, Charlie," Posey offered as they crossed the lake.

"Scary and really dumb, Pose. I should have known better. Still don't know what I was thinking back there. Hope Penny didn't see all that."

"Well, it could have been worse, that's for sure. Thanks for taking the heat, by the way. What did you think of Early Ducet?"

"Well, once he calmed down, he seemed pretty nice, I guess. Interesting guy, and once Taffy let him pet her, I figured he was okay."

They reached the south shore and followed the shoreline west. "He's like most of the people here."

"What do you mean?" Posey asked as he stepped over a large poplar that had fallen into the lake.

"Well, these folks up here like to keep to themselves. My dad always felt they had a particular sort of backwoods mentality . . . smart and quick. Kind of like a city kid living on the street, ya know?"

"No book smarts, but still clever, right?"

"Yeah. Dad mentioned Ducet to me a couple of times. We knew he had a sawmill behind his house and logged around here. I didn't know that was his house at the fork though and sure didn't know he was involved with stuff across the lake during the war."

"Say, did you notice his left hand?" Posey asked.

"Yeah. Wonder what happened. Have to ask him about that . . ."

They trudged on through the slush as the day was warming and the snow atop the ice was melting. When they reached the spit of land on the southwest corner, Charlie stopped.

"What's the matter, Charlie?"

"This is where we were hunting, Pose. Right there is where I came out of the water . . . the, ah . . . last time I saw . . ." He couldn't finish. Taffy returned from her prowl in the woods and sensed her master's sadness. She nudged his hand. Charlie knelt and laid his cheek on her warm head.

"Hey, we don't have to be here, Charlie. If this is too hard for you, let's go back," Posey offered.

Charlie inhaled and stood. "No, it's okay. I had to see this. I'm all right." He turned away and started walking into the small bay east of the spit. "Come on, this is the area my dad told me about . . ."

The boys hiked across the bay, left the ice, and followed Taffy into the woods. Before long they stumbled on a large quantity of boards and timbers stacked up on the edge of a clearing about as big as a football field. "Something was going on here, Pose," Charlie observed. "That's a lot of lumber. Look." He picked up a section of plank. US Army was stenciled on the face.

"What do you suppose the Army was doing way back here?" Posey asked.

"I don't know. Dad didn't either, but I bet Ducet will tell us."

"You think so?"

"He said he would." Charlie wandered over to what was a mountain of sawdust. "Looks like a logging camp or old sawmill, Pose."

"Then why all the secrecy and high security, then?"

"I don't know. Come on and help me look for that box . . ."

Seventeen

The white-haired watcher was frustrated. Ever since he'd found himself half-drowned on the far side of the lake many months ago, his memory of everything had vanished. At first, he wandered the far woods. Dizzy, disoriented, weak with hunger, he stumbled into one of the old log cabins back in the woods and passed out. When he woke, he took stock of his situation and decided to remain where he was for a while until his memory returned. It never did. Living off berries and roots, and drinking from the lake, ultimately he decided to explore the far side of the lake.

As his head cleared and the dizziness evaporated, he recalled the shadow of a man standing over him when he woke on the shore. The image haunted his every move. He was tormented by having absolutely no recall of anything else. He had no name, no identity, no remembrance. But, Frank Nash had somehow managed to survive that horrific evening and the bludgeoning immediately after. He was unrecognizable now, as his hair had turned pure white almost overnight. Rail thin, with dirty clothes and scraggly beard, he looked every bit the elusive wood creature Russell Posey had joked about.

Drawn to the north side of the lake. He felt he had to get to that far side. He headed east, away from Shepherd Lake. The searchers' traversing the lake looking for bodies gave up quite soon as the lake began to freeze. Nash was mostly unconscious during their searching. He did hear occasional boat motors during his brief awake periods, but gave it no further thought. His only focus was on discovery: Discovery of his identity. His past. Nothing registered in Nash except a tiny spark that led him back, ultimately, to the cabin. Somehow, the small cabin with the guest house felt vaguely familiar.

And, it was at the cabin that Frank Nash spent the winter. Everything was operable. The sheriff had left. No one bothered to shut the place down. Frank had free reign for the next six months to wander in and out of the cabin. He opened drawers and cabinets. Read through various books. Studied a journal noting particular bird and animal species. Strangely, there were no pictures around of the family. The sheriff had taken the few he could find for identification purposes if Frank's body were eventually recovered. Nash discerned from clothing left behind that the family seemed to consist of a husband, wife, and young son. Dog dishes further indicated a family pet. He did not relate to any of it, however.

Frank Nash felt empty. He could not connect the dots. Emotionally empty and dry as an old apple peel, he wandered around waiting for some sign of recognition. Until his memory returned, he couldn't force himself to establish contact with anyone. The cabin family were strangers. He did wonder in passing if he might have some connection to the cabin owners, and, if so, he felt they might be in danger if he were to reveal himself as still alive. He believed he had to be patient . . . to hope his memory would soon return. For the present, he was in no particular rush. The solitary life he was living wasn't all bad. More than once, he considered that he probably should be dead.

So, Nash settled in for the winter. He had food left in the ice box and cupboards. He discovered a 20-gauge shotgun in a bedroom closet and a couple of boxes of birdshot, and soon discovered skill with the weapon. Those acquired skills remained in whatever side of his brain drove him to eat . . . to survive. It was the other side of his brain that was blank: The most important side. The memory side. The feeling side. The side of his self that felt pain and joy and sorrow. He could feel none of that presently.

His wanderings in the woods were frequent. He killed grouse whenever possible. He cautiously hiked east to the end of the road to watch a man he did not recognize cut firewood. It was his only contact with another being.

Nash was not ready to step into the public eye . . . not ready to put himself back in danger, because the one thing he did remember was the man who struck him on the head as he rose from the water. That man represented danger, and Nash had to stay out of sight until he could figure out why someone had tried to kill him.

The gravel road to the Nash cabin, and to the neighboring cabin beyond to the west end of Shepherd Lake remained unplowed for the winter. This assured Nash complete privacy. He observed the comings and goings of the wood cutter, as he frequently trudged down the lake to his fishing shack.

After long periods inside the shack, the man sometimes left with a fish in tow . . . generally a big one, Nash observed. He longed to taste fresh fish, and occasionally visited the man's shack with fishing gear he found in a storage room adjacent to the guest house. He had to be careful, however, and always timed his fishing expeditions immediately after the man left to go home. That way, the hole in the ice was open and he wouldn't have to labor to reopen it.

In time, Frank became quite adept at catching small sunfish and crappies. He could keep the hole in the ice open quite easily, and before long, the freezer filled with small fish filets. Nash thought they were a delicacy.

Frank worried about smoke from the chimney, so he left the heat off—didn't light a fire in the fireplace, except at night. He made certain both were out early in the morning. Surprisingly, the cabin stayed fairly warm during the daylight hours as the low, winter sun poured through the front windows. *Place is plenty tight and warm*, Nash thought. Whoever built it did a hell of a job.

Frank hoped his memory would return with time, but any recollection of his previous life illuded him. He hiked through the snow on a pair of snowshoes he found in the shed, read extensively, and managed to lose about thirty pounds from his stout frame. A large man, he wondered about some of the scars he discovered on his body. Morning aches in his joints left him curious about what he might have done in his past to so abuse his body. Nothing in the cabin would reveal any of that, however.

Life was pretty simple for Frank Nash that winter. Nothing changed. Once in a while he'd notice fresh tire tracks on the road, but never actually saw a car. His only brush with a human came from the fisherman passing in front of the cabin every other day. He nicknamed the man, "Woody." Unsure why, he concluded it had to be from the single time he had seen the man cutting wood. He wondered, however, if, Woody might have been the same man that struck him on the head. The same man that left him for dead.

"Someday I'll find out, Woody. If it was you, I promise you I'll settle the score," Nash said out loud as he watched the fisherman head for home.

* * * * *

THE DAY CHARLIE, RUSSELL, and Penny arrived at the cabin was the end of Frank's sojourn alone in the woods. He had always been something of a neat freak without realizing it, so whenever he left the cabin, everything was put in place. On the day Charlie arrived, he had been away much of the afternoon, grouse hunting. Ashes in the fireplace were cold when the kids arrived. The sight of the Pontiac parked behind the cabin startled him. He hid behind a stand of white pine and watched two boys unload the car. He observed a very attractive girl dressed in a sweatshirt and blue jeans with cuffs folded up to mid-calf, helping to unload.

A tan dog pranced around and wagged at whatever it was scenting. At one point the dog lifted her head into the breeze, wagged her tail and headed Frank's way.

He prayed the dog wouldn't continue. Fortunately one of the boys called her inside. He had a sudden spark of emotion as he watched the one boy and his dog. He struggled for any sign of recognition . . . any spark of familiarity, but nothing rose. The ember died.

He shook his head and realized he had a big problem now: Where was he going to go? Where could he stay? He couldn't reveal himself to these kids as that would endanger all of them. Without knowing their plans, or how long they planned to stay, he clearly had to leave or he'd eventually be found. And . . . then what? What would happen? No, he had to remain hidden for everyone's safety.

Frank Nash left the property that evening and hiked through the woods to the west. He knew he had to find a place to get out of the elements, and the only other structure in range he knew was uninhabited, was the small cabin he discovered on one of his forays. He stuck the grouse in his pocket, laid the shotgun over his shoulder, and hiked out to the road. Most of the snow was gone so he didn't worry about leaving tracks along the road.

When he came upon the cabin at the far, west end of the lake, he approached it cautiously. He saw no tracks in the snow of humans or car tires. The cabin was dark. Curtains drawn. No smoke from the chimney. He tested the door. Locked, of course. He walked around the structure and tested all the windows. *Hate to break anything if I don't have to,* he thought.

He found a rusty screwdriver on a picnic table and began work on the door's lock. It was old, easily manipulated. It wasn't long before the old, brass lock popped. He was in.

Frank Nash set himself up in his new digs, while the three teens took over the other cabin. It proved to be a reasonable walk back down the road to observe the kids activities, and he had to be careful to stay upwind of the dog. For the most part, everything worked according to plan, except for the one time the dog tracked him down.

She was a beautiful little golden-brown long-haired dog, that actually smiled with a peculiar wrinkled lip as she approached him. "No, no," he whispered. "Go home, sweetie," he pleaded. He'd been watching the cabin from the stand of spruce trees. He lost track of the breeze, and when it changed direction, the little dog made a bee-line right to where he hid.

She was not about to leave. He knelt and took the dog's head in his large hands. "What's your name, sweetheart?" He spun her leather collar and discovered a brass nameplate. "Taffy," he declared. "Your name's Taffy, isn't it?"

She wagged furiously and licked his face, non-stop. "My God. Do you know me?" His heart pounded at the sudden revelation that the dog might be his.

Nash kept her close for as long as he could. Before long, one of the boys began calling for her, however. "Go on, girl. You have to go now," he whispered. "This will be our little secret, okay?"

Taffy hesitated, started back then returned and licked Nash's hand, as if wanting him to join her. "No, you have to go," he whispered. "Go on, go . . ."

Frank turned his back and melted into the woods. For the first time since he lifted from the water and faced the dark stranger with the club, a spark of familiarity flickered. *I know that dog. It's Taffy. And she knows me!*

133

Eighteen

IN 1944, WHEN WORD CAME via telex that General Abdelkader's work was finished at Shepherd Lake, he went beserk. "Bastards didn't even have the courtesy for a personal visit, First Sergeant." The fact that the Air Force had developed long-range flying capability to protect troop ships crossing the North Atlantic, was of little concern for Abdelkader. He had envisioned a heroic outcome for himself, and cancelling the Habakkuk project offended him greatly.

"Yes, General. Your effort here certainly deserves more than an impersonal telex," Fistric said.

"Ungrateful, short-sighted, snot-nosed sons-a-bitches," Abdelkader snorted. "Could've built this, First Sergeant. We proved it, didn't we?"

"I'd reply in the affirmative, General. Yes, sir, we sure did."

"Well, to hell with Roosevelt. Panty-waist cripple that he is. He's no commander in chief . . . that's a certainty. No balls. That's it in a nutshell, First Sergeant. While he's too weak to stand up to Churchill, our boys suffer the consequences. They haven't proven a thing, yet, near as I can tell. Long range fighter protection my ass! Those boobs in Washington have been listening to the industrialists . . . the guys who build these *supposedly* long-range aircraft. It's all bullshit and feather-bedding, First Sergeant," Abdelkader blustered.

"Yes, sir. Seems like that flight Colonel Doolittle made with the B-52s lifting off the deck of the aircraft carrier, gave Roosevelt and Eisenhower false hope to my way of thinking."

"Absolutely correct, First Sergeant. Why, none of those bombers landed safely. Hell's bells, the few bombs they managed to drop didn't prove a thing, did it? Big PR stunt of Roosevelt's if you ask me . . ."

"Yes, General." Fistric knew his general well enough to let him spout and sputter. This time proved different, however: Fistric observed a deep hatred and desire for atonement in his boss. Abdelkader showed a single-minded focus about a way to get even for having his project shut down.

After a bit, when the opportunity arose, Fistric asked, "What are your orders, General?"

"Shut it down, First Sergeant. Shutter the whole damn thing. Send the men away soon as you're done, then report to me."

"Yes, sir. And, what about Ducet?"

"What about him? Don't need 'em now, do we?"

"No, sir."

"Well, then send him home. Hell, he doesn't even have far too go . . . just to the end of the road. Aw, give him our thanks and all that for a job well done . . . couldn't have done it without him and such . . ."

"Yes, sir. Anything else, sir?"

"The rhodium. Is it secure?"

"Same spot as always, General."

"Good. Let me think on how best to, uh . . . handle that. Right?"

"Yes, sir." Fistric left the general alone in their makeshift HQ, and went to find Ducet.

* * * * *

ABDELKADER'S SCHEME TO STEAL the silver wafers was simple. He'd enlist Fistric to build a second wooden container, fill it with rock, lock it up, and ship it back to Fort Knox. A squad of troopers would accompany the shipment. All the proper paperwork would be filled out and sent along with the shipment three weeks later. He doubted if anyone would ever open the box—simply label it and stash it along with hundreds of other items in a huge warehouse someplace. Didn't matter. He'd be long gone by then.

The actual box of rodium wafers would be buried in a location known only to Abdelkader and Fistric. They planned to mark the spot with a pair of bottle caps nailed to two different trees, each one a specific distance from the hole containing the rhodium. Abdelkader had thought of everything, and one day, both would be rich.

The general told Fistric they would split the treasure, fifty-fifty. There was enough for both, Abdelkader reasoned. His only concern was to locate a source . . . off shore, no doubt, where they could quietly unload the precious metal. Abdelkader felt confident that through his years developing contacts in the service, he could find some country willing to purchase the valuable mineral.

For the short term, both would return to their home base at Fort Leonard Wood, Missouri, file the appropriate retirement papers, and muster out as was their option. Then lay low for a short while and return to the woods on the south shore of Shepherd Lake, dig up their treasure, and vanish.

The general's plan was flawless and worked to perfection. The bogus box of rhodium was never properly received at Fort Knox. Numerous snafus in the paperwork sent ahead by Abdelkader slowed everything down. In addition what became more good fortune for Abdelkader, with the increased attention given to the war effort, it meant that literally, *no one* cared much anymore about the Shepherd Lake project.

The troops that worked in the woods during the project's tenure, really had little knowledge of what their commandant and his sergeant were up to. The pulverizing of the rhodium wafers was done secretly. The formula created by the chemists was a closely held secret. Early Ducet had heard snippets about what was really going on with the rhodium recovery process, but never actually observed the pulverizing or mixing.

The prototype ice boat built by Abdelkader was constructed to be one hundred sixty feet long by thirty feet wide. With a two percent mixture of rhodium required in the slurry, only a tenth of the available rhodium was ever used to build the prototype iceberg. The remaining packages of wafers sat in a heavy wooden crate, stacks wrapped in wax paper, accessible only by Abdelkader and Fistric.

When the time was right, both men carted the crate from the general's quarters on a dark, warm night. They hauled the rhodium some distance from the compound. When they reached the appropriate spot, Abdelkader opened one of the packets of twenty-four and removed two wafers: One for each of them. In his excitement, however, Abdelkader grew careless. A third wafer slipped from the package and silently fell into the dirt at their feet.

"Shit," the general muttered in the dark.

"Sir?" Fistric shined the black-out flash on the hole. "Problem, sir?"

Abdelkader said, "May have dropped one here, Sergeant. Shine your light on the ground."

Fistric did as he was told but after a few minutes, both men concluded that all was in order. They neglected to count the remaining pieces in the broken package.

"Okay. We're good. Here, Sergeant. There's your piece." The general handed a wafer to Fistric and pocketed the other. He hurriedly rewrapped the package . . . now with twenty-one wafers, placed the bundle in the box, and closed the lid—a total of one-hundred-forty-four packages in all.

Fistric locked the box with a heavy padlock. Together they lifted the chest into the hole. "Cover it up, First Sergeant," Abdelkader whispered.

The wafer that fell was gathered up in one of the last shovelfuls of dirt. It sat unnoticed . . . partially revealed in the freshly turned earth.

"All we have to do now is muster out, lay low, and come back here when the dust settles for our reward," Abdelkader said as they hiked back to their quarters.

"Yes, sir. Foolproof plan, General. Thanks for including me . . ."

"You're welcome, First Sergeant. Guess I'll have to start calling you Barstow one of these days, right?" Abdelkader said.

"Yes, General."

Confident that the location of their prize would never be discovered—even by accident, Abdelkader believed his plan to be perfect. Furthermore, the general had also decided that he ultimately could never permit Fistric to share in the treasure. His reasoning was one of security. Fistric could not be trusted, particularly when he was drinking. Barstow Fistric had a history of getting roaring drunk when on furlough. He'd brag about all sorts of nonsense and many times wind up in a bar brawl. More than once over the years, Abdelkader had to free his first sergeant from the brig.

No, this was too big and too important. Barstow Fistric was not going to reap the rewards he thought he was. Abdelkader was going to keep it all for himself. The general had a loosely defined plan when they returned whereby he'd wait until his sergeant dug the box up, then put a bullet in his head. The hole left where they dug up the chest would become Fistric's final resting place.

Neither General Richard Abdelkader nor First Sergeant Barstow Fistric made it back to Shepherd Lake, as planned, however. Eight months after they mustered out, the two thieves were involved in a deadly collision with a freight train.

According to the *Little Falls Tribune*, Abdelkader was killed in a collision with a Great Northern freight train north of Little Falls, in late 1944. Fistric escaped, miraculously, with only minor injuries.

However, after a thorough investigation of the accident, it was determined that Fistric was culpable in the death of his passenger—the general. The sergeant was held on charges of vehicular manslaughter.

According to the paper, Fistric—the driver—and his passenger, Stephen Abdelkader, had slammed into the side of a freight train at a high rate of speed without stopping. The railroad crossing, dimly lit, had no warning lights. The train, heavily loaded, pulling seventy-seven cars, was on route to the Twin Cities carrying a load of coal from North Dakota.

Local residents indicated that Abdelkader and Fistric, both heavily intoxicated, had been thrown out of the *Let'r Rip Saloon* a short time before the collision. The bartender remembered that the older of the two, Abdelkader, made lewd and obscene remarks to one of the dancers and was punched in the face by the dancer. Security tossed both men from the premises.

In actuality, the men were on their way to Shepherd Lake to retrieve their buried treasure. A stop at the saloon and strip joint at Camp Ripley had been orchestrated by Fistric.

Details surrounding Fistric's miraculous escape—unscathed—proved suspicious. He had no explanation for how he managed to avoid being killed along with the general. The district attorney for Morrison County, Myron Entwhistle, felt justified in asking for the maximum penalty under the law as he was convinced that *intent* played a role in the death of Abdelkader.

Fistric's trial was scheduled for October 1944.

Barstow Fistric, after a great deal of consideration, had decided that because of his many years of service and loyalty to a man he *truly* despised, he alone deserved all of the loot. Fistric dreamed up what he thought was a foolproof plan to get rid of the general. What he didn't know, of course, that the general had his own plan to snuff out his first sergeant.

Fistric had indeed managed to get the old general good and drunk at the strip joint. As the driver of the green sedan, he would ensure that the general never laid his hands on any of the rhodium. Barstow would—by the grace of the Good Lord—survive a tragic accident. His plan was foolproof . . . or so he thought.

The general had passed out on the passenger side of the sedan as planned. Barstow made sure Abdelkader had plenty of whiskey to put him to sleep. After loading the general, Fistric pulled away from the saloon. Two minutes later, he pulled off on a dirt road and stopped. He left the car running as he got out.

"Wassa matter?" the general asked.

"Nothing . . . gotta take a piss," Fistric replied. He scrabbled in the ditch searching for a large rock to lay against the gas pedal. That accomplished, he climbed in, backed up and headed down the highway.

Unsure of exactly how the accident should appear, the on-coming freight train was a stroke of luck. He pulled off on the shoulder fifty-yards from the railroad crossing. Abdelkader stirred and mumbled, "Think I'm gonna be sick . . ."

"You have no idea, you pretentious prick," Fistric said.

With the door open and half-hanging out, he stepped on the throttle as the train reached the crossing. The car shot ahead. Thirty-yards, twenty, fifteen. At the last second, he maneuvered the large rock over the gas pedal and straightened the steering. Just before the collision, he rolled away from the car.

The impact was immediate, loud, and abrupt. The car promptly exploded into a huge ball of flame. Pieces were dragged down the track by the speeding freight.

Perfect, Fistric thought. He checked himself and discovered nothing broken. *Probably should look the part*, he thought, and he sat back down. He took a stick and scratched his face and arms, ripped his shirt. Then he waited for the police.

* * * * *

BARSTOW FISTRIC WAS FOUND GUILTY and sentenced to fifteen years in prison. He spent the entire fifteen imprisoned at Fort Leavenworth, Kansas.

His trumped-up car accident story didn't fool anyone . . . particularly the six-man jury. The judge gave Fistric the maximum sentence permitted under the law. There would be no parole, under any circumstance.

Fistric's dream of recovering the box of rhodium would have to wait. Because he feared a memory loss after fifteen long years, he wrote down the location of the chest and mailed it to himself in care of his sister's home in Kansas City. The letter was marked, "Do Not Open." Inside were the crucial directions:

Locate bottle cap #1 nailed to spruce tree, approximately three hundred yards south of HQ. Pace off nine steps east of the tree and make a mark. Locate bottle cap #2 on second spruce, north of mark. Pace off fifteen steps back toward the mark. Where the two lines intersect, dig!

His patience would be sorely tested for the next fifteen years as he waited for his release. He would leave Leavenworth a bitter, dangerous man. Any interference in his quest to retrieve his treasure would lead to serious consequences. He had no doubt about his mission.

Nineteen

CHARLIE AND POSEY SPENT the rest of that second day exploring the army's secret installation. Both boys were caught up in the thrill of being two of the first people, besides Charlie's dad, to thoroughly investigate what remained of a highly secret, World War II project site.

"Just think, Charlie. We're like a couple of archeologists digging up some valuable historic stuff," Posey enthused.

"Yeah, except we haven't done much digging, have we?"

"Uh, no. Ground's still frozen. That's for sure. Might have helped to have a shovel with us, though."

"Yeah, well, next time." Charlie led the way to a small barn set off from the rest of the wooden buildings. Most of the structures retained their original form, as time had not yet done enough damage to cause total collapse. The building they were currently in had one small, main room, and two smaller rooms adjacent.

"Some sort of main office, ya think, Pose?"

"Maybe. Each room has what's left of a metal bed and spring, so maybe the big cheese and his flunky slept here. Check this out," Posey declared and held up a three-ring binder half buried under the rubble.

"What is it?" Charlie asked.

"Says, *Log Book–Quartermaster,* on the front." Posey opened it up and began riffling the pages. "Just a bunch of forms that seem to be records of . . . let's see. Kinda hard to read, but it seems to be a record starting in, uh . . . November 1942. How about that, Charlie?"

"So, we'd have been involved in the war for almost a year, right? Know your history, Pose?"

"December 7, 1941. Pearl Harbor, right? Japs snuck in and bombed everything in sight. Dirty cowards . . ."

"Yep. So, these guys came in here that next year and set up camp . . . doing whatever the hell they were doing. Geez I'd love to know what was going on here."

"Well, maybe this log book will shed some light," Posey offered. "Getting late. Light's fading, Charlie."

"Yeah, we should probably go. Penny's probably wondering what happened to us. I still want to go over to Ducet's house and talk to Early, ya know?"

Charlie whistled for Taffy who was joyfully harassing a chipmunk in a large, hollow log outside. She paused, looked up, and gave one last pounce on the rotting wood. She came up empty.

"Come on, Taff. Let's go. We'll come back again. That chippy'll still be here tomorrow . . ."

* * * * *

THE BOYS RETURNED to the cabin just as the sun was setting. Frank Nash had observed the boys' leaving and a while later, Penny climbing into the Pontiac. When she drove off, he snuck inside the cabin to retrieve warmer clothing and rob the pantry of cans of food he felt certain they would not miss. He grabbed additional shells, a flashlight, and a couple of candles.

He also took the Weston's Dictionary he'd been reading to learn more about memory loss. Amnesia, he read, took many different forms. It appeared from his reading that Frank suffered from the most severe form: including both long and short term memory loss. *When would he recover?* He wondered. Maybe never, according to his reading. That piece of news was particularly depressing, but he refused to dwell on it. Instead, he had to go about the business of living and adapting. He grew increasingly vigilant now with the arrival of the teens and felt an obligation to watch over all three. He would continue to trust in a faith that had no real basis for belief: That one day his memory would return.

Currently, he had other, more immediate concerns. Power had been turned off at the second cabin he now called home, so he took a handful of candles and stuffed them in his pocket. Any small amount of light would improve his mood in the small cabin. He looked around, confident the kids wouldn't notice he had been there, and slipped out of the cabin after an hour or so.

He headed back up the narrow driveway to the road and turned west toward his new digs. A wave of sadness came over him as he realized that the cabin he just left, maybe one of the boys, certainly the dog, represented a connection to his past. He prayed for remembrance. Longed to know about his family; about his former life. But, as hard as he tried, his only memory remained of a large man stepping forward and hitting him on the head.

Why? What had I done? It had all happened so suddenly.

What Frank had no recollection of was of anything prior to getting hit on the head.

No memory of returning to the overturned boat to rescue his friend. No memory of the utter sadness he felt when he could not find the boat nor Earl. He called. He treaded water. He searched frantically. Earl and the boat had drifted away. Frank had managed to swim back to shore one more time. He crawled ashore and collapsed.

Almost immediately, he was rewarded with what should have been a killing blow to the head as he tried to rise from the water.

He had no recollection of any of that, of course. His brain was muddled, his memory gone. He lived in the moment, now. Struggling to retain his strength. Now, he had to stay close to the teens and the dog. He was certain they represented his sanity . . . and his past.

When he arrived back at the small cabin, he unloaded everything taken from the other cabin, started a fire as it was dark by then, lit two candles, and heated a can of chili over the fire. Stomach full, he made a cup of instant coffee with water he collected from melted snow down at the lake, and settled in for the night. He had to be up early the next day, to resume his vigil back at the other cabin.

His self-imposed mission gave him hope: Watch the kids, be prepared for anything. He'd try to grab whatever memories he could and try to rebuild his identity. The children might be his salvation, but before he approached them, the timing had to be perfect: He had to be sure both he and the three of them, were safe. Whoever tried to kill him, did so for a reason—the man was after something . . . something connected to the cabin maybe . . . to the kids staying there, perhaps.

Nash blew out the candles, watched the dying fire for a while, and drifted off to the calls of a great horned owl hooting just outside the cabin.

Twenty

WHEN THE BOYS RETURNED to the cabin, they had no idea a visitor-thief had been inside the cabin while they were away. Penny had returned from her trip to town. She didn't notice anything unusual either when she did.

"Had to get a few things from the store that we missed yesterday," she said.

Taffy immediately picked up on the familiar scent of Frank Nash that to her ultra-sensitive nose, permeated the cabin. She ran through the cabin whining . . . wagging her tail excitedly. She tracked him into the bedroom closet, then back to the kitchen, even into the bathroom. She looked at Charlie expectantly, as if he should know that his father was someplace close . . . had in fact been in the cabin.

Charlie was preoccupied jostling and teasing with Penny, however, as she fixed dinner. "What are we having, Penn? Sirloin steak?" Taffy's excitement went unnoticed during the playful exchange.

"You wish," she replied. "No, but thought fried potatoes and cube steaks would taste good. How's that sound?" She handed Charlie the peeler. "Here. Make yourself useful."

"What can I do, Penn?" Posey asked.

"Hmmm. Maybe set the table? Put some bread and butter out?"

Charlie told Penny all about their meeting with Ducet earlier that day, as he worked on the spuds. He was tempted to leave out the part about shooting a hole in his dark house, but hated lying to Penny. So, he confessed.

Penny was incredulous. "What's with you two? You might have killed the man." She looked from one to the other.

"I know. It was stupid, Penn. We were very lucky, I guess," Charlie said. Anxious to change the subject, he added, "On a positive note, we got to meet Early, and he asked us to stop by his house."

"Why?" she asked.

"To tell us about the military installation across the lake."

Taffy was whining. "What does she want?" Penny asked.

"Food. Forgot to feed her this morning. Right, Taff?" He picked up her bowl, spooned a large glop of Hills canned food into a cup of kibbles, and set the bowl back down. "There, now no more complaining." He washed his hands and called, "We ready to eat, Penn?"

"Almost. You guys sit down. Meat's almost ready."

Dinner was consumed in relative silence. The boys were starving. Charlie had envisioned opening a can of chili but was thrilled to eat the wonderful meal Penny prepared. "Better than chili, that's for sure, Penn."

"You know, I did look for that can you said was in the cupboard, but never found it," Penny said.

"Hmmm. Must have imagined seeing it."

"Who cares," Posey added. "This is great," as he pitch-forked another load of potatoes into his mouth.

"Take a look at this, Penn." Charlie slid the log book across the table.

"What is it?" Penny asked.

"A log book we found across the lake. Pretty interesting stuff, actually," Posey replied.

"Well, let's eat then get over to Ducet's . . . be sure to bring that book along," Charlie said.

"Right," Posey mumbled with a mouth full of food.

Charlie looked around. Something was amiss. What? He wondered. *Too quiet.* Then it hit him. Normally the sound of Taffy's eating would be noticeable and rhythmic. She ate on cue . . . always, but not now. Charlie glanced around and found her under the table.

"What's the matter, girl? Not hungry? Eat something you shouldn't have outside?" Charlie laid down his spoon, and knelt down next to her. "Taffy?" He stroked her velvety head, lifted her chin, and looked into her eyes. "Why so sad?"

Penny joined them on the floor. "What's going on, Charlie?"

"I don't know. Normally she eats like a horse. She was acting kinda goofy when we got back—running around and whining. Thought she was just glad to be back . . . hungry, or something. Now this. She's really sad, Penn. I can tell. Either that or she ate something she shouldn't have today."

"Maybe a ride in the car will perk her up," Posey offered.

"Maybe," Charlie replied with a real lack of conviction. "I know her pretty well. Something's not right . . ."

A short while later, Charlie coaxed Taffy out to the car . . . tail between her legs, head down. Normally all he had to do was mention the words, "car" or "ride" and she would stand at the door, tail flagging. Not this time. She clearly wanted to stay behind, and Charlie was not understanding why. "Come on, girl," he urged.

Ultimately, he had to clip on the leash and lead her to the Pontiac. Half-lifting, half-pushing, he got her into the back seat. Charlie closed the door carefully as she tried to slip back out, and got behind the wheel. "Never seen her like this."

He adjusted the rear view to keep an eye on her. "If she looks like she's going to barf, let me know, Penn . . ."

The short drive put them at Ducet's by 6:00 p.m. Yellow light from the house and a sodium yard light lit the area around the house. Charlie parked in front. "Stay, Taff." The three got out and went to the front door.

Ducet must have seen their lights approaching. He opened the door before Charlie could knock. "Come on in, boys," Ducet said, then noticed Penny. "Oh. Hello, miss."

"Hi. I'm Penny." She extended her hand.

"And I'm Early. Nice to meet you. See you survived your trip over to the *Ice Island Plant?*"

All three looked puzzled. Ducet chuckled, and said, "Sorry. Of course you wouldn't know what I'm talking about. Come on into the kitchen and I'll explain."

The interior of the house was neat and warm. It was evident Ducet lived alone. This was a man's home . . . clearly lacking a women's touch. Charlie couldn't help but think how his mother and grandmother would have decorated the place with all sorts of frills and ruffles.

Ducet sat at the head of a small, rectangular table. "Have a seat, kids," he said and waved them to three available chairs. "Get you something to drink? Coffee? Soda maybe?"

"No, thanks, Early. We just had dinner." Charlie turned to his friends. "You want something, Penn? Russ?"

"I'm fine, thank you, Early," Penny replied.

"Me too. Thanks," Posey said.

"I don't get many visitors here. Kind of deserted most of the year. My old Blue passed on last year, and I sure miss that old dog." Ducet scrubbed at the bristle on his face with the remaining fingers of his right hand.

"Say, where's that pretty little dog of yours, Charlie? She could have come in, ya know."

"Oh, thanks, Early, but, Taffy's been acting kinda funny. Something's not right with her, so I left her in the car."

"Oh, I'm sorry to hear that, son. Sure hope it's nothing serious. Dog's are funny about puttin' stuff in their mouth. She could've found something kinda rank over at the project site maybe didn't agree with her. Ya, think?"

"Maybe. We never leave mouse poison around because of her, but I suppose there could have been something over there . . ." He drew in a breath and sat back. Worry filled his face.

"Don't fret, Charlie. Dogs have a way of working themselves out of trouble. Why, I remember one time old Blue got messed up with the wrong end of a porcupine . . . got quills stuck in his mouth and nose. Lordy, he was a mess. Hurtin' so bad he wouldn't let me near him for nothin'."

"What happened," Posey asked.

"He spent three days down at a pond behind the house . . . buried up to his eyeballs in muck. I watched him stick his head under water every so often to let the cool water and mud soak on those quills, and wouldn't ya know, after about a week they worked their way out, his fever dropped, and he was fine. So, don't you worry, son. She'll be fine."

Ducet stood and said, "I gotta have something sweet. 'Scuse me, folks." He crept over to a cabinet and pulled down a cookie tin. He reached in and pulled out a handful of jellybeans. He flipped a couple in his mouth, and carried the tin back to the table.

"There ya go. Help yerselves . . ." He stuffed the rest in his mouth and chewed noisily. After thirty seconds of chewing, he said, "Had a girlfriend once by the name of Box Car Boni. She got me started on these jellybeans. Cute gal, Boni was. Didn't do me any favors by getting me hooked on these things, though. Only got a few teeth left after all that sugar."

Posey couldn't resist asking, "Why Box Car, Early?"

"Hah. Funny thing about Boni. We'd go park in an area next to the railroad tracks." He smiled at the memory, then continued. "Humph . . . anyway, we'd be kissin' away and stuff and when a freight would pass by, she'd have a fit and want to leave. When I asked her what she was afraid of, she said she always worried that someday she'd be walking along the tracks near her house and some old bum would jump out of a boxcar and grab her. Ever since then I called her Box Car Boni. Not to her face, a course."

The teens chuckled at Ducet's anecdote, and waited politely for him to talk about Shepherd Lake.

"Okay. I can see in yer faces that you want me to stop blabbin' about Boni and tell you all about the *Shepherd Lake Project*, don't ya?"

* * * * *

AN HOUR LATER, Early Ducet had finished his tale. Without interruption, the old man managed to describe in great detail the events he knew to be true, about the project on Shepherd Lake. His only pause in the telling was to excuse himself to go to the bathroom or get more candy.

"That's about it. Once Churchill and FDR pulled the plug, that nasty General Abdelkader shut that plant down quicker than a cat's kerchu. I was paid off and show'd the door. Never even got to say 'So long' to the general, even. Just, 'Adios, and thank you very much.'"

Charlie was first to ask, "Did it work, Early? Did the sawdust island actually float?"

Penny chimed in with, "Could it stay in one piece and not melt?"

"And, what about Nazi torpedoes?" Posey asked all wide-eyed and energized.

"Whoa, now. Hang on. I'll answer your questions best I can. Yes, they actually had it in the lake and camouflaged case someone happened by. Matter of fact it stayed in that lake of yours, Charlie until it sunk over a year and a half later. I only found out about most of what I'm telling you sometime after they closed it down. I knew a little and was never fooled by their claims that they were experimenting with that ethanol nonsense."

"Wow! But, if it worked, why didn't they build the big one, the, uh, what's it called?"

151

"*Habukkuk*," Posey answered. "I found that word in this log book, Early." Posey lifted the heavy binder off the floor and laid it on the table.

"Let's see that, son." Ducet reached across and dragged the binder to him. He began paging through it. "I'll be damned. Look here." He spun the binder and pointed to a signature at the bottom of the page. "That's my 'John Henry', boys. Well I'll be damned, that's for sure." He shook his head and smiled.

"And the torpedoes?" Posey asked. "How did you test for that?"

Ducet chuckled. "First off, I didn't test diddly-squat, Russell. Remember, I was hired to head up the logging operation. I was the lumber and sawdust guy . . . that was it. I was happy to serve my country right then 'cause as you remember from your history, we'd just got our butt's kicked by a surprise attack by the Japs at Pearl Harbor. We were fat, happy, lazy, and fell asleep on the rest of the world." He shook his head at the memory.

"So, whatever the general and his flunky, Fistric, did to test their floating island against bombs and torpedoes and such, I have no first-hand knowledge of that. Whenever the munitions guys came around, I was escorted off-site until they were done. I can tell you, I heard plenty of rumbling and banging coming from back there in the woods. Sounded like the Fourth of July is what. Could hear it all the way back in town which is where I was escorted to."

"But, you . . . uh, they were convinced the island could withstand any sort of shelling or impact from torpedoes?" Charlie insisted.

"Yes, sir. They were and I was too. That damn floating pile of sawdust was the damndest thing I ever saw. Snuck through the woods one Sunday just to see the thing with my own eyes. Why, I was so excited to be a part of it, I was ready to try for a second time to enlist and go fight Nazis." Ducet waved his broken hand at them, and finished, with, "'Cept for this, I would have."

"What happened, Early? Your hand, I mean," Penny asked.

152

"Careless, missy. Like most accidents . . . operator error. Runnin' that old saw blade back there when I was a youngster. Wasn't paying attention . . . probably dreaming about some cute gal in town like Boni or some damn thing." He smiled and continued. "Before I could say, 'shit on a stick,' I lost both fingers. Bled like a stuck pig, I did."

Wide-eyed with awe, Posey wanted more detail. "What'd ya do?"

"Picked up the two fingers, wrapped them in wax paper, stuck my hand in an old glove, put a twist on my arm with a rope to stop the blood, and high-tailed it to Walker. Only doctor for miles around here's in Walker. Remember that if you ever do anything as stupid as me . . ." He glanced at Penny. "You okay, miss. Look kinda green over there." Ducet smiled and grabbed another handful of jellybeans.

Twenty-One

THERE WAS ONLY ONE more thing to discuss with Ducet that Sunday night. It was the elephant in the room: "What about the silver or whatever it is?" Charlie finally asked as Ducet yawned for the sixth time.

"Silver? What, sil . . . .oh, you mean the rhodium," Ducet replied and yawned again.

"What's rhodium?" Posey asked.

Ducet hesitated. He had a question of his own. "You said, 'silver,' Charlie. Rhodium *is* silver in color, but how did you know about it being silver?"

Charlie had no way to evade Ducet at this point. "'Cause, a few weeks before my dad died, he was over there grouse hunting and stumbled on to a box buried in a hole. Taffy dug it up, actually. It was a very heavy wooden box, he said, that had US Army printed on it."

Ducet was wide awake now. "Wait a minute here. You mean to tell me the general and his flunky buried that stuff? They never shipped it back to Washington?" He scratched his chin and reached for the log book. "They were supposed to box up all the remaining rhodium . . . it was stacks of these little wafers kinda like small tea cookies. Did your dad see what was in the box?"

"He couldn't get it open, and it was too heavy to haul back across the lake by himself, but he found one of the wafers sticking out of the dirt."

Ducet inhaled sharply. He sat back, puffed his cheeks, and exhaled. The teens heard a slight whistle as air passed his lips. "Do you, or, did your Dad give you . . . ?"

Charlie reached into his jeans. "You mean, this?" and laid the wafer on the wooden table.

Ducet stared at the wafer for the longest time. "I never saw any of that stuff first hand. Never permitted to even talk about it. Can I see it, Charlie?"

Charlie, laughed. "Oh, sure, Early. Guess you of all people have a right to touch it." He slid the wafer closer.

Ducet picked it up with his good, left hand and stared at it. "Pretty light, isn't it?" he commented. "Guess I expected this stuff to be heavier." He thought for a moment and added, "You know, if your Dad said the box was too heavy to carry, and as light as this little piece is, why . . . you have any idea how many of these . . ." he waved it in the air and continued, ". . . how many must be in that box?" Ducet whistled. "Holy Moly, Sadie Mae, you guys are millionaires many times over if you can find that box."

"Well, we don't exactly have the box in our possession. I was kinda hoping you'd help us find it, Early. You'd be entitled to a share, of course." Charlie offered.

Ducet nodded his head. "Be glad to help jest for the excitement of it all. Anything you folks'd like to pass this way would be appreciated. Did your father ever know what this was going to be used for?" Ducet asked.

"No. Not that I ever heard. He and his business partner, Earl Foster did some research and had someone from, the 3M Company look at it to find out what it was. I don't think they ever heard back, though and thought it was silver," Charlie answered.

"Well, I found out later that one of the problems with the pykrete sawdust in its original form, was that as it froze in the block of ice, it was too brittle and also melted sooner than the engineers liked. So they dug around and experimented with all kinds of stuff, and came up with this." He held out the wafer.

"What was it supposed to do?" Penny asked.

"Just exactly what they needed it to: Raise the melting point to strengthen the pykrete. It was added to the slurry as a powder—a one to two percent concentrate I was told, and they were all set."

"Where'd it come from," Charlie asked.

"Gold. And silver, I think. It's found in small quantities and mined as a by-product. Extremely valuable, everyone always said. More than gold itself, even."

"So, somehow they separated it out of the gold, melted it down into these wafers, then pounded the wafers to get the powder?" Charlie said.

"Yep. One of those wafers was exactly the amount needed for each block of ice they made. It was pretty slick. After studying on it, I'm convinced it would have worked." Ducet handed back the wafer. "Bet if I look at this log book a bit, I'll find where the general dummied up the paperwork with the inventory and such."

"Whatever happened to the general?" Posey asked.

"Don't know exactly. He was angry, that's for sure. Fit to be tied when they abandoned his pet project. Word was he had visions of being appointed to Eisenhower's staff or some such blather. Not surprised at all to hear he rigged a bogus box to ship back, then buried the real stuff. Something must have happened to both him and Fistric. Otherwise they'd a been back lickty-split to dig up these wafers, and your dad never would have found the box."

Charlie was getting tired. He was also worried about Taffy, hoping she wasn't sick. "I think we should go, you guys. Thanks for telling us all about the project, Early. Now we need to get back over there and see if we can find that box. You want to come with us tomorrow?"

"You bet, Charlie and it's real generous of you to let me in on this," Ducet replied. "Be happy too, Charlie. Have to get my chores done first though. Got a problem with one of my mules . . . came up lame yester-day."

"Probably the least I can do, Early, after shooting a hole in your darkhouse," Charlie replied.

"Yesterday's news, young man. Already forgotten. Here, put this back in your pocket." Ducet handed Charlie the silver wafer and walked them to the door. "What time you kids up in the morning, anyway?"

"Uh, how about nine?" Charlie offered.

"Nine? I've already put in a full day's work, son. Seems to me you boys especially, need to learn something about a hard day's work. Next summer you come to work for me here at the sawmill, Charlie. Bring your buddy, here. Pay you a decent wage and build up those skinny frames on you two." Ducet laughed, patted both on their backs, and finished with, "Good night. Git on home, now. I enjoyed our little visit. I'll be over at 9:00 if I get my chores done and don't have a problem with that old mule. Anyway, if I'm not there by 9:00, then something's come up and I won't make it. Okay?"

"That's fine, Early," Charlie said.

"Good night, Early," all replied and headed for the Pontiac.

"Oh, say, I'll bring the log book with me tomorrow, okay?" Ducet called.

"That'll be fine, Early," Charlie replied.

Taffy perked up as Charlie climbed into the car. She gave a slight wag and settled back on the seat with Penny.

"She any better, you think?" Posey asked.

"I don't know, Pose. Don't really think so. Let's get home and see if she'll eat . . ."

The Pontiac left Ducet's property and headed west toward the cabin.

Tabor Splinter was parked in the darkness a couple hundred yards away. He wondered about the relationship between the old man and the Nash boy. This complicated matters, certainly, and might have to be dealt with. But first, he had to separate the dog from the boy. Just a while ago as he tried to get close to the green house to hear their conversation, the dog sensed his presence and barked. Splinter had to retreat.

He was more convinced than ever that if he was to succeed with his mission, the dog had to be eliminated. But first, he needed to know what part the old man was playing in the Shepherd Lake drama. Problem was, he never liked to expose himself . . . unless the end result was part of his contract. In this case, the old guy was of little concern, and Splinter wasn't prepared to take him out—unless he had to. Tabor was perplexed: A condition a man in his business couldn't afford. He'd already deposited the poisoned meat back at the cabin while the boys visited with the old guy. Confident no animal could resist a chunk of top sirloin, Splinter was certain the dog would no longer impede his plan and be dead by morning.

So, decision made, Splinter waited until the Pontiac's taillights vanshed before he started the car. He coasted into the yard. Ever cautious, he kept a wary eye peeled for resident dogs. *Every farm has at least one mangy mutt,* he thought.

He waited. No barking. Good. He felt exposed by the bright sodium yard light, but he was planning a frontal approach at any rate. He and the old boy were going to have a little chat. One way or another, he'd find out what his involvement was. *Gettin' tired of pussy-footing around.*

Tabor Splinter had been trained well. He knew how to extract information from stubborn individuals. His first teacher had been a master.

158

Twenty-Two

TABOR SPLINTER WAS SOMETHING of a ghost. Born in 1930, just outside of Berlin, Germany. He grew up one of Hitler's, *Jungfrau:* A soldier in the Nazi youth movement. Tabor excelled at all levels of his training: Hand to hand, weapons—both light and heavy, academics, and he rose to the top of his class with special tutoring from Herr Joseph Manheim, a top Nazi doctor specializing in both physical and psychological interrogation. Splinter was an apt pupil, and were it not for Manheim's astute predilection for forecasting events yet to unfold, Tabor would have risen to become a star in the Nazi regime.

Manheim was particularly prescient when he predicted Hitler's fall—he held his prediction close, however, and only shared it with his protégé, Tabor.

"You must leave," he said.

"Why, Herr Manheim?" Splinter asked.

"Because the war will be lost as soon as the United States enters the conflict. Adolf Hitler has no chance of succeeding . . . and once the world finds out about the labor camps? No, Tabor, I'm doing you a favor by sending you away. I have a sister in Chicago, USA. You will stay with her."

"And, what about my family?" Splinter asked.

"They are of no consequence. You are your own person . . . soon a man. I have trained you well, and who knows how you will come to utilize those skills. Perhaps I will join you in the USA, Tabor. Wouldn't that be a good thing?"

"Yes, Herr Manheim," the boy replied.

So in 1941, at the age of ten, Tabor Splinter sadly left his homeland and his family and traveled by steamship to the United States. He had all the proper papers and a passport forged by one of Manheim's aides. It showed Tabor Splinter to be an adopted child of one Gertrude Manheim, a resident of Chicago, Illinois. Splinter had a pocket full of money, directions on how to get to Chicago, spoke English fluently thanks to his tutors, and traveled by train to Chicago with little trouble.

When he arrived at the Union station, Gertrude Manheim met him at the train. Splinter would soon discover that the Manheim bloodline included a very stern and rigid adherence to discipline . . . at every level. Tabor was seldom permitted out of the house. Only very brief forays to the corner store were allowed by Gertrude . . . only to purchase essential food and cigarettes.

Splinter did not attend public school. Gertrude, his aunt to anyone that cared to ask, became his teacher in all things: math, literature, history, even personal hygiene. Tabor had no privacy. Gertrude bathed him, supervised his toilette, and lectured the boy on the evils of, *touching himself*. In short, Tabor was a prisoner of Gertrude Manheim, and in time, he'd come to understand what had to be done to escape her grip.

As the boy grew he also became bitter. He dreamt and plotted how to escape the claws of the evil Gertrude. When he was sixteen, it was clear Herr Manheim was never going to follow him to Chicago. In fact, after the war, all communication and discussion about Gertrude's brother ceased. Tabor never learned what happened to his tutor.

The last straw dropped on Christmas 1946. Splinter had just received his only present. It was sitting on the side table with his name on it. They had no tree, of course, nor any other decoration of relevance.

Just the one present from Gertrude. Silently, Tabor took it upstairs to his room and closed the door. The present was wrapped in brown paper. No ribbons or bows. The object was small, about the size of a package of cigarettes.

Tabor stared at the package for the longest time. He was afraid . . . afraid for one of the first and last times of his young life. Suddenly he froze. He sensed movement, and looked over his shoulder. Aunt Gertrude had silently glided into the room as was her want. Tabor had no privacy. There was no lock on his door. It was one of Gertrude's many rules, that Tabor must be open and visible in every way. "Aren't you going to open it?" his aunt asked.

"Yes. Of course," Splinter replied. Dread filled his voice.

"Well, go ahead then, silly boy. It won't bite you . . ."

Tabor carefully unwrapped the package. His heart was pounding. He could hardly breathe. Inside he discovered a black box. Gertrude joined him on his bed. She sat very close, her stale nicotine tainted breath gagging.

"Open it, Tabor," she commanded.

He opened the package as commanded. He didn't want to. Somehow he knew that a gift from Gertrude would be unpleasant. Inside, carefully cushioned on red velvet, was a large, curly lock of hair—Gertrude's hair.

"Now, whenever you want to think of me . . . to feel close to me, all you have to do is open the box and . . . touch me, Tabor. Won't that be special?" she asked with genuine sincerity. She laid her fingers on his thigh and began stroking him gently. Recently, Gertrude had found many different ways to stroke her nephew . . . all repulsive.

Splinter doesn't remember much of what happened next. He did recall slamming his elbow into Gertrude's face knocking her off the bed. She was bleeding profusely and unconscious. Once he regained his composure—once he willed himself to remember all Herr Manheim had taught him, he went into action.

The police and the fire marshal later determined that the tragic fire was due to an overloaded electrical circuit in the owner's bedroom. Neighbors recalled a boy coming out of the house occasionally, but had never been introduced to him and had never any conversation with the woman who lived inside. They surmised the boy was an infrequent visitor and made no effort to find him.

Tabor Splinter became a ghost. He didn't exist for all intents and vanished into the streets of Chicago. He didn't own much so didn't have to take much with him. A small suitcase with a few clothes, all the money and jewelry he could find in the house, and left with the satisfying knowledge that the evil, sick Gertrude died a horrible, fiery death.

For the next number of years, Tabor Splinter drifted from town to town throughout the Midwest. A quiet boy, many said, but a hard worker and, as some found out, not one to mess with. He had a very short fuse when aroused and, when alone, practiced many of the skills taught by Herr Manheim.

In time, he would learn to utilize every one of those peculiar skills in his new line of work.

* * * * *

"COME ON IN HERE, SPLINTER. Got a job for you." Bernie Jackman said.

Jackman owned a saloon on Chicago's west side. Splinter had been working for Bernie for over a year, performing various, very private and singular tasks. Most were illegal, but Splinter was the perfect choice for the type of work Jackman sent his way. As far as Bernie could tell, the young man had no conscience. Jackman loved that about him—along with his loyalty. Thus far, the jobs were simple enough: debt collecting from numerous deadbeats (Bernie ran a bookmaking operation out of the back room of the saloon). Modest enforcement was utilized—meant to *remind* the forgetful few, not to mess with Bernie. All such tasks were designed to retain Tabor as a low-profile employee. Tabor relished the enforcement part.

Now Bernie had a different job for the eager youth. "How old are you, Splinter?" Jackman asked.

"Twenty-two," he replied.

"You been working for me for what, a year now? Maybe more?"

"About that, yes." Tabor answered.

"Like working for me?"

"I guess. Why?"

"Oh, I just think it's time we graduated you, so-to-speak. Think you're ready for graduation?"

"Depends on what you have in mind, Bernie. Can't say yes to anything until I know more," Splinter replied. He had grown to be tall, broad shouldered, thin at the waist. A daily regimen of exercise in his spartan room built and maintained his sinewy strength. And now, anticipating a new chore to perform for his employer, his dark brows furrowed as he studied Jackman.

"Close the door and grab that chair," Jackman demanded. He opened his top desk drawer with a key, and lifted out a folder. When Tabor was seated, Jackman opened the folder, laid it on the desk top, and spun it around to face Splinter.

Tabor glanced at the photo of the man in the folder. "Who's this?" he asked.

"That's the man you're going to eliminate," Jackman replied and sat back in his chair. He watched Tabor's reaction very carefully. If the young man made any sign whatsoever of reluctance or abhorrence, if he hesitated in any way, Jackman would pretend to be kidding and close the folder. Tabor Splinter would then cease to exist—for real. It was a gamble, but Jackman was a gambler.

He saw nothing in Tabor's body language other than a slight tensioning of his shoulders. Splinter's skin seemed to redden and boil, Jackman observed. For the first time since meeting the young man, Jackman noticed that his eyes were of two different colors. The left eye black, the right eye light green. The green eye seemed to glow now . . . *almost like it's excited, thrilled.* Good, he thought. *This kid is perfect . . .*

Twenty-Three

SPLINTER'S FIRST KILL was a small-time hood named, Boots Brown. He'd been caught muscling in on Jackman's territory by taking bets out of his mother's house. Previous warnings had gone unheeded. Greed got in the way of common sense. He could have easily packed up his penny-ante operation and moved just about anywhere, but Boots suffered from the same ailment most young men his age at that time suffered from: A youthful feeling of invincibility.

Unwisely, as it would prove, Boots Brown also thought he was a tough guy. A few fistfights, a slugfest with his mother's landlord, these insignificant conflicts gave Boots what he needed least: a false sense of his own bad-assness. He was not a tough guy. The tough guys in Chicago in the 1950s were guys like Bernie Jackman. Guys like Tabor Splinter. Boots came to realize the error of his ways . . . too late, to do him any good.

Splinter was a good-looking young man. Tall, Aryan featured, graceful in every movement. His handsome, soft face could be misleading, however, and Boots would mistakenly misread the kindness in Splinter's face as his easy out.

Tabor had followed Boots one cold, spring day as he made his collection rounds. He tailed him beneath an ELL overpass and paused to observe Boots relieve one of his customers of a wad of cash. He waited until the customer left, then approached his target. "Is your name, Boots?" Splinter asked.

Splinter didn't yell. He never yelled. As a matter of fact his voice was level . . . barely audible.

Boots turned, pocketing a wad of bills as he did. "Huh? Yeah. Who are you?"

"Name's not important, Boots. My mission *is*, however . . . least as far as you're concerned."

Boots spit out a wad of gum. "Yeah? What mission, punk."

"Oh, boy. Another tough guy. Good. That makes this lots easier. I'll take that money, first of all, Boots." Tabor's green eye flickered.

Boots laughed, but he had a worried look on his face. Something about the guy didn't ring true. Something about his weird eyes . . . "Forget about it," Boots snarled. "Get the hell out of here." Boots's bravado was unconvincing, hollow.

"Hmm. Okay, let's try this," Splinter said. "My employer, Bernie Jackman, requests that you give me all your money. There, how's that for polite?"

"Jack-off Jackman? That smuck? He thinks he's gonna strong arm me? His days in the sun have ended, my friend, so tell him he can go piss up a rope."

Splinter put his right hand in his pocket and stepped close to Boots. "I am not your friend, Boots. Matter of fact I'm about as far from a friend as you can get." With that Splinter withdrew his hand, flicked open a six-inch knife, and before Boots could utter a word, Splinter opened a long gash in his throat—from one ear to the other.

Boots grabbed at his neck with both hands. Wide-eyed with horror, he looked down to watch his life spilling down the front of his cheap suit. Within seconds, his legs weakened, and he dropped to the dirty pavement. He remained on his knees as his heart ceased to beat. His jugular had been severed as cleanly as if a surgeon had done it with a scalpel.

"Nighty-night," Splinter said. He stooped to retrieve the wad of cash from inside his coat, wiped the knife blade on Boots's sleeve,

166

nudged his torso with his foot, and watched the man collapse in a heap. "Nice boots, Boots."

Splinter glanced around to be certain no one had seen the murder, shrugged his shoulders, and walked away.

Splinter would perform many more similar tasks for Bernie Jackman. As word spread that Bernie had acquired a true, hard-to-find *specialist*, a man without conscience or moral turpitude, Tabor began hearing offers from other parts of the country.

One such offer was from Duane Silk in Minneapolis in 1959. Restless, anxious for a change of scenery, Tabor felt it was time for a little free-lance work. He drove to Minneapolis.

* * * * *

ON THE MONDAY MORNING in March, the day the teens were supposed to meet with Ducet, the boys were up early. Surprising to both—as they had told Ducet they'd be ready at 9:00, it was 7:30 when they woke. Penny soon joined them.

"How about some eggs and bacon for breakfast?" Penny asked?

"Sounds good. I'll make some toast," Posey offered.

Charlie had Penny make a couple of extra pieces of bacon and mixed them into Taffy's dish along with her other, regular food. She promptly gobbled the entire bowl as Charlie watched.

"There. Knew you had to be hungry," he said. He was relieved nothing appeared to be wrong with her. Certainly her hunger that morning was a good indicator. "Wanna go outside? Take care of business?" Together they went to the only door in the cabin. Charlie opened both the main door, then the combination storm, and let her out.

Charlie watched Taffy wander to the edge of the yard and sniff at something in the weeds. Then, he closed the door and went back to the kitchen to eat with Penny and Russell.

Outside, Taffy approached the tainted chunk of meat cautiously. She was alarmed. The odor was peculiar . . . sweet. It was wrong. Her master hadn't left it for her, she was certain of that.

A dog's nose is ten thousand times more sensitive than a human's, and even though the sirloin was tempting—she did salivate—the meat gave off too many other bad smells. Primarily, an unknown human aroma proved most alarming.

She left the meat lie momentarily, and began circling the area—following some faint scent left from the night before. It had a familiar odor, similar to one she'd picked up the other day just outside the cabin. She followed the trail out to the road where it vanished. She would return to the tempting piece of meat later . . . after she took care of her business.

She squatted, kicked up some leaves to cover her scent, turned to go back to her find, and suddenly stopped.

Taffy's tail rose. She froze. Something else on the wind. A familiar, yes . . . a friendly smell. Her tail wagged as she identified Frank. She headed into the breeze, west down the road. The scent increased in strength. She broke into a trot. As she crested the last rise before reaching the end of the road, she spotted Frank coming toward her.

Taffy broke into a full lope and crashed into his arms as he knelt to greet her. "Taffy? What's going on, girl? How come you're out here?"

Suddenly alarmed that the teens might be following the dog, he jumped the ditch and hid in the woods. Taffy followed, certain a game of hide-and-seek was in play.

Nash pulled her close as he knelt behind a juniper. He watched the road to the east and waited. Taffy licked his face. "Shhh," he said. Unsure of what he'd do if the boys did appear, he carefully slid further into the thick brush.

After fifteen minutes, Nash was convinced the boys were not following the dog. "So, what are you doing here, anyway?" he asked the golden retriever. His brief time with the happy dog was intoxicating. He hadn't felt such warmth and joy in a very long time.

Nash went back out to the road. "Let's head back the other way and see what's going on . . ."

By the time they got back through the woods to the edge of the yard, Charlie opened the door and called, "Taffy?"

He whistled, then called, "Here, Taff. Come on, girl." He waited.

Taffy looked at Frank for some sign that together they would join Charlie. She couldn't understand why he was not with his boy. She wagged and started toward the cabin.

"Go on, girl," Nash whispered. "It's okay . . ."

"Taffy! Hey! Come here," Charlie insisted.

Obediently, Taffy stepped from the woods, trotted toward the cabin. She hesitated as she passed the tainted meat. Then stopped.

Charlie noticed she pulled up in the same spot he had last seen her and wondered what she had been sniffing. He went back inside, put on his boots, and went to investigate.

"What's so darn interesting over here, Taff?" He approached and stared into the weeds.

She wagged and nudged the chunk of sirloin with her nose. She looked up first at her master, then glanced deeper into the woods where Frank was hiding, then back at the meat.

"What's this?" Charlie asked, and leaned over to stare at the meat. Something about its appearance and being so out of place just lying in their yard, alarmed the boy. "Russell!" He yelled. "Hey, Pose. Come out here a minute."

Posey had his sneakers barely on his feet and shuffled across the lawn toward Charlie and Taffy. "What's going on," he asked.

Penny followed close behind.

"Look at this," Charlie said and toed the chunk of meat with his foot.

The pair leaned over and stared. "What the hell?" Posey straightened and looked at Charlie. "Looks like prime beef, Charlie. Where'd it come from?"

"Damned if I know. She was sniffing at it when I let her out before breakfast, and I didn't pay any attention. Then, just now she was still looking at it. Something's wrong."

"What?" Penny asked.

"Well, why is it here? Who put it there? And . . . look at what's sticking out . . . " He took a couple of twigs and pried the meat open. "Look here. What's this blue stuff?"

"Know what I think?" Posey said.

Penny gasped and covered her mouth in alarm. "Poison?"

"Yeah. Think so. Someone's trying to poison Taffy. There's no other explanation for why that piece of meat is lying in our yard, full of rat poison or some other damn thing. It's bait for Taffy . . . to eat."

Posey shuddered and knelt to stroke the golden. "Good girl, Taffy. You're too smart to eat that, aren't you?" Posey looked up at Charlie, and asked, "Seriously, why didn't she eat it, Charlie? You think she knew?"

"You know, I'm probably prejudiced or something, but I've seen some things with her before that I always wonder about. Remember I told you about the accident? After Dad and I swam to shore?

"Of course. Scary as hell, Charlie."

Charlie continued. "Well, right at the end, before I reached the decoys, I grabbed Taffy's tail. Didn't think I could make it. She never hesitated. Just kept right on swimming and chugging. She pulled me in, you guys. I really don't think I would have made it without her help. I believe she knew I wouldn't make it, otherwise."

Charlie scratched her head, and continued. "So, yeah, I think she's that smart. She smelled something here that wasn't right so she ignored the meat. And, thank God 'cause look at all the blue stuff inside . . . enough to kill a horse."

"What are you going to do with it?" Penny asked.

"Throw it in a bag, and find some place to dump it. Ground's frozen so I can't bury it. Maybe Early'll know what to do with it."

Twenty-Four

FRANK NASH OVERHEARD the entire conversation from his hiding spot in the woods. His blood chilled, and it wasn't from the cold air. He was certain that the same person who tried to kill him had been at the cabin recently, and made a brazen attempt to kill the boy's dog. The killer's ultimate target? It had to be one or all of the kids. But, he was clueless as to any motive. What he had become convinced of was that the boy named Charlie was Taffy's master, and if true, because of the dog's familiarity with Nash—well, then Charlie might just be his son. That revelation alone evoked a strong sense of affection for the boy.

It was also quite frightening to consider that the man—or men trying to poison Taffy, didn't seem too concerned about raising alarms about their presence at the cabin. *If they had succeeded in killing Taffy, no one would have found the meat chunk—or what was left of it. They might have wondered who as after the dog . . . certainly no neighbors, as there weren't any. No, it was just too desolate out here. A crime . . . murder even, could easily be committed, the body or bodies hidden forever in the woods, and not a soul would ever know.*

Frank would soon be faced with a decision. At some point if the teens were indeed in danger, he'd have to reveal himself to protect them. If they were already in danger, then it didn't matter if he revealed himself. He would stay close and wait for the right opportunity.

172

He was certain of one thing now. The boy named Charlie was the thread that would lead him back to his former life. Charlie represented the way home for Nash.

* * * * *

THE TEENS WENT BACK INSIDE. Charlie returned with a bag and picked up the meat. He brought it back into the house and threw it in the garbage. He glanced at the clock and it was well past 9:00 a.m.

"Wonder what's keeping Early," Charlie commented. "I'd like to ask him about that poisoned meat and see if he has any idea who would want to kill Taffy."

Posey looked at his friend from across the dining room table. "Ya know, as much as I liked listening to Early last night, you did almost kill him, Charlie. You don't suppose he, uh . . . dropped the meat?"

"No. You really think so?" Penny asked.

"I can't believe that," Charlie replied. "He's a nice guy. Remember how he talked about missing his dog, Blue? Guy who misses his old dog wouldn't go around poisoning other dogs, Pose."

"Yeah, I guess you're right. Has to be someone else around here wants Taffy gone—or us out of here." Posey concluded.

Penny asked, "Charlie? What're you thinking?"

"I don't know, Penn. Taffy hasn't been acting quite right since we got here. Remember the other night when she took off after something? And, then this morning? She was gone for twenty-five minutes after she poked at that meat. Where'd she go?"

"Not so sure I like the implication, Charlie. Sounds like somebody around here doesn't want us here." Posey answered.

"Who else do you know except, Ducet?" Penny asked.

Charlie hesitated. "No one, really." He glanced at the wall clock. "It's 9:45 and no Ducet. I tell you what. Maybe I'm way off base, but I think someone's been watching us the whole time we've been here . . .

almost like we are intruding or something. It's weird, you guys. Really weird . . ."

"What should we do? Think we should go home?" Penny asked.

"Absolutely, not! I want to find out what's going on. This is our cabin, not anyone else's. We're staying. And we're taking that damn .22 with us when we go back across the lake. The three of us are staying together. We're going to be very alert. Keep our eyes peeled. I want to find out who's watching us."

"What about Early?" Posey asked.

"Something else he had to do, probably. Some other chore. He said not to wait. We can't wait. He knows where to find us. Let's go."

The boys threw on their coats. Penny layered with a heavy wool shirt she found in the closet. She pulled a dark-blue stocking cap down over her head and drew on a pair of Charlie's gloves. "What can I do, Charlie?"

"Carry the .22 for starters, Penn. Let's go out to the shed and grab some tools."

They rounded up a shovel, an ax, and a crowbar. They put them in the toboggan and set off across the lake.

* * * * *

AFTER THE TEENS LEFT Ducet's the night before, Tabor Splinter made his move. No dogs sounded an alarm, the man in the green house appeared to be alone, and Splinter had to find out what the kids were up to.

Splinter kept his blade palmed, hidden as he knocked on the screen door. After a bit, Ducet answered.

"Good evening, sir. My name is Victor . . . uh, Steven Victor. May I have a few words with you?"

Ducet stepped back. Something about the man, the time of night, his strange bi-colored eyes, didn't seem right. "What's this about?" Ducet asked.

Splinter dove in. "It's about the two boys and girl who just left, sir." He edged through the door. Quickly scanned the room. *Alone. Good.* "I've been retained to keep an eye on the three. Seems someone might be out to harm one or all."

"I see." While Ducet was uneasy, he didn't feel he could simply tell the stranger to go away . . . not if the kids were somehow in danger. "Pardon my rudeness, Mr. Victor. Don't get many visitors out here. Come in, please." Ducet stood to one side as Splinter stepped into the room.

Splinter stopped and faced Ducet. The blade tucked into his sleeve. "What was your name, sir?"

"Ducet. Early Ducet. Here, have a seat." Ducet pulled out a chair for his visitor at the kitchen table, waited until the man was seated, and sat down across from the man. "And, who'd you say you're working for, Mr. Victor?" he asked.

It was getting late, but Splinter had made his move and was all in now. "I didn't say, did I?" His green eye sparked just a little. "Actually, I'm employed by the Nash family attorney and business advisor, Mr. Ducet. That's all I'm at liberty to reveal. What I can tell you is that a disgruntled former employee is apparently out to exact some sort of revenge. The man's made numerous threats to the family. You'll have to accept my word—that we are concerned about the Nash boy's safety—and that of his friends."

Early Ducet didn't trust this man. His eyes revealed little truth and what he had been saying sounded far-fetched. "You say, 'a disgruntled former employee' of the deceased father is out to get revenge? How so?"

Splinter sighed and looked around the kitchen. "Once again, I'm not really at liberty to say anything more. In fact, we are risking some retaliation from this man if he finds out I'm on his trail. It would be extremely helpful to know what you and the Nash boy discussed earlier. Perhaps there is a clue that would lead me to the individual making the threats."

"I see," Ducet said, unconvinced. "Jelly bean, Mr. Victor?"

He slid the can toward the stranger.

"No, thanks," Splinter replied, growing impatient. "Now, it would be helpful as I've previously stated, if you'll tell me what you and the boy discussed this evening. It's terribly important that we stay ahead of the kids, for their own protection, don't you see." Splinter slid the jelly beans back across the table.

He felt for the switchblade, which was currently in his pocket. Ducet wasn't cooperating. Splinter felt he might have to resort to a more aggressive form of interrogation if the old guy didn't start talking.

"Well, as I've already said, me and the Nash boy jest met. Today, actually. Over at their place . . . out on the ice. I was, uh, in my dark house waiting for a northern to swim on by so I could . . ."

Splinter interrupted. *Enough* . . . "Yes. Okay, I get that. But how did that lead to your invitation for coffee and two hours of conversation? What did you talk about?" Splinter demanded as his voice rose.

"Look here, Mr. Victor. I've tried to be accommodating with your requests, but I'm not sure I like the tone of your voice. Nothing was said between those three and me that would cause the earth to shudder. Trust me. We were jest getting acquainted. Period." Ducet replaced the top to the jelly bean jar. "Say, you mean you sat out there all that time watching my house? Not sure I like the thought of that, Victor."

Splinter studied the old man. *Smart as a fox,* he thought. *Uh, uh, he knows something. And, he's not talking. One more try, then we move on to plan B,* Splinter thought. "Look, it's late Mr. Ducet. I've come a long way and frankly I'm out of my element out here in the wilderness. My only concern is the safety of the Nash boy. I hesitate to threaten you, sir, but if you are in any way interfering with the job I was hired to perform, you and I will cross swords, and that's not something you want to do. Do you understand?"

Ducet had enough of this strange looking guy with the green eye. He pushed his chair back and stood. "What I understand is this: I invited you in to my home . . . at your request. I've been as honest as I can possibly be answering your somewhat puzzling questions. I detect an urgency in you that makes me wonder. Not sure it has anything at all to do with Charlie's safety. I suspect some other motive entirely, so given all that, I'd suggest you leave. Now."

Ducet glanced at the shotgun hanging over the door, then headed in that direction. As he did, Splinter reached into his pocket and slipped the knife into his hand. He'd be across the small kitchen in three steps and before Ducet could turn and grab the shotgun, he'd be at the man's throat.

Splinter stood to make his move. As he did, a loud knock sounded at the front door. Splinter stopped. He palmed the knife.

Ducet had reached the door and quickly threw it open. Eyes wide, he declared, "Why, First Sergeant Fistric. What a pleasant surprise. What brings you to this part of the world after so many years?"

"Ducet? Early Ducet?" Fistric asked. His mouth fell open. "What the hell? Thought you'd be dead by now, Duce. I'll be damned. And, Just the man I need right now."

"Come on in, Sergeant. Can't tell you how good it is to see you. We've got a lot of catching up to do," Early said.

Fistric noticed Splinter. "Oh. Didn't mean to interrupt anything, Duce."

"Oh, no. This gentleman was just leaving, right Mr. Victor?"

"Yes. But, we still have some unfinished business, do we not, Mr. Ducet?"

"No. I don't believe we do. I have nothing more to tell you. Good bye, sir." Ducet held the door wide.

As Splinter passed, he whispered, "I'll be back, old man. We aren't finished . . . not by a long shot." A cruel smile crossed his face. He turned and walked to his car.

Ducet slammed the screen door none too gently.

"What brings you back here, Sergeant?"

"Well, I had some time to kill after my most recent, uh . . . employment was terminated and thought I'd come back to go out and visit the old project site. Nostalgic, I guess. Must say, I'm surprised to see you here, Duce." Fistric looked down and noticed the mud he'd tracked in. "Aw, shit, Duce. Sorry about that."

"No problem, Sarge. It'll clean up. Where you been, anyway to git all that crap on yer feet?"

"Well, that's the hell of it, Duce. Tried to drive back to the site and promptly got stuck . . . really stuck. Forgot all about the weather up here and such. Thought maybe with that old John Deere I saw out back, you could get me get unstuck?"

* * * * *

BARSTOW FISTRIC HAD seriously miscalculated his chances of recovering his hard-earned treasure. Fifteen years earlier, he and the general had gotten as far as Little Falls, Minnesota, in their quest for the buried rhodium. Each man had already planned to eliminate the other, and it became a question of who made the first move. That proved to be Barstow.

He felt his ill-conceived plan foolproof—especially considering the neighborhood. The local yokels couldn't possibly be very smart, so his plan would easily work. However, an overly aggressive district attorney somehow managed to sift through what was left of the general's car and put together a rather convincing argument for a conviction of the first sergeant.

Lucky ass-hole, Fistric thought. *Who in their right mind bothers to investigate to the nth degree a simple collision between a couple of drunks and a freight train? No one but that jerk-water DA.*

Unbelievable, thought Fistric. *Plan was perfect . . . right down to the rock on the throttle. So what if I wasn't injured. Guy can get lucky once in a while, can't he? Ah, well, I did my time and now I get the reward.*

So there he was many years later, on the last Sunday in March, headed for Hackensack driving a 1952 black Chevy coupe. Low slung, two doors, the perfect old car for a couple of teens to strip down and turn into a street rod. Not exactly the type of off-road machine to go burrowing through mud and bog in northern Minnesota, however. Barstow forgot how sloppy it always became as the heavy snow melted each spring. The Army's high slung trucks and jeeps managed to travel the logging road without trouble, but not the low-hanging Chevy.

He really had felt prepared. Even purchased the necessary tools to dig with at a small hardware store in Brainerd. He virtually languished behind the wheel on the leisurely drive from there, then turning west out of Hackensack, relishing what was soon to be his, and dreaming of what he'd do with all the money coming his way.

His plan called for a late, after dark arrival to mask his presence. He had slowed at the fork, made the slow turn, passed through the familiar old gate, and managed to drive all of fifty-feet before getting stuck in the mud.

"Son-of-a-bitch!" Fistric shouted. Once he realized his miscalculation, he slammed the steering wheel and looked back over his shoulder to see if anyone was around who could help.

More importantly, if he couldn't make the long, winding drive back to the project site until the road dried out, how the hell was he going to claim his prize? *How am I gonna get it out of the woods? Shit on a stick.*

Fistric opened the door and stepped out. Immediately his brown oxford sank a foot into the mud. "Dammit! Only got but one pair of shoes."

Why didn't you bring some boots, moron? He pulled his foot out of the sucking mud, made a weak leap to solid ground, almost made it, then tipped back and settled with his fanny in the wet goo.

"Nooo," he shouted. "What'd I do to deserve this?"

Fistric turned to one side, put both hands into the mud, pushed himself up, and stood. Now both shoes were covered in slimy mud as were his slacks. He slogged to the edge. Directly ahead, about three hundred yards away, was a dark-green house with a black sedan parked in front. Further investigation revealed an old John Deere tractor beneath a shed behind the house. *Perfect*, he thought. *That guy'll help me for sure . . .*

And that was how Barstow Fistric became re-acquainted with Early Ducet. Luck was on his side after all. Why, once he thought about it, why not recruit old Duce to help him dig up the box and maybe give him a small share. Or? Well, he'd deal with that when the time was right.

Twenty-Five

BACK IN MINNEAPOLIS, Duane Silk had lost all patience in dealing with Marsha Nash. Every attempt to pry information from her had failed. Clearly she had been listening to her son, who had stone-walled all his attempts to get his hands on, not only existing Nash monies, but the treasure Frank Nash discovered, a treasure he was certain existed—someplace.

It was time to take matters into his own hands. He had heard from Splinter the night before but was not satisfied with the progress. With the impasse with Marsha Nash, Silk felt he had to find out for himself if indeed the silver-colored metal was valuable enough to proceed. Most importantly, was there more of the same?

He still needed proof from Splinter that a treasure was buried up north someplace. If he had to go up there himself, he would—if he was convinced of the value in such a distasteful journey.

Duane Silk was many things, but one thing he was not was a nature boy. The outdoors brought on every allergy known to man for Silk. He began scratching and itching at the mere thought of stepping into the woods. *Ticks, spiders, chiggers . . . uh, uh. Ugh. If I have to go, Splinter's doing the heavy lifting. After all, I'm the brains of this outfit,* he thought.

His frustration led him to track down, George Burbank Weston. The same Weston whose name he discovered in Earl Foster's files. The man from the 3M Company. He drove to the man's home after a brief telephone conversation. Weston lived west of Minneapolis in the village of Victoria.

Silk spotted the house, a small Cape Cod on a quiet street. A couple of street lights illuminated the short street. Silk parked the Cadillac and got out. He approached the house with his briefcase in one hand, his business card in the other.

Weston had seen Silk approach from the front window. He opened the door before Silk could knock. "Mr. Silk?"

"Yes, sir. Duane Silk, Mr. Weston. I'm so glad to finally meet you in person."

"Please come in, Mr. Silk. I just got home. Can I get you something to drink? Cocktail? Soda, perhaps?"

"What are you drinking, George? May I call you, George?"

"Certainly, Duane. And I'm drinking a whiskey and soda. Been a long day."

"That would be perfect. Thank you," Silk added.

"Have a seat in the living room. I'll fix the drinks."

"Thanks, George." He chose the couch, looked around the room, and asked, "You married, George?"

Weston returned with the cocktails and replied, "No. Never been. Too busy, I guess. Minnesota Mining can be a pretty cruel employer sometimes. They demand quite a commitment from their employees."

"I'm sure," Silk replied. "Cheers, George." He held his glass up.

"Thank you. The same." He took a sip and asked, "Now, what can I do for you? I think I told you that my findings could only be revealed to members of the Nash family, or their legal representative. Unfortunately, my report wasn't complete before, uh, before the accident. The assayed findings have been locked in my drawer ever since I heard of Frank's and Earl's deaths."

"Yes, I completely understand," Silk answered, "And that's why it was imperative I see you in person." He paused and took a drink. "You see, I've been given power of attorney for the Nash family as well as legal guardianship for Charlie Nash, should anything, uh, well, if anything should ever befall his dear mother. Someone had to look out for the boy's interests, you see."

"Well, I guess that changes things, then. May I see the documents? Have they been notarized?"

"Oh, yes. Of course." Silk withdrew papers from his briefcase and handed them to Weston. "Uh, do you still have the, uh . . . sample, George?"

Weston studied the documents. He looked up. "Huh? Oh, no. After we ran all the tests, I gave the sample back to Earl. I presumed he returned it to Mr. Nash."

"Oh. Yes, of course. I believe Mrs. Nash did mention the sample was locked away in a deposit box downtown." Silk straightened his sleeves waiting for Weston to finish reading.

"Did you notarize this yourself, Duane? Looks like your name here. Kinda fuzzy though . . ."

"Oh, no. That's my brother, uh . . . Dave. We often get confused."

"Well, everything appears to be in order, I guess." He handed the papers back. "Let me go fetch a copy of the final report for you."

When he returned, he handed the report to Silk, who hurriedly read the salient details, and promptly asked, "Rhodium? Not silver?"

"No, no. Not silver. We knew immediately it wasn't. It's a derivative of both silver and gold, however. Very rare. Very valuable. Those of us involved in analyzing this sample are very curious about where it came from. As I'm certain you and the family are," he added.

"Oh, yes. Indeed yes. We are very interested in finding out much more about this, ah, rhodium, George." Silk polished off his drink, stood up, and said, "You've been extremely helpful, George. I'll be sure to tell the Nash family about your willingness to help. One last question, though."

"Yes?" Weston asked.

"What's the value of, say, an ounce or gram of rhodium . . . say, compared to gold." Silk held his breath for Weston's answer.

"I was afraid you'd ask that question. As far as we know, there is a limited market for rhodium. It's much like palladium—another extremely rare metal. We were able to discover more of an international market, primarily Japan. For some unknown reason, the Japanese have feelers out now to purchase all the rhodium they can acquire . . . at almost ridiculous prices. We have no idea what they are doing with it."

"How ridiculous are those prices?" Silk asked. His eyes bulged.

Weston gave him an estimate, and followed up with, "That's a ballpark guess, you understand."

Silk was totally unprepared. He was shocked at the number. He sat back down to collect himself . . . Without thinking, he muttered, "Son-of-a-bitch!" Realizing what he had just said, Silk followed with, "Oops. Sorry, George. Kinda caught me by surprise there, you know?"

Silk's first thought once he gathered himself was that he simply had to go north. There was too much at stake to leave everything to Splinter. This matter required the deft touch and handling of the first team: Namely Duane Robert Silk, Esq.

Silk smiled, gathered up his papers and briefcase, and stood. "Thanks a million, George. You have no idea how helpful you've been."

"My pleasure," Weston replied.

* * * * *

CHARLIE, RUSSELL, AND PENNY slogged through the melt and slush as they dragged the toboggan across Shepherd Lake that Monday morning. Taffy followed, although unlike most any other time she'd been out anyplace with Charlie, she would have been wandering off investigating every scent passing her nose. Not this morning, however. She lagged, occasionally looking back as if expecting someone else to be coming along.

"What's the matter, girl?" Charlie had observed her dawdling, and knew it was strange. "Almost like she's waiting for someone, ya know?"

"Geez, I hope the guy with the bad meat isn't going to follow us. This is starting to give me the heebie-jeebies, Charlie," Posey said.

"Yeah. It is kind of creepy, Charlie," Penny echoed.

"Just remember, we've got that rifle, just in case." Charlie's comment was not all that reassuring to either friend.

Posey followed up with, "Still think we should've called the sheriff, or something."

"And tell him what? We found a piece of bad meat laced with poison? What's he gonna do, Pose? Nothing, that's what. Come on. We're almost there," Charlie added.

When they reached the center of what was left of the compound, they split up and began canvasing the area. They were looking for any sign that the leaves and earth beneath the tree canopy had been disturbed. The recent span of warm weather had melted most of the snow in the woods except for small piles on the north side of larger trees. Now they could see the bare ground quite clearly.

"Try to cover a section about forty yards out–back and forth, Pose. Penny, you do the same on his right. I'll be on your right doing the same."

Got it," Posey replied. "And I'm looking for . . . ?"

"Disturbed ground. A spot where Dad would have dug up the ground and recovered it. It's our only starting point. He said he couldn't carry the chest, so he buried it back in the same hole until he could come back with me and Earl Foster. I'd think it should be pretty obvious where he dug, don't you?"

"Depends," Penny replied. "What if they originally buried it a long ways away? Did your dad say anything about landmarks, or how far away from the camp he found it?"

"No. And, Taffy found it, remember?"

"Well, can you get her to go hunt for it . . . again, somehow?" Penny asked.

"Not a bad idea, actually. Let's keep looking. If she suddenly gets interested in an area, we'll check it out," Charlie replied.

The three covered every inch of ground in the clearing for over two hours without finding anything. Taffy was no help, as she parked herself facing the trail back to the lake and never moved.

"All right, now what?" Penny asked.

"I've got to get Taffy up and hunting, that's what. We're going to move off deeper into the woods. That's where I would've hid it anyway, wouldn't you?" Charlie stated.

"Good point." Penny said.

"Come on. Follow me and let's keep looking. Taffy!" Charlie whistled. "Birds, Taff. Hunt 'em up, girl."

Charlie had said the magic word: "Birds." Bored with the day so far, she had lost interest in watching for Nash senior. Besides, her master had his gun and that always meant hunting so she bounded over to Charlie and immediately began sniffing and wagging.

"There she goes. She'll cover a lot of ground. We have to keep up."

Charlie laid the .22 on his shoulder and watched as Taffy ranged from right to left, ten to twenty yards in front of them. Charlie directed Posey and Penny to walk abreast of him about thirty yards apart, or just the distance Taffy roamed in front of them.

They marched through the woods for three-hundred yards, then Charlie directed Taffy to turn around. They swung east, then back again and around. In thirty minutes they had covered a great deal of ground.

"Whoa, Charlie. Let's take a break. You bring anything to drink?" Posey asked.

Charlie was wearing his hunting vest and had a plastic thermos of water. "Here, Pose." He handed him the container. The three failed to notice Taffy nosing in a nearby pile of brush.

As Posey raised the thermos to drink, he tilted his head back a bit and stopped. "Hey, look at that," and pointed.

"What?" Charlie asked and looked toward a tall red pine Posey indicated. The angle was different, so he didn't immediately see what he was pointing at. "I don't see anything. Just a pine tree . . ."

"No. Move over a bit, and look about six feet up the trunk. What do you see? Can you see it, Penny?" Posey asked.

She took three steps and stopped. "Yes . . . ah, it's an Orange Crush cap!"

Charlie took two steps and declared, "What the heck? A bottle cap nailed to a tree? You don't suppose . . . ?"

"Why not. How else to mark a spot that won't go away," Penny said.

Posey added, "But, that's a big tree, Charlie. They couldn't have buried it beneath the tree. Too many roots and the ground's hard and undisturbed all the way around it."

"Yeah, but what if it's a marker used to point in some direction . . ." He looked around and spotted Taffy now completely beneath a large pile of brush. "Look, you guys? Look at Taffy . . . I think she's found it!"

Charlie noticed that the brush covering the spot was still semi-green; the twigs still had leaves attached. That meant it was fresh; cut the previous fall. That meant his father had been here. So had Taffy. *And she remembered the spot.*

Charlie couldn't speak. Tears filled his eyes as he watched Posey and Taffy furiously reveal the earth. Penny noticed and took his hand.

"What is it, Charlie?" she asked in a whisper.

"I don't know, Penn. Something just hit me, I guess." He inhaled and knelt down next to his dog. He suddenly realized that this very spot was where his father had been digging last fall.

Penny knelt with him. Posey dropped down on the other side. "You okay, Charlie?" he asked.

"I'm okay, Pose. Thanks. Why don't you run and get the shovel. Shouldn't be too hard to dig this up . . ."

All of this activity did not go unnoticed. Frank Nash had followed the teens to the shore below the cabin and watched the three through a pair of strong binoculars he found in the cabin. When they moved deeper into the woods, he waited until he was certain they couldn't spot him, and ran across the lake to get closer. It was a risky move, but he felt compelled to stay close to the kids.

His lungs were burning when he reached the far shore. It took five minutes for his breath to return and heart to slow. *Must've been a smoker,* he concluded.

He entered the woods down the shore—east of where they went in, struck out on an angle downwind—to intercept their track. He worried that Taffy would pick up his scent and reveal his presence, so he stayed well out of range. Always downwind.

Within fifteen minutes, Nash heard the first faint sound of the kids' conversations. He could only pick up brief words and phrases on the wind, but it didn't take long for him to understand what they were doing.

It was clear they were searching for something in the woods. He had no idea what it was nor did the conversation he overheard reveal much in detail. He stayed well away when they decided to spread out . . . much further when they managed to get Taffy involved. At long last, they settled on one particular spot that strangely held a spark of familiarity for Nash.

He shinnied up a poplar tree to get a better look. This would keep his scent high off the ground. Then he waited. Waited to see what they were so interested in . . .

Twenty-Six

THE PREVIOUS NIGHTS' VISIT to Ducet's had left Splinter extremely upset. He was very angry. He had rules. Rules, in Tambor's book, could never be broken. Not when the rules pertained to a contract. Never. In his line of work, mistakes proved very costly. Not only had he challenged his own rule by showing his face to Ducet and failing to interrogate him, but Ducet's visitor also saw his face. That was a mistake that would have to be corrected.

The entire contract was becoming very messy. Chances were increasing by the minute, of Splinter's making one mistake too many. A mistake of the sort made at Ducet's house could be fatal. He would have to rectify both before he left town.

He decided to sneak over to the Nash cabin after leaving Ducet's and see what the kids were doing. If the dog had taken the bait from the night before, they should be off looking for a local vet in a futile attempt to save the dog. If they were indeed gone, he'd get inside the cabin and see what they'd been up to.

He climbed in the Plymouth, started it, and, as he turned around, he noticed the black Chevy stuck in the mud a ways down the road at the turn-off. Now that he thought about it, the guy arrived at Ducet's on foot . . . so, the Chevy must be his. *Wonder what he was doing trying to get down that muddy road? That's the road I took last fall.*

Splinter thought about the guy Ducet referred to as Sarge. *Clearly a military guy. Somehow they were acquainted from years past, but what was the guy doing dropping in now? At this time of year? At night? Dressed as he was? His clothes looked new. Store-bought. Cheap. Hardly fashionable. Pale complexion . . . guy was either in a cave for the past number of years, or? Hmmm.* Splinter would have to question this new guy as well.

Damn! This is getting way too complicated. Need to talk to Silk. Speed this thing up and get the hell out of here . . .

Splinter drove on past the gate to the Nash cabin. He slowed and strained to see down the narrow path to the cabin beyond. *Shit. Can't tell. Have to park and walk in . . .*

He pulled ahead and off to the side. If anyone stopped and questioned him, he'd invent a story about car trouble. *A real estate guy from the Cities checking out lake property. Something.* He climbed out, quietly closed the door and hiked back up the road to the gate.

Splinter stopped and listened for any sound coming from the cabin. All he could here was the wind soughing through the fir trees. He passed the ACHELESS ACRES sign. *Right. Like to put all these yahoos into a permanent state of acheless.*

When he reached the cabin, he was startled to see the white Pontiac parked in back. That meant the kids had been to town and back with the sick dog. Or, were they still inside? Never left because the dog was dead? He listened carefully and decided to back off.

Splinter just couldn't take any more chances. Instead of lingering, or forcing his way in, he chose to retreat. Hopefully, the dog was gone and the poison worked its magic. He'd return to town, call Silk, and figure out what to do next. Clearly, some one or more of these people were, *going to have to be eliminated . . . and soon,* Splinter vowed.

* * * * *

"I think I hit something, Charlie." Posey threw down the shovel, got down on his knees, and began clawing at the loose earth with his gloved hands.

Taffy sat next to Penny, looking in the hole and sniffing. Suddenly the wind shifted. She stood and turned around. Her nose into the breeze.

"What's the matter, girl?" Charlie asked.

"Charlie? Help me . . . I . . . think . . . I've got the box," Posey called.

Charlie leaned over and felt through a thin layer of soft earth. "This is it, Pose. I'm sure of it."

"See if there's a handle on your end . . . yep, gotta handle over here." Posey said.

"Me too. Think we can lift it out? Penny, keep track of Taffy?"

Penny looped her fingers through the dog's collar and leaned over to peer into the hole Posey had dug.

"Let's try on the count of three, okay?" Charlie said.

"Yep. One, two, lift . . ."

Both boys strained with the effort and slowly the box released. It was heavier than they thought, but between the two boys, they managed to lift it out. When they reached the edge of the hole, they slid it to one side and sat back.

"Holy shit! Look at that," Posey declared.

All three stared at the US Army stencil—black print on olive drab paint. "It looks kinda spooky doesn't it?" Posey stated.

Taffy had slipped from Penny's grip and wandered off. She was following her nose into the wind directly toward the tree where Frank Nash had been hiding. He had noticed her looking his way, so when Penny grabbed her collar, he lowered himself, and quickly ran back away from the project site.

Taffy picked up his scent five minutes after he left and followed his trail . . . tail wagging, ears up, happy to be playing the hiding game once more.

Before long, Nash and Taffy vanished in the heavy undergrowth.

Penny saw Taffy leave, noted the direction, and turned back to the green box.

Charlie, so focused on the box and its contents, completely forgot about his dog. The teens excitedly chattered about what to do next.

"Get the toboggan, Pose."

"Be right back," he said and ran away.

Charlie gave the lock a whack with the shovel . . . to no avail. "We need a bolt cutter, Penn. Bet Ducet would have one."

Posey returned with the sled.

"Okay, let's get this thing on and take it to back to the cabin. Early has the tools we need to open it. We'll take it to him, later, I guess." Excitement filled Charlie's voice.

Penny held the rifle. She looked in the direction Taffy had gone. The boys were occupied with the box so she set out to find the dog.

Charlie and Posey heaved the box up onto the toboggan. Both boys looped the rope attached to the front over their shoulders, and set off toward the shore. Charlie noticed Penny had wandered off. "You see where Penny went, Russ?"

Posey was struggling with the loaded sled. "Uh, uh." He looked around. "Probably went ahead with Taffy, I bet."

The two boys started off. Dragging their load through the woods was difficult as most of the snow was gone. They finally reached the shore. There was no sign of Penny or Taffy.

"Now what?" Posey asked.

Charlie cupped his hands to his mouth and whistled. He followed that with a loud shout, "Taffy. Here, girl." Nothing. "Penny? Can you hear me?"

The woods were silent. "What the hell?" Charlie dropped the toboggan rope and walked back inland. "Something's wrong, Pose. Come on, let's . . ."

Suddenly, Taffy appeared at a full lope and crashed into Charlie. She was panting heavily and promptly dropped to the ice and began licking and biting the slush for a drink.

"Okay, but where's, Penny?" Charlie asked.

"Right here," she said as she appeared from behind a stand of jack pine. She was breathing heavily and still toted the rifle. "That dog was on the scent of something pretty interesting, Charlie. I couldn't get her to come with me for anything. Finally I had to loop my belt through her collar and drag her back."

"What was it?" Posey asked.

"Never really saw. Heard it crashing through the brush, though."

"Maybe it was a bear," Posey offered.

Penny shuddered at the thought.

"Yeah, maybe. Bears're coming out of hibernation right about now, Penn. Was Taffy growling?"

"No. She was wagging her tail and kind of smiling. It was weird."

"Well, no harm done. Let's get this box back to the cabin," Charlie offered and picked up the rope.

Taffy rose from the slush, and looked back into the woods.

"Leave it!" Charlie commanded her.

* * * * *

NASH REALIZED TAFFY had caught his scent. He ran as fast and as far as he could before he ran out of breath. His zig-zag trail slowed Taffy down, but only slightly. The chase and her capture took a while. Frank turned and saw her coming, he leaned against a maple tree, slid down to the ground, and opened his arms as the panting golden charged into his lap.

"You certainly are persistent, aren't you, girl." He scratched behind her ears. She licked the back of his hand. Nash looked up, realizing they were now deep into the forest, well south of the shoreline, and quite a ways east of the project site. He listened to hear if the kids were calling for Taffy, but he heard nothing. At least at first. Suddenly he heard the sound of a female voice calling the dog.

He was tempted to give up and yell at the girl and reveal himself, but knew he shouldn't. He stood and commanded, Taffy to, "Speak!" The dog looked at him, then barked once. Then a second time. "Good girl." *Now for the real test,* he thought. "Stay! He held his hand in front of her face, palm forward, and backed away. He repeated the command. "Stay!"

Taffy was sitting quietly waiting for the game to begin anew when Penny found her a few minutes later. She was looking into the woods. Penny couldn't tell what had her interest. "There you are!" she exclaimed. "We've got to get back. Come on, girl."

Taffy didn't budge. Wouldn't leave. Penny tugged on her collar and reluctantly, the dog came along. She'd walk a few steps, then sit again. Penny undid her coat and slid her leather belt from her jeans. "Okay. Let's try this." She slipped the belt through Taffy's collar and retraced their steps back through the woods.

Nash kept moving away from Taffy as quickly as he could. After a few steps through the brush, He came across what looked like an old logging road. It seemed familiar. It lead back toward the site where the boys were digging. *The old logging camp?*

There had been a cabin in the clearing where Nash had dried out and spent a few days when he emerged from the lake. It was sparse, rain tight, but he found some old sacks to wrap up in. He huddled in a corner. Nibbled on a stash of nuts and berries a resourceful chipmunk had stored in a drawer. Drank rain water from an old pail.

When he felt strong enough, he'd left the shelter and followed the trail east to the gate outside of Ducet's. He watched the road for a long time. The few cars that came by all came from the north and headed east. Nash decided he'd go left, west down the gravel road. It was late that day. Days were short and the sun was just disappearing below the horizon when he finally reached the Nash cabin—his cabin.

This recent history of his life was quite clear. He remembered everything from the time he left the lake. All prior to that was fuzzy.

Now, he wondered: *What were the kids digging up?* Something stirred in his head. He waited for more information to surface, but nothing came. He knew he had been in the area of the dig site when he came out of the lake, but, *did I work over here? What, dammit? What?*

Nash hesitated. It was late. He had watched the kids cross the lake with the box. The sun was gone. Only a bright orange glow remained. He stared at the sky and noticed the first star in the west. What was it? It had a name, he was sure. It would be full dark soon. He had to stay close to the kids. Something about the box was worrisome, but he didn't know why. Right now, he had to watch the kids . . .

* * * * *

"WHERE WERE YOU?" Charlie asked as he stroked Taffy's flank. "What was she doing, Penn?"

"Not much. Just sitting and looking off into the woods."

"Well, let's go," Charlie declared.

Posey and Penny had turned along with Charlie, but Taffy hesitated—still looking back. Ultimately, she felt obliged to obey her master. She trotted out on the ice.

Nash had observed the kids and Taffy from a distance. He leaned against a thick poplar and watched Charlie and friends lug the toboggan across the ice. "Charlie," he whispered. "Charlie." *Is that my son?*

It was almost totally dark now, and Nash was struggling to see the boys clearly. He felt safe venturing out on the ice toward their cabin. But, then he stopped and dropped to the ice. He lay prone in the slush. The kids had made a detour toward the fish house. *Now what?*

Posey had raised a question of concern. "You think it's safe to just have this box lying around the yard, Charlie? I mean, think about the poisoned meat and all. What if someone comes around and finds it?" Posey had stopped, waiting for his friend's response.

"Good point," Charlie said. "We can't open it anyway . . . don't have the right tools. We need Ducet for that." He looked around and spotted Early's fish house. He pointed. "How about we stick it in there?"

"Perfect," Posey replied.

"What do you think, Penny?"

"Kind of obvious, but maybe that's good," she said.

They veered left and headed toward the dark house. Once there, Posey propped the door open with a chunk of ice. The three dragged the green box inside, then closed the door.

"Okay. Should be safe there, right?" Posey said.

"Yeah. For sure," Charlie said. "Come on, I'm hungry. Then I want to go see what happened to Early."

* * * * *

BARSTOW FISTRIC COULDN'T believe his luck as he stumbled across Early Ducet that Sunday night. Yes, he'd made a slight miscalculation regarding the weather at that time of year, but sometimes *if you just hang in there*, he thought, *luck finds a way*. "Yes, sir, Duce, this is my lucky day to have found you still here after all these years," he commented to Early Ducet.

Ducet had still been greatly disturbed by Victor, his earlier guest that night. And, while he welcomed the sudden appearance of his old boss, the man was now becoming a bit of a bother. Even though it was late and very dark, he had to try and free the Chevy from the mud and get rid of Fistric. The man's insistence that Early haul him back to the project site made sense now that he knew the box had never been recovered by either Fistric or the general. Ducet had to keep Fistric away from the site. After all, hadn't he and Charlie worked out a deal to go to the site themselves and look for the rhodium? *Why all of a sudden had Fistric appeared on the scene? And what about this Victor character, the man from the Cities? The nasty looking guy with the goofy eye kept insisting that I knew something about something—which I did, of course. But, how did the guy know that?*

Ducet felt on edge . . . had a bothersome itch, but, didn't know how to scratch it. He needed to piece everything together. Fistric's presence was intrusive. He had to get rid of him that night.

One thing he knew for sure: He wasn't lugging Fistric back to the site, no way, no how. He didn't trust the man, either. No. He had to get rid of him and go find the three teens.

"Getting late, Sarge. 'Fraid all I can do is drag you out of the muck. Got chores to do. Have to feed my mules, and, uh, clean the barn. Life of a farmer, eh?"

"Yeah, I understand, Duce. Well, we got more time to talk about the good-old days and the ice boat, later, right?"

"Yeah, right, Sarge. Come on. Let's get you outta the mud and on yer way," Ducet coaxed. He pulled on a pair of rubber boots, then a canvas jacket, and held open the door for Fistric.

Fistric kept wanting to reminisce, however. "Say, Duce. I ever tell you what the guys used to call you? Behind your back, of course." He was following Early out to the shed where the tractor was stored.

"Matter or fact I do, Sarge," Ducet said as he climbed up and sat on the metal seat. "Deuce-and-a-half, right?"

"Yeah. Son-of-a-bitch. You knew."

"I knew." He held up his left hand and wiggled the remaining two and a half fingers. "Pretty clever, actually, but I heard worse over the years." He replaced his glove, stepped on the starter, and the old Deere came alive.

"Climb up, Sarge, and park your butt on the fender there." He waited until Fistric was aboard, put the tractor in low, and drove out of the shed. They bounced down the road to the gate . . . and Fistric's car.

"Hop off, Sarge." Ducet left him standing on dry ground while he attached a chain to the rear axle. He had to crawl underneath, unfortunately, and wound up with mud all over his overalls and coat, but he had no choice. *Gotta get the guy out and send him away,* he thought.

Back on the tractor, Early ground the gears into reverse and slowly backed off. It only took a few seconds for the Chevy to break loose. "Jump in the car, Sarge. I'll keep pulling but you gotta steer."

Fistric reluctantly stepped back into the mud, opened the door, and climbed behind the wheel. He turned over his shoulder to steer as Ducet increased the throttle.

In minutes, they were back on solid ground. Ducet removed the chain, climbed back on the tractor, and yelled, "Good to see you, Sarge. Take care, now," and sped off back to the shed.

Fistric waved goodbye. *I'll come back tomorrow—maybe bribe the old goat to help me. Sure as hell, not going to walk back there in the damn mud.* What choice did he have though, if Ducet wouldn't help?

Twenty-Seven

BARSTOW FISTRIC HAD CHECKED in at the Northstar Motel after leaving Ducet's Sunday night. A hot shower and a steak at the Chat & Chew Café revived his spirits. He wasn't sleepy so he headed to the only saloon in Hackensack, a watering hole known as, The Muni.

Fistric had many, not-so-fond memories of nights spent in Hackensack many years earlier during the war. Inevitably, in his attempt to escape the constant and demeaning influence of General Abdelkader, Fistric would overindulge, get stinking drunk and be dragged back to the project site by the MPs.

True to form, Fistric drank himself into oblivion that night. He became so obnoxious and cantankerous the sheriff had to be called. Once again, Barstow found himself back in jail. He was hauled off to Walker. Fistric made such a commotion that night the sheriff had to promise the old soldier that he'd call his close friend, Early Ducet, to spring him first thing in the morning.

* * * * *

THE SHERIFF WAS TRUE to his word. He dutifully called Ducet Monday morning. Ducet wasn't happy about this turn of events and asked the sheriff to, "Keep the fool on ice for the rest of the day."

"No can do, Early. Gotta turn him loose," the sheriff declared. "You'll have to come get him this morning."

So, Ducet had to drive to Walker on Monday instead of meeting the kids as planned. Fistric would have a world-class hangover, so after picking him up. Early would dump him back at his motel. Fistric would be down for the day and out of his hair. He still had to tend to, Jilly, his mule, but thought he might catch up with the kids, later.

* * * * *

FISTRIC'S SECOND NIGHT in Hackensack took a familiar turn for the old sergeant.

After sleeping away most of Monday, Fistric returned to The Muni and picked up where he had left off the night before. Shots of bar whiskey chased by Hamm's beer soon left Fistric in a semi-conscious state. A pair of local natives, members of the Chippewa tribe, were sitting at the bar along with Fistric.

"Never met an Injun I couldn't whup!" declared Fistric to no one in particular. He had failed to take note of the two members of the Chippewa nation down at the end of the bar.

"Shut the hell up, old man," The bartender cautioned, remembering the troubles from the previous night.

"Why's thad?" Fistric asked.

"'Cause you're about to get the living shit pounded out of yer stupid self by those two boys over there." The bartender nodded to his right toward the pair of Indians.

Fistric's eyes weren't too sharp after years of incarceration. His advancing age didn't help either. He squinted in the direction indicated. About all he could discern was the indistinct shapes of two individuals some distance away. "Aww, hell. They can't hear me anyways." He threw back the whiskey, slammed the glass on the bar top, and demanded, "Another, barkeep!"

200

"Nope. That's it for you, old timer," said the bartender.

"Bullshit to that, bub. My money's jest as good as those two yahoos over there. 'Sides, I'm gonna be rich by tomorrow and you might jest wanna be nice to me, ya know?"

By now the pair on the end had taken particular interest in Fistric. One nudged the other after listening to him, and both stood up. They grabbed their beers and headed toward Fistric.

"Take it easy, boys," the bartender said. "He meant no harm to you two."

"No harm taken, Norm. We just wanted to say 'Hello' to the old timer and buy him a beer . . . just a friendly, 'Injun' sort of gesture. A peace offering, ya know?" With that, he threw an arm around Fistric and sat on the stool next to him. "What say, mister? Can we buy you a shot?"

Fistric, as drunk as he was, had enough sense to see that not only was he out-numbered, but at his age and as drunk as he was, he was in no condition to take on the two young men he'd just insulted. "Yeah, sure. Nothing personal there, chief. Matter of fact, I'm feeling so good about my future prospects, I'll buy the whole joint a drink!" He waved his empty glass around the saloon and received a few, whoops from the scattered customers.

The pair parked on either side of Fistric. They waited for their drinks. "What's your name, bud?" the fellow on the right asked.

Fistric turned and said, "Huh? Oh, Barstow. What's yours?"

"I'm Sammy and my friend over there is Jay," he replied.

"Pleased to meet you fellas. Let's have a toast: To the Indian Nation—The Chippewa!" Fistric raised his glass to salute his new friends, and downed its contents.

Sammy and Jay sipped their beers. "What are you doing up here, Barstow?" Jay asked.

Fistric nodded and smiled. "Oh, jest going to recover something that belongs to me, thas all."

"Really? And what might that be, Barstow?" Sammy pressed.

SHEPHERD LAKE

"Oh, I shouldn't really talk about it . . . is top secret stuff, know what I mean?" Fistric thought about what he'd just said, and wondered if the two new friends might be of some help. "Say, you fellas wouldn't maybe have a big truck would ya? Maybe, a truck that could slug its way through mud and shit?"

"You need some help hauling something, Barstow?" Sammy asked.

"Yeah, sure do. Say, forget what I said earlier, boys. I been away for awhile and plum forgot my manners. Get a few drinks in me and I'll say most anything, know what I mean?"

"Sure we do, Barstow. Don't you worry about it," Jay replied and winked at his friend. "And, we'd be happy to help you out. 'Course it'll cost you. Gas ain't cheap, and we're pretty busy. You can pay, right?"

"Oh, yeah. I can pay all right. Don't you boys worry 'bout that. There'll be plenty to take care of you for all your trouble."

"Well then, when do you think you'll need us, Barstow?" Jay asked.

"Tomorrow, chief. We go tomorrow . . ."

* * * * *

CHARLIE, PENNY, AND POSEY had spent an uneasy Monday night worrying about their hiding place. "Not good enough," Posey concluded.

"Yeah, I think you're right. It's pretty much out in the open, isn't it?"

"Think we should move it now?" Posey asked, knowing it was pitch dark outside.

"I'd say, 'yes' if I knew where to move it to. Any ideas? Penny?"

"Do you really want to drag that box around in the dark?" Penny asked. "Why not go get it first thing in the morning?"

"Yeah, but where do we move it to?" Posey insisted. "This is your country around here, Charlie. I don't think it should be close to the cabin, though. Do you?"

202

"No. I don't. Let me think about it tonight. I'll come up with something. But we do need to get up really early tomorrow and move it, right?"

"Yeah, for sure," Posey answered.

It was too late to hunt up Ducet after dinner, so they decided to wait until after they'd hidden the box again. Posey went to bed while Penny and Charlie played cribbage.

After a couple of games, both were yawning, but each reluctant to make a move toward their respective bedrooms. Penny finally broke the ice. "I'm kind of spooked tonight, Charlie. Do you suppose we could . . . uh, sleep in the same room?" Her cheeks were already red from their day outside, but flushed a bit brighter now.

"Sure. Come on, Penn." He stood and held out his hand. "It's okay. I'll take dad's bed and you sleep in the other one." Charlie's parents slept in twin beds.

Penny took his hand and pushed away from the table. She stood close, then kissed him ever so softly. "I really do like being with you, Charlie Nash."

Charlie knew what she meant as he felt the same way. He wanted to know more, though. "Why, Penn?"

"Why, what?"

He led her into the bedroom, turning out lights as they went. "Well, we've been really close for so many years . . . what's different now? I mean, I can't think of anyone else I'd want to spend time with besides you . . . girl wise I mean, but now that we're older, well it's just . . . different."

They reached the bedroom. "I know," Penny replied and stepped into the bedroom. Charlie closed the door. She turned to him. They stood close. Penny leaned in and wrapped her arms around his neck. They kissed again. This time the kiss was longer, much more passionate. They sat down on one of the beds. Penny fell back and looked up. She reached for him and pulled him to her.

Sometime later, Charlie sat up and looked down at Penny. He stroked her cheek. She grasped his hand and tugged it down. "Penn, we had a deal, remember? I mean, I told you not to worry, that I'd never take advantage of you. Remember?"

"Oh, Charlie. You're so sweet. What we're doing right now feels so right. I'm not at all bothered by this. It feels good, and I know you're the only boy I'd let touch me like this." She took his hand and placed it on her chest. She kept his hand covered and pulled him to her.

Just then, there was a loud knock on the door. "Charlie? Penny? Maybe you should leave the door open, okay?"

Charlie and Penny laughed and pulled apart. "He's right," Charlie said. "Come on, let's get some sleep." He kissed her briefly and pulled her to her feet. "You get the bathroom first . . ."

* * * * *

THE NEXT MORNING, as it had been decided, the teens were up at the crack of dawn. After a quick breakfast of scrambled eggs and toast, they were out the door headed for the dark house.

Before they reached the target, Charlie said, "Think I know just the spot, you guys." He dropped the toboggan and moved off.

"Yeah? Where?" Posey asked.

"Come on. I'll show you . . ."

* * * * *

BY TUESDAY MORNING, Ducet was finally able to drive to the Nash cabin in search of the kids. He pulled into the yard in his pick-up, turned off the ignition, and climbed out of the truck. He closed the door gently. It was 7:30 a.m. and he feared the teens might still be in bed. He looked around, walked over to the Pontiac, looked inside, then straightened.

It was too quiet. Dog should be barking. He walked toward the only door into the cabin and paused. He looked in the window to the dining room. Empty. He knocked, fully expecting sudden barking from Taffy. Nothing. No barking, no anything. *What the hell?*

Ducet opened the screen door and tested the knob of the main door. It turned easily. He twisted the handle, opened the door, and called, "Hello? Charlie? You here?" There was no answer so he stepped inside and walked into the kitchen.

A glance around the cabin indicated the kids had been up quite early, made breakfast, and had left . . . on foot. Ducet walked to the living room and looked through the bay windows facing the lake. He didn't see the teens, but did see a strange man standing down near the dock, looking west—toward his dark house. *Wonder who that is?* He couldn't see his fish house as a stand of birch blocked his view.

Ducet continued to watch. Curious about the man and his purpose, he sat down and stared out the windows. *Something weird about all this,* Ducet thought. The dock was some distance from the cabin, the man unrecognizable.

Suddenly the stranger turned and looked back at the cabin.

Ducet bristled and stood. He quickly backed up into the kitchen, stumbling as he struck a rocking chair near the doorway. He ducked around the corner and peeked down toward the lake.

He didn't want to let the man see him . . . he had no weapon, was unarmed. Had no idea who he was. Maybe a friend or partner of the guy from last night—Victor. More importantly, *where were the three kids?*

After a second quick glance toward the dock, Ducet realized the stranger was gone. He stepped out into the living room and looked again. Nothing. He wasn't there. Then . . . where was he?

* * * * *

THAT SAME MORNING, Duane Silk pulled into Hackensack. His sky-blue Cadillac was quite conspicuous in the small town, but Silk enjoyed that. He loved playing the big-shot, and the way things were going, he could afford the Cadillac and much more before too long. He checked in to the Northstar Motel, and asked the clerk for Victor's room number.

"Mr. Victor is in room 221. Down at the end, Mr. Silk."

"Thank you. And I'm in which room?"

"We're kinda full today . . . strange 'cause it's not a busy time of year, so I can't get you close to your friend. Best I can do is 211, all right?"

"Sure. Whatever. Do I just dial his room number?"

"No, ask the operator to assist you. She'll ring him. Actually, that'll be me." She giggled and handed Silk his key.

When Silk got to his room, he asked the clerk to ring Splinter. The phone rang once and was immediately answered. "Yes?"

"Victor, it's me," Silk said.

"What's up, boss man?"

"I'm surprised to find you in right now, Victor. Figured you'd be out watching the Nash kid."

"Well, I'm just full of surprises, aren't I?"

"Well, I'm here to take charge of this affair now," Silk said.

"What do you mean, 'Here'?"

"In Hackensack. In your motel. Room 211. Let's meet and discuss what to do next. Clearly we need a plan, don't we?"

"We? You think you're up to this, Silk? Could get kind of messy, you know."

"I can handle it. Don't worry about me, Victor. Come down to my room and let's talk."

"Nope. Don't want to meet. Don't want to be seen with you. Obviously, if you were able to call my room, then the clerk now knows we're acquainted, right?"

"I guess. So what?" Silk asked.

"So what? That's precisely why I choose not to meet face to face with my employers. Because of you, I've just violated rule number one, Silk. I'm not at all happy about that."

"Who gives a rip, Victor . . . Splinter? I'm paying the bills. I'm in charge. You'll do as I say and like it, understand?"

Splinter didn't answer right away. He'd already decided how to deal with this idiot. He'd play along, keep his distance, and when the time was right . . . after his big payday, well, *too bad—so sad, Silk.* "Okay, Silk. Go ahead and play the big cheese. I'll fill you in on the details, we'll come up with a plan, but we will not meet face to face, understood?"

"Fine. Whatever."

"I'm gone from here, Silk. I'll find another place to stay and call you when I get there. You'll pay for my room and tell the clerk I had a family emergency. Stay by the phone." Splinter hung up, packed his bag, left the room, and drove away from the motel.

"How did I ever get involved with this character," Silk muttered. He called the front desk, told the clerk to put Victor's bill on his account, and told her his friend had to leave. Then he flicked on the TV and discovered only one channel with decent reception—CBS. *As the World Turns* was on. Actually one of his favorite shows. He flopped on the bed and waited for Victor to call.

Twenty-Eight

FISTRIC HAD BEEN ESCORTED to the Northstar Motel by the two Indians, on Monday night. They poured him into his room, number 219, and booked the adjoining room, number 217 with a common pass-through door. Neither Sammy nor Jay were going to let Fistric out of their sight.

The next morning, they woke Fistric at 8:00 a.m. It wasn't easy. The old sergeant had a colossal headache, and was still half-drunk. He barely remembered the events of the previous evening, and had little recollection of his night in jail. It took Sammy carefully explaining what the three had decided, before Fistric put everything together.

He did remember shouting insults at the Indian Nation in general, so he quickly applauded the pair's efforts to help him recover the treasure box. He'd give each a few bucks and send them on their way, he figured.

"You ready to go, Barstow?" Jay asked as he handed the old man a paper cup of steaming coffee from the front office.

"You bet. Let me take a crap, drink my coffee, and we're out of here," Fistric replied.

A while later, when the threesome arrived at the entrance to the logging road, Fistric pointed at Ducet's house. "That's the guy who was *going* to help me. His tough luck and your good fortune, boys. Just head on through the gate and keep trucking down that shitty road."

It took quite a while for Sammy to slog through the mud and ruts until they reached the buildings at Shepherd Station. "What the hell is all this?" Jay asked.

"This is where I was in charge of a top-secret project during the war. We were working on a plan to build a floating island—an ice berg that was indestructible. Could've ended the war if Roosevelt and Churchill hadn't pulled the plug on the whole thing."

Sammy and Jay looked at each other. They were more than a little skeptical. The names mentioned had little impact on either man. "Okay, so what was so valuable here, Barstow?" Sammy asked.

"Well, they were little squares kinda like cookies, made of a mineral that was . . . *is*, very, very valuable. The box we are looking for is worth plenty, boys. Trust me on that."

"Great. Where is it?" Jay inquired.

"Follow me. And bring that shovel . . ."

* * * * *

CHARLIE, PENNY, AND POSEY had just finished moving the box to a new location, when the sound of a heavy engine echoed across the lake. It was Fistric and his new friends as they drove closer to the old buildings.

"What's that, Charlie?" Posey asked.

"Sounds like a truck. Heading to the buildings over on the other side. Wonder if it's Ducet? We missed him yesterday. Maybe he got confused and went over there to meet us?"

The kids finished hiding the box and returned to the cabin. The truck noise from the other side faded, then stopped. Charlie leaned the toboggan against the house. "That box should be safe now, you guys."

"I'd say. No one will ever think to look there, Charlie. What now?" Posey asked.

"Well, I guess we should . . ." He glanced behind the cabin and spotted Ducet's truck. "Say. Is that . . . ?"

Just then, Early Ducet stepped out from the cabin. "Charlie. Russell. Young miss. Sure glad to see you three, that's for sure."

"Early?" Charlie turned to look across the lake. "Then, who's that over there?" He pointed to the other side of the lake.

"What do you mean, son?"

"We just heard a truck moving over there and thought it might be you. If not you, then who?" Charlie asked.

"I don't know. Fella came to my house Sunday night . . . fella I used to know way back then. It was the first sergeant I told you about—Fistric. Tried to drive in there in a Chevy sedan . . . damn fool. Got hisself thrown in jail after that. Had to drag him out Monday morning. Never did have any time to get over here after that. Anyway, he wanted me to take him back there with my truck. Can only guess he came back to recover the box. And now, seems like he found someone else to drive him over there. Wonder who?" Ducet scratched at his stubble, then blurted. "Say, there was another feller that came by . . . nasty guy who threatened me if I didn't tell him what we had discussed."

"Who was that?" Charlie asked.

Ducet told the kids all he knew. "Said his name was Victor. Ring any bells?"

"No. Never heard of him," Charlie replied. "We dug up the box."

"You did? No shit! And, did you open it?"

"No. Need a pair of bolt cutters for that."

"Where is it?" Ducet asked.

"We hid it."

"Twice." Penny added.

"Why twice?"

"Didn't think your dark house was safe enough, so we just moved it this morning."

"Okay. Whenever you're ready, we can open it. Always carry bolt cutters in my truck." Then Ducet remembered the stranger. "Say, there was *another* guy here down by the dock when you guys were gone."

"Who was it?" Charlie asked.

"Don't know. Never seen him before. White hair, tall. Thought at first it was that guy Victor from last night, so I ducked out of the way. Next thing I knew he slipped away. All of a sudden, there's all kinds of people around here. Weird, huh?"

"I guess," Charlie said. "S'pose they're all looking for the box?"

"Maybe. Hard to know who yer dad and the other feller might have told. Could be most anyone, I guess and maybe not so friendly either."

"So what do we do now, Early?" Posey asked.

"I think you three should stick close to me. Got a funny feeling about all this. Too many coincidences for my liking."

"You think any of these guys would . . . you know, hurt us, Early?" Penny asked.

"Who knows. The mere thought of great riches can turn most men from civil to evil in the blink of an eye and if that box is *full* of all those wafers, why it's got to be worth a bunch of money. What did ya do with that pea shooter of yours, Charlie?"

"It's in the house. But I've also got my shotgun . . . no, that's at the bottom of the lake. I forgot. Wait!" He darted into the cabin, dug through the closet, but came back empty handed. "Crap. I know that old 20-gauge was here last fall, but now it's gone."

"Who could have taken it?" Penny asked.

"Got me," Charlie replied.

"Look, I've got an old 12-gauge back at my house. Let's stick together and go get it. I'm thinking it might be time to bring the sheriff in on all this," Ducet said.

"Sounds good to me," Posey said. "Charlie? What do you think?"

"That's fine, but let's keep the box hidden for now. Okay?"

"I agree," Ducet replied. "Come on. Let's go."

* * * * *

Nash had been observing the boys for quite some time. Ducet's arrival alarmed him at first, but when he recognized the old guy as the fisherman he'd been watching all winter, he was relieved. And, as it was obvious that the kids felt comfortable and safe with the man, Nash was satisfied.

He'd watched the three remove the box from the dark house and move it to another location. Their choice raised a smile on Nash's leathery face. *Pretty clever*, he thought. *Leave it to kids.*

Now he sat on his haunches beneath a towering Norway and observed the kids and Ducet leave the cabin. Taffy paused and raised her head. *Nuts. Forgot to stay downwind.* He ducked behind the massive trunk and held his breath. *No. Stay, Taffy. Please?* He willed.

Just as she was about to head his way, she stopped and turned ninety degrees. Her tail flew up, and the hair on her back stood straight. She growled and took three steps toward something or somebody standing in a stand of jack pine.

Nash peered around the trunk to see what had alarmed her. He saw movement. Heard a click. Then a man stepped from the grove and marched toward the cabin.

"Hold that dog or I'll shoot her!" The man shouted.

Twenty-Nine

PLINTER HAD NEVER INTENDED to drag Silk along with him. Tabor was a loner. He relished all the little details inherent in his craft. Cleverness, stealth, brazen thinking—these were *his* skills. He felt it imperative that each employer leave him alone to ply his trade. Silk could wait forever, if he wanted, but he would never be permitted either to meet Splinter or work with him.

So, instead of checking into another motel—Walker being the only other town within range—Splinter made a choice: End it—now. Confront the target, extract the information, and eliminate whoever he needed to. Kids and dogs included.

Splinter had parked the Plymouth down the road and hiked back through the woods to the Nash cabin. He stood and watched for a brief time. Ducet's presence was unexpected, but posed no real problem. He only needed to get to the Nash boy, force him to reveal the location of the treasure, then clean up the mess.

The teens had left the cabin with Ducet. *Time to move*, Splinter thought.

After shouting the warning about the dog, he stepped forward at a brisk pace until he was fifty feet away. "Better get a grip on that dog, boy, or she's dead." Splinter pointed the Colt at the dog. He hated guns—much too cumbersome and sloppy to his liking—but he was taking no chances with the dog. Idly, he wondered how she had survived the poison.

Charlie grabbed Taffy's collar and dragged her back. She was barking furiously by now, snarling and prancing as Splinter approached.

"Put her in the car young man or I shoot her right now," Splinter commanded.

"Taffy! Come on, girl," Charlie said as he struggled to get her into the Pontiac. Once the door was closed, he returned to Posey, Penny, and Ducet.

"Victor. What the hell is this? Guess that's not your name, but who cares, right?" Ducet called.

"That's right, old man. No more pussy-footin' around. You all know what I'm after, and one of you is going to tell me where it is, right?" He pointed the gun at Posey. "I'll take four-eyes here out first, as he's of little value to me."

Posey's face turned slate-gray, but he never backed up or ducked. Splinter fired, and the retort echoed through the tall pines. The bullet struck Russell high in the shoulder. He staggered back and fell to the ground.

"Now. Do you believe I'm serious?" Splinter asked.

"Yes, for God's sake, man! These are just kids!" Ducet exclaimed.

Charlie knelt next to his friend. "Early? What should I do?" Tears filled his eyes and he trembled. He had never felt so afraid in his life.

"Put your hand over the wound, son, and press hard." Ducet removed his jacket and handed it to Charlie. "Here, cover it with this and keep pressure on it."

By now, Taffy was going crazy in the Pontiac. She was clawing and biting at the canvas fabric of the convertible top.

Splinter fired another round through the side door of the car. Taffy gave a high-pitched screech, then continued barking.

"No! Don't!" Charlie shouted. "Please don't hurt her. I'll tell you where it is."

"That's better. But, if you send me off on some wild goose chase, the old man goes next. Then the girl."

214

"No! It's right here . . . close by. We dug it up and brought it across the lake yesterday. Honest. You can have it . . . all of it. Just don't hurt anyone else, please?"

Splinter knew he'd made his point. The sight of blood will do that most times. "That's better. Old man, throw me the keys to your truck."

Ducet did as he was told. "Here." He tossed the keys.

"All right, kid, where's the stuff?" Splinter asked.

Charlie pointed beyond the cabin to the east. "Over there. In the woods. In a big box."

"In the woods? Where?" Splinter demanded.

"I'll have to show you," Charlie replied.

"Let's go. Leave four-eyes here. You, cutey pie . . . you're coming too." Charlie took Posey's good hand and placed it over the wound. "Keep pressing on it, Pose. The bleeding stopped, I think. We'll be right back, okay?"

"Sure, Charlie. Hurry though . . ." Posey's voice tailed off. He was weak and losing consciousness.

* * * * *

BACK BENEATH THE GIANT Norway, Frank Nash was frantic. He'd witnessed the entire episode and was helpless to do anything to stop Splinter. The shotgun was back at the cabin. He had no weapon . . . no knife, even. He looked around and picked up a heavy broken limb. It would have to do.

But, now what? He couldn't just bust out of the trees and run towards the cabin. The man with the gun would shoot him down in a minute. No, he'd have to wait for the right opportunity.

The boy who had been shot needed medical attention, but so far he was still alive. Nash believed he had to stop the man from shooting–killing–anyone else . . . including his son. *Just wait. Get in closer and wait.*

As he watched, the group moved around to the front of the cabin. Nash quickly dashed to the guest house in the rear. There was a tool room adjacent. Maybe some sort of weapon in there. He slipped inside, into the dark. Once his eyes adjusted, he picked up a machete used to clear brush. Silently, he snuck back outside and around the far side of the cabin.

The group had now moved off into the woods east of the cabin. He knew where Charlie was leading the man: To the spot he and the other boy chose to hide the box. Clearly, the man with the gun wanted what was in the box.

Now that he knew where they were going, he would take a more direct route to the hiding place. He'd get there first. *Wait! What about the other boy?* He had to see to his wound. He had to.

Nash turned back and hurried over to Posey. He knelt down and laid the machete in the grass. "Can you hear me, son?" Posey's eyes were closed. His breathing ragged.

When Posey looked up, a very strange man with white hair and a heavy beard was looking down at him. "I . . . uh . . . who are you?" Posey mumbled.

Nash hadn't spoken to another human in a very long time. His voice cracked as he said, "I'm pretty sure I'm Charlie's dad." He put an arm beneath Posey's head, and lifted him into his arms. "Let's get you inside and get some help out here."

Nash carried Posey inside and laid him on his bed. After checking to see that the wound had stopped bleeding, he covered Russell to keep him warm, and said, "Rest now, son. What's your name?"

"Posey. Russell Posey. I'm Charlie's friend."

"Yes. I know. I've been watching you. I have to go now and help Charlie. I'll call the sheriff before I leave to get you to the hospital. Rest easy now, okay?"

"Yes, sir. Mr. Nash?"

216

"Yes, Russell."

"Charlie's going to be awfully happy to see you."

"Me too." Nash hurried from the room, picked up the phone, and waited for the operator. Once he had made the call, he hung up and dashed from the cabin. He ran towards Charlie's hiding spot and prayed he wouldn't be too late.

* * * * *

THE INDIANS SAT IN THEIR TRUCK drinking beer while Fistric searched for his treasure. "Lookit the old fool," Sammy muttered and lifted the can of Hamms to his mouth. "Dumb's a box of rocks, that one."

"Hmmm," his partner crooned. "What we going to do with him?"

"Shhh! Listen." Sammy rolled his window down all the way. "Hear that? Gunshot from across the lake . . . from the place out past Ducet's. Where those duck hunters died last fall."

"Nobody's up there this time of year, right?" Jay asked.

"Dunno. I was out there couple days ago lining up timber leases, and I remember seeing a strange car on that road."

"Well, I'm thinking this fool's had too many drinks in his life and has no idea what he's doing. Crazy as a loon. Here he comes . . . this'll be good, you bet."

Fistric stormed up to the truck and threw the shovel in the back, disgusted. "It's gone. Someone stole it!"

"Who'd steal your box, Barstow?" Sammy asked.

"How the hell do I know! The only other person who knew where it was died a long time ago. Hell, I jest spent fifteen years in jail 'cause I kilt him!"

Sammy looked at Jay. Jay looked at Sammy. They'd heard enough. they nodded to each other. Jay rolled up his window. "Okay, then, old timer," he said. "Guess we'll be on our way. See ya around . . ." He put the truck in gear, spun the wheel, and gunned the engine. "Nutty as a fruitcake," Sammy muttered.

Fistric watched in disbelief as the truck chugged back down the road. "Hey! What about me?"

* * * * *

DUANE SILK WOKE WITH A START. *As the World Turns* had failed to hold his interest, and Splinter never did call as promised. *Time to take control of the situation*, he thought.

Silk picked up the phone and waited for the girl to answer.

"Yes, what number please?" she asked.

"No number. Just some information, miss."

"Yes, Mr. Silk? How can I help?"

"Two things: Where's the next closest motel, and can you direct me out to Shepherd Lake?"

The clerk told him where the motel was, but had never heard of Shepherd Lake. "I'm sorry, Mr. Silk. This is the Land of Ten Thousand Lakes, you know," and she giggled.

"Lord save me from these people," Silk muttered as he hung up.

Thirty

DUANE SILK DROVE TO WALKER and inquired at the Starlite Motel about the elusive Splinter. After being told no one had checked in that morning, he drove the Caddy back to Hackensack and stopped at the Standard Oil Station.

The attendant filled up the blue beast, checked the oil, and scrubbed the huge windshield. He walked to the driver's side for payment. "Quite a car you have there, friend," he offered in a small-town sort of way.

"Yeah, right," Silk grumbled. He handed over a twenty and asked, "Say, any idea how I get to Shepherd Lake?"

The attendant removed his Standard Oil cap, passed a greasy hand through sparse hair, and replied, "Seems to me it's out west of town, mister."

"Think you could be a bit more specific?" Silk snarled sarcastically.

"Hmm. Well, that whole area was jest opened up a few years ago, ya know. Most folks around here don't know much about what's out there. Hang on a minute, and I'll make a call as soon I get yer change for ya."

Silk fumed as he watched the man pick up the phone in the office.

"Holy cow, where do these people come from?" Silk asked no one within earshot.

The attendant returned, handed over Silk's change, and offered, "Best I can do for ya is this. See that road that branches off 371 there?" He pointed back down the street.

Silk craned his neck around in the direction the man pointed. "Yeah, and . . . ?"

"Well, ya turn there and follow that road as far as you can until ya come to a fork . . . bear left and that should lead to Shepherd Lake. Good luck and thanks for stopping," he concluded.

"Lord help me," Silk mumbled as he put the Caddy in gear, spun the wheel and laid dual black streaks of rubber making a u-turn.

The pride of the GM fleet quickly climbed to sixty miles per hour and fish-tailed down 371. Silk slammed on the brakes so he wouldn't miss the turn, barely skidded past an old lady crossing the highway, and pounded down the dirt road leading west out of Hackensack.

"Finally got directions from an old gink with bad teeth. Good grief! How I hate northern Minnesota. All right, Splinter or Victor or whatever the hell you want to call yourself, I don't need you anymore, and, because of that, I don't have to pay you one damn cent!" Silk muttered outloud as the heavy Caddy barged through the thick sand on the roadbed. "You just go ahead and play the tough guy, Splinter. I have my own plan on how to extract the needed information from the Nash kid . . . it's called cleverness and finesse, Splinter. Words you certainly aren't familiar with."

Silk droned on as he steered the unwieldy Cadillac down the dusty road.

* * * * *

ONCE NASH WAS SATISFIED the Posey boy would survive and he had made the appropriate call to the sheriff, he ran out of the cabin. Taffy had continued to bark and chew on the canvas top and by now had managed to tear a hole in the top big enough for her head.

Frank Nash stopped next to the Pontiac. He couldn't leave her in the car as she would certainly escape in just a few minutes. Somehow he felt Taffy might be helpful . . . but not unless she was under control. He grabbed a length of clothesline from the tool shed, opened the car door, and tied the rope around her collar.

"Come on, Taff. We have to hurry." They started off together to intercept his son and the others. Taffy led the way, straining at the rope, as she knew precisely where her master had gone. It was all Nash could do to hang on to the rope. He thought about tying the loose end around his waist to be certain she wouldn't get away, but decided against that.

As they entered the woods east of the cabin, a shot rang out and echoed through the woods. "Oh, no," Nash said. "Please, not my son."

* * * * *

TABOR SPLINTER HAD HAD enough. The Nash kid was leading him on a wild-goose chase . . . he was sure of that. "Hold it, kid." He leaned over to catch his breath. "What do you think . . . that I just fell off a turnip truck?"

Charlie faced the man and said, "Huh? What do you mean?"

"What I mean is I think you're full of shit! Maybe shooting your buddy wasn't proof enough how serious I am. So, who's next? Oh! Guess what? There's only you and the girl and the old man left. Hmmm." Splinter reached in his pocket, pulled out a quarter, flipped it in the air, and caught it. "Heads it's the old man. Tails it's the girl. Choose, kid."

"No! You can't . . ." Charlie yelled.

"Okay. I'll choose . . . heads! Sorry, old timer . . . that's you" Splinter pointed his gun at Ducet who by now had figured out what Splinter would do, so he decided to become a moving target. He started running through the poplars. Too late. Splinter fired. Ducet fell. Hard.

Charlie tried to run to Ducet, but Splinter caught his arm. Without thinking, enraged and tapping into a side of him that he had grown familiar with lately, Charlie reached down and picked up a heavy, dead oak branch. With just the one free hand and arm, he swung it at Splinter's head.

"Penny! Run!" Charlie shouted.

She tripped and fell as Splinter stuck out his leg. As he moved, he stepped into Charlie's swing.

With a loud *crack* the limb struck Splinter directly on the bridge of his nose. Blood gushed. The killer let go of Charlie to cover his nose. Tears clouded his eyes. He spun wildly searching for the boy . . . all the while waving the gun.

Charlie grabbed Penny's arm and dragged her into the woods with him, toward the old man. Ducet had crawled deeper into the woods. Wounded in the leg, he was able to crawl and drag his bad leg. "Early! Here, let me help." Charlie bent to put an arm around Ducet and helped him stand.

"Leave me, Charlie. Run!" Ducet begged.

"No! Not without you . . . come on . . . hurry."

* * * * *

WHEN FRANK NASH heard the report from Splinter's gun, his heart froze. Taffy bolted at the sound of gunfire and tore out of Nash's grip. She ran off toward the gunshot.

"Taffy! No!" Nash hollered and followed the dog into the poplar.

Just ahead, Splinter shook his head to clear the fog and circling stars. Droplets of blood flew as he did and marked the white bark of a large birch.

"Son-of-a-bitch!" he shouted. "You can't get away, kid. I'll find you," he hollered. "And when I do, I'm gonna gut you like a fish until you tell me where my box is! Hear me, kid?"

Splinter's bellowing echoed throughout the leafless forest.

Taffy was slowed only slightly by the long length of clothesline. Downwind of all the activity in the woods she knew so well, she quickly picked up Charlie's scent and headed directly for her master.

Charlie had caught up with Penny. Together with Ducet in tow, they managed to put about fifty yards between themselves and Splinter. They paused behind a large, fallen log. All three were breathing hard.

"You can't keep dragging me, Charlie," Ducet whispered raggedly. Save yourself and the girl," he pleaded as they listened to Splinter's shouts.

"No, Early. We'll be . . ." Charlie's words were interrupted by Taffy crashing from a clump of alder. She tumbled into Charlie's lap. "Taffy? How'd you get here?" Then he noticed the rope around her neck. "What's this?"

Ducet shrugged.

Penny stroked the golden's head. "How'd she get out, Charlie? Who tied the rope on her?"

Thirty-One

SAMMY TWO FEATHERS and his friend, Jay Silverheels were members of the Leech Lake Band of Chippewa. Reservation kids, they grew up near Walker learning to cope with the woods, waters, and city folk who were buying vacation property in the area. Over time, and particularly after the federal government opened up the Chippewa Forest to homesteaders and logging, Sammy, Jay, and most of the other Indian tribe learned how to get along with the growing white population. Up to a point.

Neither Sammy nor Jay could abide the white man's stupidity, however when it came to the ways of the woods. In ever increasing numbers in the late 1950s and 1960s, they witnessed carload after carload of folks moving into the area around and south of Leech Lake. The vacationers' mission seemed to be uniform: Build, then occupy their dream cabin on Leech or on one of the many small lakes dotting the area. Then, spend money like there was no tomorrow.

Sammy, Jay, and the tribal leaders weren't fools. While they might privately resent all the intrusions and crowding and noise, they weren't about to turn away from a new source of money flooding the area. The white man's money spent well, and any enterprising Indian with an ounce of brains soon learned how to separate the fools from the flock. Playing the "Indian Game" in the 1950s meant dressing in authentic garb and dancing at weekly Pow-Wows, creating cheap souvenirs to be sold along the highway, and waiting for opportunities to make easy money.

Sammy was just such an opportunist. He learned at an early age how best to survive with the white man and derive various sources of income.

Finding cheap—make that free—logging leases provided by the federal government was just one of the ways Sammy cashed in. He never actually did any wood-cutting himself, but "rented" the timber rights to the many loggers who lived in the area now. It proved to be one of many cash cows Sammy and Jay milked.

One of the first things Sammy determined was that he needed to be, "In the know," to be the first to hear about opportunities and the best way was to purchase a combination cb/two-way radio and mount it in his Ford F350. Once he had the radio, it was a simple matter to join the Leech Lake sheriff's posse—a volunteer group often called upon to help with searches, boating accidents, and sometimes even criminal apprehension. His buddy Jay tagged along, although not officially one of the posse.

And now, after Sammy and Jay abandoned Fistric back in the woods on the south side of Shepherd Lake, they picked up a call from the sheriff requesting help—medical and police—just across the lake from where they had been, the same area of the earlier gunshot.

"Let's go, Sammy," Jay hollered. The big truck roared and spit gobs of dirt and mud as Sammy drove to the end of the Shepherd Lake logging road.

They tore past the gate and just about t-boned a blue Cadillac. Sammy slammed the brakes. "Another dumb-ass whitey," Sammy declared. He rolled down the window as the driver of the Cadillac, Duane Silk, stopped his car in the middle of the road.

Silk had been driving up and down the road for a good while. He rolled down his window, stuck his small head out the window prior to stepping out. But, he then noticed the mud and thought better of that idea. He yelled instead. "Say, either of you fellas know how I can get to Shepherd Lake?"

Sammy backed up, then pulled alongside the Caddy. "Tell him to drive back where we just came from, Jay. If he's lucky, he'll meet that boob Fistric hiking back out."

Jay directed Silk to drive through the gate and to keep going. "After a while, you'll come to the lake. Can't miss it, sport." Jay smiled and rolled up his widow. "Let's go. That Beaner will get that Caddy hung-up for sure."

"Thanks, guys. Have a good day," Silk said. "At last, someone with an ounce of intelligence and respect to give me solid information." He turned into the muddy road and began slithering off down the trail into the woods.

Sammy gunned the engine of the big truck and roared off down the road toward the Nash cabin.

* * * * *

CHARLIE, PENNY AND DUCET were exhausted and could go no farther.

"Leave me," Ducet said for maybe the tenth time.

"No. I won't. We have to figure out how to get the guy's gun." Charlie looked at the rope around Taffy's neck. "Gotta idea, Early."

Charlie untied the rope, found a poplar adjacent to the path they were on, and tied one end about knee high. He laid the rope across their trail, covered it with leaves, and threaded the other end through a V made by a branch and trunk of another tree fifteen feet away.

Penny held on to Taffy as she watched Charlie lay the trip rope.

Ducet nodded. "Might work, Charlie, but only if he walks the same route we took."

"Let's get you over here, then. Make it so he has to walk directly to us and over the rope. When he gets to the rope, I'll yank it and trip him up," Charlie said.

Ducet didn't voice the obvious, but in truth, feared what would happen if Splinter didn't walk directly in their same path—or close enough to be tripped up. "Good thinking, son. Can you keep hold of Taffy, young lady?"

"Yes. Think so," Penny answered.

Charlie took off his belt, threaded it through Taffy's collar, and handed it to Penny. Suddenly, they heard thrashing and swearing as Splinter came closer.

"Time to pay the piper, folks. I'm like the nursery rhyme . . . how's that go? Oh, yeah. 'Fee, fy, fo, fum . . . I . . . smell . . . well looky here. Guess what? I found you!" Saying that, he barged ahead directly toward where they were hidden. "Gotcha now, you little . . ."

Taffy leapt and snarled and pulled loose from Penny's grip. Splinter reached the rope. Charlie yanked it taught. The crazed killer stumbled and fell forward. The Colt discharged for the third time that day. Charlie felt a white-hot pain in his arm. He spun around from the impact. Penny screamed as blood poured from Charlie's arm.

Frank Nash suddenly broke through the underbrush and dove on top of Splinter. They rolled back and forth . . . throwing punches and grabbing for anything within reach. Splinter still had the gun and swung it against Nash's temple. Frank was dazed . . . millions of white flecks floated in front of him. He lay prone looking up at the brilliant blue sky.

Splinter stood, pointed the gun at Nash. Just as he pulled the trigger for the fourth time, Taffy attacked and grabbed the first area of Splinter's body she could reach: His crotch.

The shot went wild. Splinter bellowed with a loud howl and clubbed the dog away. His breath left him then, and he leaned over in great pain. No one moved for the longest time. The woods were deathly silent.

* * * * *

SAMMY TWO FEATHERS and Jay Silverheels pulled up just outside the gate to the Nash cabin. The men heard another gun shot as the truck's engine wound down.

"Shit, Jay. That's close by," Sammy said. He reached behind his head and unclipped the .30-06 hanging on the rear window rack. "Let's go!"

The two Chippewa men piled out of the truck and struck off in the direction of the shot. It didn't take them long before they came upon three men, a teenage boy and girl, and a dog. It was a chaotic and bloody scene. One of the men was wounded and propped against a tree. Another man with white hair lay on his back looking at the sky—apparently stunned. Blood covered half his face. A small brown dog had a grip on a third man's upper thigh and was thrashing back and forth. That man had a gun. He pointed it at the teenage boy. He was yelling, "Get it off me!"

Splinter spotted Sammy and Jay. He snarled. His green eye glowed like a laser as he twisted around and pointed the gun at the Indian pair.

Sammy never hesitated. He pointed the rifle and fired.

As the .30-06 slug entered Splinter's left eye—the green one, his last thought was of his Aunt Gertrude. *Strange . . . to think . . . of her . . . now.* Darkness closed in.

He had been slammed back into a bunch of prickly ash. He settled into the nasty nettles. His heart stopped. Tabor Splinter, the ghost, died almost instantly.

Taffy had loosened her grip and trotted over to Charlie. Jay knelt and attended to the man with the bleeding leg, while Sammy checked on Nash, saw the superficial wound, then turned to the kids. "You all right, son? No, I guess you're not." Charlie was losing a great deal of blood. The Indian grabbed the nearby rope. He sliced off a short length with a large sheath knife, fashioned a tourniquet with a stick and twisted it on Charlie's arm. "There. How about you, sweetheart? Any injuries I should know about? No? Well, I want you to loosen this stick every few minutes, then tighten it up again, okay?" Sammy commanded.

Charlie was speechless, and growing weak. So was Penny. She was frightened beyond words. She clung to Charlie. His blood covered much of her clothing. Mouths wide open, eyes wide with fear, the teens looked at each other, then glanced down at the man with the white hair lying at their feet.

Nash was coming around. He turned his head to the side so the unbloodied side of his face was visible. He looked at Charlie. Then at Penny. Frank smiled a smile that felt just wonderful. He winked at Penny and said, "Hi."

Charlie squeezed Penny's hand as Taffy lay down next to his father and gently licked his face. In a raspy, whispering voice audible only to Penny, Charlie asked, "Is any of this real, Penn? Is it a dream?"

Epilogue

CHARLIE AND FRANK NASH were reunited sometime later at the Brainerd Lakes-Area Memorial Hospital. The third of Splinter's gun shots had nicked an artery in his forearm, and he lost a great deal of blood, but Sammy's quick thinking saved his lilfe. Charlie would spend the next ten days in the hospital recovering.

Russell Posey was taken to the same hospital, but later transferred to Methodist Hospital in St Louis Park, Minnesota. His injury proved more serious. Posey was in and out of consciousness for many days, and underwent multiple surgeries to save his right arm.

Early Ducet proved too tough to die at age sixty-seven. He spent only a few days at the Brainerd hospital, then was driven home where he convalesced with an old girlfriend who had heard of his misfortune and came calling when he got home. Her name was Boni Lesard: Box-Car Boni. They had known each other since childhood. She brought him a large jar of jelly beans.

Charlie had a steady visitor during his stay in the hospital. He and his Dad had plenty to catch up on. Frank's memory was still quite foggy, but Charlie would help fill in the blanks.

Penny was too upset to drive, so Sammy drove her and Taffy to the hospital that night. Both were exhausted. Penny felt Taffy had been truly heroic. She hated to think what might have happened if she hadn't broken loose that day.

Marsha Nash arrived that night. She and Penny checked into the Paul Bunyan Motel in Brainerd. They spent the following days at the hospital. Taffy was permitted to visit at will. Penny's parents arrived a few days later and brought her home.

Duane Silk did ultimately meet up with Barstow Fistric that day in the woods. Silk tried to enlist the stranger's help in getting the Caddy unstuck. Fistric flipped him the bird and kept walking. He managed to walk out, hitched a ride to town, and headed for the Muni.

Silk was arrested a few weeks later in his home town of Brown Valley, Minnesota. Having spent a couple of days in the woods dealing with all sorts of terror, Silk eventually lost touch with reality. He was later committed to the Fergus Falls Home for the criminally insane.

* * * * *

LITTLE WAS MENTIONED about the US Army box of rhodium. Technically, the mineral wafers belonged to the United States government, but because of a peculiar statute of limitations ruling in 1947, minimal claims could be made by the government that were, "Not to exceed twenty percent of the value of property or goods previously declared as lost or stolen." No such claim was made to the Nash's for the rhodium, but they would offer up the twenty percent anyway.

A full year later, Charlie and his dad decided it was time to go and dig out the box. They felt it appropriate that the following parties be involved and share in the prize: Russell Posey, Penny Tercel, Early Ducet, Sammy Two Feathers, and Jay Silverheels would all be given a share.

They met at the Nash cabin on a bright March day and strolled— or hobbled as was the case with Ducet, down to Shepherd Lake. They followed the shoreline east for about a hundred yards. Charlie, Penny, and Posey were leading. They stopped when they came to an old beaver house.

Charlie pointed. "It's in there," he said. "At least it was."

The boys dug it out with a shovel and pick. Early had his bolt cutters. They gasped as one voice as the contents were finally revealed and the wax packages spilled out onto the ground.

"My, oh, my," Early declared. "Ain't they pretty, though . . ."

* * * * *

THE RHODIUM WAS SOLD at auction on the international market to the highest bidder. There was sixty-seven pounds of the stuff and fetched a remarkable sixteen million dollars. The successful bidder: A Japanese company named, Mitsubishi. The Nash's found out sometime later that the rhodium was to be used to complete a new, very special circuitry called, "A Mother Board." This became an integral part of wireless telephones.

After twenty percent was given back to the government, Penny, Ducet, Posey, Sammy, and Jay all received one million dollars, each. Charlie and his Dad kept another four million.

The balance was used to fund the Shepherd Lake Foundation. Tom Warner was hired as CEO. Its mission: To provide underprivileged athletes, both boys and girls, scholarships to attend college and pursue their chosen sport. The foundation had an additional mandate: to include children from the Indian reservations of northern Minnesota.

Warner continued to coach hockey in his spare time.

Russell Posey purchased a pair of contact lenses and tried out for the West High Cowboys hockey team. He became their starting goalie his senior year. A brand new world opened up for the young man.

The Cowboys had a great year with Posey in the nets. They not only won the Minneapolis City Conference title, they went on to compete in the state tournament in Saint Paul, where they finished second.

The team that beat them for first place? A team from Walker, Minnesota.

In her senior year at West High, Penny was accepted to Boston College University. Charlie received a hockey scholarship to the University of Minnesota, Duluth, but declined. He told the coach he'd love to play hockey for "The Bulldogs" but asked that the scholarship be given to another boy. He would pay his own way . . .

Charlie and Penny remained, "more than friends . . ."

The End

Author's Note:

While Shepherd Lake is a work of fiction, a few elements are based on fact. The hunting accident actually happened to me along with two friends and a young boy. We were very, very lucky no one died that October day. The event was written as a short story, "Accuse Not Nature," *and published in an anthology titled,* Stories of the Unexpected.

The Habakkuk project was indeed a real event directed by Sir Winston Churchill. A prototype was constructed of Pykrete at a secret location near Lake Louise, Alberta Canada. It was built as described in the novel and hidden in a large boathouse. For more information, Google "Habakkuk Project."